Arthur Lynch

Human Documents

Character-sketches of representative men and women of the time

Arthur Lynch

Human Documents
Character-sketches of representative men and women of the time

ISBN/EAN: 9783337370558

Printed in Europe, USA, Canada, Australia, Japan

Cover: Foto ©Raphael Reischuk / pixelio.de

More available books at **www.hansebooks.com**

HUMAN DOCUMENTS

CHARACTER-SKETCHES OF
REPRESENTATIVE MEN AND WOMEN
OF THE TIME

BY

ARTHUR LYNCH

AUTHOR OF

"RELIGIO ATHLETÆ, "A KORAN OF LOVE," ETC.

LONDON

BERTRAM DOBELL

77 CHARING CROSS ROAD

1896

PREFACE

THE whole man thinks. The brain itself is only part of the apparatus by which the individual, sometimes consciously, sometimes unconsciously, guides himself amidst his surroundings. In a thousand fashions day by day he is making the test of his powers, and Nature is returning to him her inexorable verdict. The man's intellectual work is determined in great measure by his physical constitution and his emotional quality. Byron's lame foot and Carlyle's dyspepsia have become classical, and the examples of Swift, Rousseau, Luxembourg, Turenne, Plotinus, Kant, and a thousand others could be cited by way of showing how physical peculiarities may give a cast to a man's whole intellectual life.

But these cases are only the more striking exemplifications of the general law of that continual interaction of mind and body, of character and circumstances, which has given rise to various apothegms containing the same meaning in their central truth—"Character is Fate"; "How shall a man be hid ?"

In the estimation of character, and in the estimation of the products of human activity, such as art and literature, there are certain broad bases which form the veritable canons of criticism— the intellectual grasp, the emotional calibre, the physical base, the knowledge of the field; and from these the drift and tendency, the moral and purport of the whole work may be deduced.

The analysis of character requires not only the laying bare of the strong points and the weak points of the individual, his various forces and faculties, but also the due estimation of the relative weights of his different motives, the due proportioning of his powers. These may be thrown into different perspectives in different circumstances; but there is a continual tendency for the individual, even amid his restrictions, his exaggerations, his want of balance, to assert the type of his own character.

.   .   .   .

Read, for example, such a book as Bain's "Criticism of John Stuart Mill." That work may be thought by many to be dry in style, and even captious in its criticism ; but if the whole scheme of its analysis be grasped, and the eclectic method of the estimation of character be appreciated, then not only will it be seen to give a conception of Mill far clearer than any even elaborate biographical sketch, but also Mill's character, with all its limitations and faults, arises far grander and more unassailable than from the most impassioned and eloquent eulogy.

The lack of this kind of analysis is the reason of the futility of the great part of our histories, biographies, novels ; and any man who has had those experiences of life that force him to look steadily upon the motives that have guided himself, and to endeavour to assert the vital things of his own character—any man of the world, then, will understand the impatience which seized upon Abraham Lincoln upon one occasion in reading a "Life of Edmund Burke," flinging the book into a corner in disgust at its "orthodoxy," its sophistication, its shallowness.

.   .   .   .

In this regard the question of "personalities" may be discussed. A public man's personality is public property, and we have a right to weigh his powers and estimate the energy of every faculty, physical, mental, emotional, upon which his career and influence depend. We strip recruits for the army to test their fitness. We have as much right, and more reason, to strip off the moral trappings of our Prime Ministers.

The French, ever in the van of civilisation, and the Americans, with their disrespect of all that is not intrinsically valuable—the first with their exquisite literary style, the others with their genial audacities—make no scruple of personalities. The tendency of the New Journalism in this respect is not a bad one; we must pull the trappings and shams off institutions and men to see them as they are.

   .   .   .   .

The manner in which these " Human Documents " are regarded by the author is simply that of interesting studies of character analytically considered, and from an objective standpoint.

A further interest arises from the fact that in the course of these studies we are also forming an image of the physiognomy of our own time, of which these characters are representative. The age also must be eclectically considered. Its features must be seen gradually developing, and it is curious to compare in this respect one generation with another, and to endeavour to form an idea of that gradual evolution of human Society upon which we may imagine the good Gods to look down, sometimes with approval, sometimes with wonder, sometimes with a strange Gargantuan amusement.

ARTHUR LYNCH

ERRATA

The reader will please to correct the following errata, which are due to the absence from England of the author while the book was passing through the press.

Page 1 (first line of quotation), "konnte" *should be* "könnte."

Page 212 (lines 7 and 8), the clause, "as distinct . . . fibre," *should be in brackets* ( ).

Page 214 (line 3 from bottom), "Kiplinguesque" *should be* "Kiplingesque."

Page 215 (line 9 from bottom), "of watching" *should be* "in watching."

Page 222 (line 15 from top), "some" *should be* "a most."

Page 224 (line 15 from top), "blackboard" *should be* "backboard."

Page 252 (line 8), "suffer" *should be* "strive."

CONTENTS

		PAGE
H.R.H. The Prince of Wales	. . .	1
Kaiser Wilhelm II	. . . . .	17
John Burns	.	44
Tom Mann	. . . . .	59
Mr. A. J. Balfour	. . .	79
Joseph Chamberlain	. . . .	108
W. T. Stead	. . . . .	138
T. P. O'Connor	. . . . .	156
Zola	. . . . . .	176
Rudyard Kipling	. . .	203
Sara Bernhardt	. . . . .	232
Ada Rehan	. . . . .	245
Herbert Spencer	. . .	261
Alexander Bain	. . . .	285

HUMAN DOCUMENTS

H.R.H. THE PRINCE OF WALES

> " Es konnte kaum ein herz'ger Närrchen sein
> Er liebte nur das allzuviele Wandern,
> Und fremde Weiber, und fremden Wein,
> Und das verfluchte Würfelspiel."
> —*Faust.*

> " A better hearted wight you never knew,
> But for his love of haunts not over nice
> And women, don't you know, and drinking too,
> And then that cursed fondness for the dice."

NEXT to Her Imperial Majesty the Queen, and much more prominently before the eyes of the British public, we find as the head and ornament of the State H.R.H. the Prince of Wales, K.G. . . . .

He is to English eyes the most familiar representative of royalty in these latter days. He may be taken as the peculiar embodiment of that supreme glory of the British Constitution. In the natural course of events he may soon be the final arbiter of legislation for all that mighty Empire on which the sun will never set. At every hour of the day and in every day of the

A

year prayers for his welfare are sent up to the
throne of heaven. His fame resounds throughout
the civilised globe, and for one man who has
heard the name of Herbert Spencer ten thousand
are familiar with our Prince's claims to hold the
highest place in the convocations of all the illustrious of the nations. Our weak pen can barely
hint at the sources of all his prestige ; but for the
proper understanding of the Prince as a man an
attempt must be made not merely to realise the
greatness of his position but also to indicate the
profound influence of that greatness upon his
subjects.

Even as all roads were said to lead to Rome,
so in England and in other nations governed
after well-approved constitutional methods all
manner of human excellence reaches its summit
near the foot of the throne. The soldier finds
himself the machine of his sergeant, and knows
that his commander is again but the slave of the
captain, and the captain the slave of the colonel ;
and when at last he has mentally ascended, leap
after leap, and finds "dynastic reasons" at the
top of the mighty structure, can it be marvelled
at that his judgment is lost in the dazzle of light ?
Those who hunger and thirst after righteousness
look up to their curate, their vicar, bishop, arch-
bishop, and at length are fain to bow in reverence

before their Defender of the Faith, King, by the Grace of God. The man of commerce, beholding interminable grades in the temples of mammon, can hardly realise how far the best representative of his class is below, a world below, a Prince. Let the Prince but touch with his sword the kneeling form of the highest of poets—that is to bestow upon him a yet higher rank, a conceded place near himself ; and the Carlyles, the Faradays, and the Mills are lost in the inferior grades. He is, in a word, the supreme personage of the most civilised nation of earth.

The Prince of Wales is in person a short, *pansu* (to avoid saying paunchy) German-looking little gentleman of fifty years. Though stout he is by no means particularly well set up, and as is often the case with the patrons and amateurs of sports, racing, and the like, his own "points" are limited as to athletic pretensions—short in the reach, ineffective in stride, hopeless in class, and what one would in another case without ceremony call "tubby." A certain finicking style of walking with a weak knee gives the hint, often confirmed in the Prince's appearance and manner, of the little German gentleman being overlaid by the influence of the French school—say, of Louis XV. The osseous frame, though projected upon no distin-guished lines, is sound enough ; but the muscles, probably never of good quality and suffering from the sins of luxury, are flaccid and unwholesome. The circulatory system is fairly good, but doubtless the strong point of such a constitution is the assimilative power. With this constantly borne in mind, much of the Prince's popularity and no small part of his political success may be fairly explained. "Not on morality but on cookery let us build our stronghold : with stupidity and sound digestion man may front much." This is the extreme position, as speculatively referred to by Herr Teufelsdröckh in "Sartor Resartus" ; but we do not mean to apply it to our particular subject too closely. It has been hinted of late that the Prince's digestion is not what it used to be ; only a pungent little Teufelsdröckh could ever suggest stupidity ; and if morality be asserted as the peculiar forte of the next succession we may well preserve a discreet silence. True it is that a sound digestion may be overtaxed, and the privileges of an unadventurous intellect are rather such as are fostered among men than prevail in the favour of the Gods. The poor Prince, we fear, is a victim of his own bourgeois Paradise.

A glance at his countenance discovers the sad records of bilious attacks—the dull flesh, the sallow complexion, the eyelids fatigued, the unlustrous eye, the weary wrinkles, the harassed unintellectual forehead, the scanty hair of the head, the manner of a man who finds no great stimulation from within,—all these are the judgments of nature on a foolish life.

The wrinkles and the worn cheek of the thinker and the worker are as honourable, surely, as the battle scars of the veteran. Look at a portrait of Pascal or of George Eliot. The countenance even in repose is full of eloquence ; every line is graven with a history, and the shades as well as the depths of expression make a study possibly more delightful than even of the chiselled features of beauty. Look at the Prince. He is exhausted at a glance. The countenance is that of the mediocre man. If that definition be but insisted on, it may be in every act the complete explanation of his conduct, everywhere the fair appreciation of the man. The lines of his countenance are those of good-heartedness, even beaming good nature, sensual pleasures, barren fatigues, unrespected worries, boredom. Withal there is the shrewd look of the man about town ; and the deportment, far removed though it be from the antique type, is nevertheless capable of assuming a bourgeois dignity, and is serviceable if not very imposing even in the most pompous inanities of a Prince's life.

Our pen, we are fain to confess again, can only

dimly sketch the Prince. There is but one man we know of who could fill in the picture. The Prince is a perfect study for Zola.* How he would delight in him—that heavy-handed master. All the elements are there. The *milieu* is a treasure—the sumptuousness, the bourgeois comfort, the upholstered paradise, all the setting of this diamond, the splendour of the halls, the banqueting chambers, the glittering of lights, of jewels, decorations, the brilliance of the ball-rooms, the indescribable distinction of the throng of titled guests, the beauty of the ladies who circulate about this idol, their emulation and their envies, the *flamboyant* magnificence—all this would rise and expand and become enormous, accumulating, with the scintillating and the garish colours flung on, until at length it opened out into the crushing irresistible effect—*épatant*, smashing! Then for the Prince himself—the very sun of this great human galaxy, the bourgeois little personage flattered and bored, with the *teint mat* (dull skin), the *paupières fatiguées*, (dragging eyes), the mediocre little man about whom the whole comedy is played behind these masks.

"It is my trade to be a Prince"—and excellences

---

* *Vide* Nana where the Prince is sketched under the title "Prince d'Ecosse": "d'une distinction de viveur solide"; and, "Il est un peu de mufe tout de même."

and limitations contribute to aid him to play that part to a certain high degree of excellence. Though the Prince is not of an active habit, nor under any stimulus likely to be better than a moderate man, yet he is not badly adapted to long-continued exertion at low pressure ; and if genius be, as it has been defined, the " capacity of being infinitely bored," he may aspire to a distinguished place amongst the Knights of the Bauble.   An attempt to analyse the intellectual parts of the Prince of Wales is useful only as a psychological exertion.   Naturally, he is a cosmo-politan man.   He has travelled much, he speaks many of the European languages, he has met men of every kind, eminent in every sphere of intellectual activity, well-informed upon all the topics of interest in the old world and the new ; and at length in his later days, in utter weariness and emptiness of spirit, he is glad to wile away the evening playing baccarat in no distinguished company.   This is bad, we needs must own, for " fifty years of Europe."   But the result, though lamentable, is not surprising.   A walking-stick traverses the world and is a walking-stick still ; and though the Prince is anything but a stick, yet what he may have done in the " green leaf " has certainly not been conducive to intellectual power in the " dry."

What a Prince sees in his own sphere bears about as much relation to the whole scheme of life as do the pyrotechnics of a popular chemical lecture to the understanding of the depths of the science. Superficial interest soon palls; and a study only commences to be, as we say, "fascinating" when the mere contingencies have ceased to occupy attention and we are beginning to uncover the springs of the wonderful machine. The poor Prince once declared pathetically that he was always interested in chemistry, but never had time to learn it. This we fear was but a temporary wistfulness on the part of His Royal Highness, for the course of life of a man enjoying such great privileges must be mainly determined by the drift of his own interests and tastes, and there is reason to believe that the Prince's attention has been willingly occupied by matters involving considerably more time and less brains than the acquisition of a moderate amount of chemical lore. And similarly with respect to the Prince's companionship—for he who has the opportunity of the society of the best intellects of the land again finds himself, by the inevitable conditions of his tastes, his calibre, and the solicitations of vanity, not the particular friend of the Spencers, or Huxleys, or even of titled poets, but rather of the "smart set," men about town, and not infrequently jockeys and gamblers.

Nor is all this more remarkable than his lapse from the devotion to chemistry. There is no royal road to any kind of distinction except, indeed, if the wonder and admiration of the vulgar be called distinction, that of an adventitious rank. In what sense could the Prince be said to be of the society of Huxley, or Gladstone, or of an Edison, or a Pasteur? To be sure he may walk familiarly, even ostentatiously, with a man of this quality; he may chat with him "affably," and even offer him a cigar; he likes to decorate himself occasionally with a great man, just as he likes to wear a big diamond in his shirt front, or to exhibit himself in the costume of an admiral; but after all, to enter that society is a privilege only to be attained by that determined self-cultivation in knowledge and wisdom that has made these names illustrious. No one will imagine that the Prince of Wales is ever likely to have a throne amidst the " Kings of Thought."

The Prince, and this is also a natural outcome of his environment, has a great memory for details, and trifles. A face once seen, especially if it be that of a good-looking woman, does not readily slip from his recollection; and though he has not risen to the intellectual height of inventing a buckle, yet he would not be far behind George IV. in the appreciation of a bow.

The Prince, then, is not a genius : he has no great ambitions, nor wild enthusiasms. He does not dream of gaining glory on the tented field, nor of emulating Nelson on the perilous waters of the deep, nor of discovering a new land, nor of finding a North-West passage, nor of probing deeply into the profound world of science, not even of chemistry, nor of attuning his people to noble thoughts, nor of witching them with great accomplishments. No. He is far, far away from this. His *forte* is common sense. He wishes to eat, drink, and be merry. There are not the delicate viands of the *gourmet* in the regions of the Poles ; there are no boon companions at the sources of the Nile, nor horse races in Sirius, nor fair women on the bleak heights of science, nor the mollified flesh of content amid the Greek ideals. There is another—a nearer model—Sancho Panza ; and the Prince's "set" have sedulously developed and expanded that cult round his own congenial figure. It is all there.

Yet the Prince is not without reputation among the most cultured of the nation. He holds the pride of place at the annual dinners of the British Association of Literature ; he opens the International Congress of Hygiene and Demography ;

and on the occasion of his presiding at a meeting of distinguished medical men to discuss the question of leprosy, Sir Andrew Clarke made the wisdom at least of his *public* displays the occasion of a remarkably effusive oration.

The emotional side is the Prince's real strong point. In this respect no words but his own German can graphically describe him. He is *wohlbehagen, gemüthlich, gutmüthig.* The meaning may be indicated by saying that these words represent comfort and good nature in German embodiment. Live and let live is his motto. He is on the best of terms with the good people who have made him their model; and his affability, condescension, easy manner, so disengaged from the possible august and severe accompaniments of Royalty, has no parallel in history, and must rather be mated in the freer atmosphere of fiction, as in that creation of an amiable brain, the King in La Mascotte—"You may kiss my royal hand." He is a rare appreciator of good things, a lover of sports, a lover of a good horse, of good music, of opera bouffe, of burlesque, of the circus, a lover of good wine, and choice dishes and good cigars, and all those dainty pleasures of the flesh conceded to so exalted a position. He is bland, conciliatory, tolerant, beaming, and benevolent, and what lends an indescribable charm to his discourse, and makes one forget its peculiar guttural utterance, is that he seems—even when one knows that one is within the atmosphere of greatness—familiar. Translate a Charles II. into the modern Teutonic habit, and you have a fair representation of the Prince ; nor do his subjects reciprocate with any less corresponding degree of loyalty.

We used the word loyalty with shrewd advice in this place, to indicate at one stroke that we are not dealing with the ordinary race of men ; for all the affections, and all the thoughts and intentions that impinge upon the state of a Prince have their distinct and subtle quality. We may be friendly to a man of our own type ; we are *loyal* to a Prince, for in his favour we live. Nor can anything in the previous discourse, even where the hard fact may have seemed to be recalcitrant, be considered in any degree disloyal to England's future sovereign. For loyalty and its obverse, with respect to the Prince by the grace of God, are not matters, we repeat, of ordinary affections, but come to all men and to himself respectively at the very moment of his birth. He becomes our King not because he is wise, or virtuous, or great, or because he is in any human excellence superior to the least considered of his subjects ; he is our King by right of birth ; and the study and criticism of his human faculties, though an instructive and commendable exercise in itself, can have no bearing on prerogatives which by no means take them into account. Yet as in these days scepticism has so far advanced that we reason upon articles of Faith, it is not unnatural, though it may seem inconsistent, to discuss the nature of loyalty. The great excellence of a monarch in this enlightened age is that he interferes not at all in the course of government; and if the flippant ask what then is the advantage of that which merits praise only when altogether useless, the reply must be that there are affections of the soul not to be measured by the standard of a utilitarian philosophy, nor to be subdued to the tyranny of reason. Loyalty is of such a kind.

Nor in this particular is the Prince likely to strain its endurance. For that principle of government which some who are reckoned amongst the wisest of men have excogitated as the best, and which becomes a fair measure of the civilisation of a nation, the Prince has accepted from sheer indolence of temper—*laissez faire*. It is after all the man with a "mission" who, if he be very zealous, becomes at length either the victim of despair or the object of hatred—the man who is inclined to look askance at the amusements of the people, who would curtail the opportunities of vice, and set upon their spirits a discipline of self-improvement ; the man who holds out to them unfamiliar ideas of virtue and greatness, and demands of them an appreciation of principles, which he may have been led to esteem sacred, but for which the whole manner of their upbringing has made them unfit. A Carlyle may amuse himself with appreciations of respectability, and fling about the term "gigmanity," but that is a practical position not to be disturbed by the laughter even of the Gods. A Carlyle may enrage and disport himself like a leviathan because the hero as prophet or the hero as poet is not accepted as the great man ; but a nation whose prosperity and prestige are greatly founded upon commercial pursuits is inclined to think that these careers of heroism are, after all, bad trades ; and not the words of wisdom of a Mill or a Spencer, nor the satire of a Swift or a Thackeray could, even if understood, divert the minds of the majority of men from the worship of a sumptuous show. The bourgeoisie is the bulk of the nation, and the Prince is a bourgeois "writ large." Hence his strong point is his great social influence. He becomes a paragon. Not so much "everybody who is anybody" as everybody who is *nobody* feels the power of society's unwritten laws.

It is true that there was an outcry against the

Prince on a certain occasion ; for it appears that His Royal Highness, then staying at a country house, and being somewhat tired after a hard day's racing and surrounded by somewhat "mixed" society, sat down at length, as we have said, in sheer ineptitude of spirit to play cards for trifling stakes. A scandal arose, and it was hinted that the Prince was in the habit of doing this thing. Philistia rose into dignity, and for a few days the newspapers were deluged with outpourings of cant scarcely less ridiculous than the obverse and habitual kind which is as the very cement to the British constitution. However, it was but a squall, and the Prince emerged with no detriment, not even, one can gravely aver, a diminution of personal dignity. A few days later he figured in the great pageant of the German Emperor, and he was already in the heart of villadom restored ; and when he read his elaborate presidential address to the International Congress of Hygiene and Demography, it was with enthusiasm that the cultured made his rehabilitation complete. He is in a word the most popular man in England. His gainsayers may remember the escapades of his protracted youth, but he is a grandpapa now, and the more active of his follies have ceased to scandalise him ; and if any remain they are but the incidents to be expected in regard both to his

position and his age.   And with this we must
retire satisfied, that, compared with the illustrious
line of British monarchs who have preceded him,
he can hardly fail to be a good and popular King,
an intelligent and doughty Defender of the Faith,
and a typical and peculiarly interesting figure-
head of "our glorious constitution," at what we
sincerely hope may be an epoch-making crisis
of its expansive development.

KAISER WILHELM II

WHOSOEVER, in Berlin about four years ago, had accidentally fallen in with and remained unaware of the rank of the personage who now bears the title Kaiser Wilhelm II, would probably have been content with the simple reference—a young German. But even at that time it needed no great prescience to be able to say that if this young man were ever to ascend the Imperial throne of Germany, where his nod could set in motion all the mighty armies of Europe, and whence his whispers would be telegraphed "in capital letters" to every part of the world—then truly he could not but loom up to the wondering gaze of his contemporaries as a giant, a Titan. . . . The personal appearance of the Kaiser, apart from his usual surroundings, is certainly somewhat insignificant ; but the accoutrements, the sumptuous vestments, the dazzle of decorations and gold embroideries, the brilliant *entourage*, all the pomp and circumstance of an Emperor, must assuredly form in the eyes of men, and

especially in the eyes of his subjects, a spectacle
irresistibly imposing.   This effect of mere exterior
adjuncts it will be important to bear in mind,
not only as being inseparably bound up with
the Kaiser's sway and prestige, but as having
a natural reflex upon his own character.   For
it would be idle to assert that in general a monarch rules the multitude by virtue of superior
gifts or exalted purposes ; and, correspondingly,
we may expect to find him less solicitous for the
philosopher's ideal of the perfecting of the soul
than for the garish shows, the fantastic tricks of
authority, the excursions and alarums that appeal
most effectually to the standards of the mob.   A
man who changes his dress five times in a single
day may excite the contempt of a Brutus, but
may nevertheless, in view of the people whom he
governs, be straining thereby to the eminence of
semi-idolatry and unquestioned right of life and
limb.

Hence for the purposes of our criticism it will
often be necessary to make digressions, on the one
hand to refer to popular judgments, and on the
other to seek out some more justifiable criteria.
To one who has grown up apart from all considerations of royalty it is indeed actually impossible to realise in how far that superstition
may emasculate the intellects of men ; and those

displays of what is called loyalty—still the uneasy propensity of so many—must appear not so peculiarly repellent and despicable as, in a sombre way, pitiable, or at other times undeniably amusing. Particularly is this the case in the atmosphere of Deutschland, where a high standard of intellectual culture has not yet destroyed the traditional tone of servility in the Press and in all expressions of public opinion ; and to give a closer indication of our meaning we will be content with one mild example. The *Vossische Zeitung*, one of the " Freethinking " journals of Berlin, and really just about as Liberal as it is safe to be in the police-ridden Fatherland, had a considerable article describing the enthusiasm which the Kaiser produced at Kiel shortly after his succession to the throne—by appearing in an admiral's uniform on the steps of the Town Hall *an hour before* the promised time. It concluded quite an excited little peroration by the assertion, triumphantly flourished out, that conduct of that kind could not but be regarded as the happiest augury for the future success of the now-so-proud German navy.

Therefore, throughout one's study of the Kaiser it is not sufficient to keep in view merely the man ; but to understand his position and the position of the people whom he governs it is necessary to interpose between any merely human picture we may arrive at a sort of mirage-producing medium that makes his proportions and his acts appear almost fantastic in their magnitude.—When the Kaiser puts on his cap with an air of authority then from "manchem schlichtem munde" (from many a sleek smooth mouth) we are told the words are heard "Das geht," "Das geht"! (That will do, That will do!).

The Kaiser is a small man, not more than 5ft. 5in. in height, slight, but compact. His military training has so far aided the development of his physique as to make it at least fairly serviceable. His countenance has been made familiar to all. One would be curious to know what Lombroso, the author of "l'Uomo Delinquente," and the student of the types of the Roman Emperors, thinks of that countenance. Courage is there undoubtedly, even a certain aspect of aggression. Courage of the type there indicated is a very dangerous quality in the commander of four million fighting men. The dome of the skull is contracted, and there is a disproportion very displeasing between the narrow forehead and the broad and powerful jaws. The forehead is smooth and marked by no lines of deep thought. The countenance on the whole is somewhat shallow in expression and of no great intrinsic interest. Were it not a Cæsar's image it would appear commonplace, and that is all. . . . The temperament of the Kaiser belongs mainly to the class sanguine. But here it is necessary to make certain reservations and explanations. The sanguine temperament, somewhat unscientifically defined, as indeed are all the classes of temperament, is distinguished usually by fair complexion, full-blooded habit, large osseous and muscular systems, considerable physical strength, and general robust health, though with a liability to inflammatory diseases. In the case of the Kaiser, however, this constitution has been vitiated and cheated of its free development by the taints of a bad heredity. The strumous characteristics are not to be concealed—the sallow greyish complexion, the dull eye, appearing at times as though congested, the "wooden look," the impaired energy of movement, the paralysed and atrophied left arm, the chronic disease of the ear—the whole aspect, in short, of a physique of good original type, struggling with a deadly blight. The Kaiser is the unfortunate product of the too close intermarriage of unsound stock.

With perfectly healthy persons the marriage of even first cousins is not necessarily productive of degenerate offspring. The tendency of intermarriage, however, is to intensify morbific elements of the constitutions of the parents. The records of royal families, and of exclusive aristocratical families, especially on the continent, exhibit to a very remarkable extent the dire results of such alliances—struma, phthisis, cancer, insanity, pseudo-hypertrophic paralysis, and neuroses of every kind.   The blood that flows in the veins of Kaiser Wilhelm II is only too imperially "blue," for Nature, knowing not titles, has found no means of eliminating its infused subtle poisons. The race of the Guelphs have that predisposition which expressed itself most violently in the insanity of George III of England.   The mother of the Kaiser is the offspring of a marriage of first cousins. His father died at a comparatively early age of cancer.   The result is, and this has been aided also by the circumstances of his education, that in the son the sanguine temperament has been overridden by the nervous or rather neuropathic factors, with their febrile and ill-regulated activities.

The Kaiser's mental energy is certainly in excess of his physical energy, though both are somewhat deficient.   This judgment is so much at variance with that which has become fashionable that it is necessary to be explicit and circumstantial. Therefore, after referring to some examples of current literature, where we may discover the source rather than the reflex of popular impressions, we will endeavour to set forth at least certain standards of appreciation of intellectual work, and on that basis to arrive at an estimation of the character of the Kaiser's mental acts. Turning, for instance, to the *Review of Reviews*, one finds a " Character Sketch " of Kaiser Wilhelm II, and in these pages of popular reading he figures successively, and with all manner of sensational and preposterous adjuncts, as a Kubla Khan, the Switchback of the Continent, A Hair Trigger, A Toro, A Latter-Day Journalist, A supreme type of the most vigorous type of latter-day journalist, A Prussian Lord Randolph, A Second Napoleon, A General Gordon, A man whose immense vitality seems unable to exhaust itself in labors at which relations and neighbours stand aghast, A Shouting Emperor, A Summus Episcopus, An Educational Reformer, A man who uses a combined knife and fork with one hand, *in this resembling Lord Nelson;* and so on throughout the whole range of tumid and vapid display of, probably, the supreme example of the "supreme type of the most vigorous type of latter-day journalists."

The *Daily News* rushes in, according to the adage, to declare the Kaiser to be a *miracle.* The *Daily Telegraph* has absolutely revelled in its meretricious finery, and the *Times* has laboured dutifully beneath a cumbering load of platitudes. And in the end, "after cloying the gazettes with cant, the Age discovers"—that following hard upon the campaign of a procession in the London streets, and a visit to the Opera House in the evening, this unquenchable little Hannibal has been well enough to take stock of a squad of volunteers in the early part of the day, and finally, with little more preparation and *brouhaha* than requisite for the sailing of a Channel Fleet, has swept away for a three weeks cruise in his yacht. One morning it was possible to read a telegram in the *Times*, in which it was gravely announced as a proof of the astonishing energy of the German Emperor, that, after holding a review of troops at Spandau in the morning, he had ridden to Berlin (a distance of about twenty miles), and was so little exhausted at the close of the day that he was able to take tea (fact) with his mother.

Finding ourselves then somewhat confused in the mirage, it is at this stage that we will divert our immediate attention from the "miracle" in order to search in a somewhat wider scope of things a possible clearer guidance. The highest types of thinkers—though we assert it dogmatically perhaps it would be well, in view of current opinion, to acknowledge certain misgivings—are men like Newton, Darwin, Pasteur, Spencer. A main characteristic of their minds is the con-

firmed habit of analysis and generalisation, the
seeking of the causes of events, and the tracing of
the sequence of events with regard to the law
involved in their occurrence ; all in fact that may
be summed up by saying that they think in *general
propositions.* It becomes their habit of thought to
regard particular circumstances not only for their
value in themselves but also as exemplifications
of more widely applicable principles. No manner
of vagueness is implied herein ; but rather a discipline of thinking is indicated by which the
scientific mind is able to grasp a vast and otherwise impracticable mass of details. Further, in
minds of this character the intellectual energy as
a motive power in itself is very high. The course
of their life's work exhibits synthetic form. The
research of causality, the resolute following out
of inferences, the regard for ethical conceptions
and applications, all grow into a passion.

It is in great measure to men of this class that
the main distinctive features of our modern civilisation are due. Suppose now that we assume
the standard of type to be in this case, as indeed
throughout the whole range of life, not mass but
synthetic development ; then of another type of
intellect next in development to the first we
might cite Napoleon and, in a less degree, Lord
Beaconsfield as brilliant examples. Here, though

we still find of course abundant intellectual activity, the stimulus arises more directly from occasions of immediate importance. The whole project of intellectual life is less cogent, less coherent. The whole scheme, or the series of schemes, of such a life is generally felt even in a popular view to be of lower structure. As we descend the scale we observe that considerations of practical outcome become more and more the pressing matter. The concrete incident is held in relatively greater importance as compared to the principle involved. The attention becomes more devoted to detail. There is less plan and less coherence, and in the sum total of things less importance and less consequence in the products of the mind of less developed type. The philosopher may be a guide a thousand years after his death. Only the material results of a Napoleon, except in so far as he may be a philosopher also, are of great importance to a succeeding generation.

All this may seem to be far away from the discussion of the character of Kaiser Wilhelm II, and indeed we are of opinion that it will be necessary to descend to a level not very exalted to contemplate him. But before referring directly to the acts of his reign, it will be well to throw a glance at the conditions under which alone high intellectual work is possible. Turning, for example, to a subject in which the Kaiser has interested himself—Education—our studies would be greatly aided by consulting the authoritative text-books, and of these the highest place may fairly be assigned to that masterpiece, Bain's "Education as a Science." That book is more than a discourse on the principles of education : it contains implicitly a beautiful exposition of logical methods. The field is a vast one, yet it is adequately grasped ; the problems are deeply based and intricate and involved, but a rare power of analysis has drawn them well into order ; and withal there is in the attack of the whole matter something greater than logical method or perspicacity : there is the clear survey of a great project of intellectual work, and the due regard to proportions and perspective. All the life's labours of a profound and energetic thinker like Bain might, without undue forcing, be considered subsidiary to this achievement ; and in making a study of "Education as a Science" we become convinced that no man of less calibre could have threshed out anything more than tentative views of the subject. What then must we conclude respecting the value of the Kaiser's thoughts upon matters of so great intricacy ? . . . And what has been here suggested

Human Documents

about education has a much wider application, for at a certain level the processes of intellectual work in diverse fields attain a considerable outward similarity. The great jurist with his classifications, his tabulations, his habit of analysis, and his habit of generalisation, endeavours to make his labours as effective as possible by the aid of methods that equally serve the great neurologist or the great botanist. That work again implies long training, and that training in turn implies persistent exercise of thought and a continued endeavour towards logical principles. The knowledge of any particular field, be it jurisprudence, nervous diseases, labour problems, or education problems, implies an assiduity, an *immersion*, in the subject of study.— Every man in his own domain is vehement in vouching for this. The very conditions of a Kaiser's life are therefore fatal to any considerable intellectual status, for that as we note everywhere presupposes a development of brain only to be arrived at by the patient and persistent discipline of thought.

Let the matter be brought to the test of experience. The Kaiser, as a matter of fact, is at one with Bain on an important point in the curriculum of the gymnasia. They both say that the classics have been assigned an importance absurdly out

of proportion to their uses in modern life. Bain
indicates to us how this overweening pretension
of the classics has become recognised. Fostered
legitimately enough at the Renaissance as being
the sole avenues to a learning that had been
neglected for centuries, the classics subsequently
became established by direct endowments; and
now that their advantage has in great measure
passed away, the enormous value of the vested
interests involved gives to that kind of learning
an artificial prestige. Accordingly a great part
of our collegiate course is spent on objects that
are detrimental rather than otherwise, if we
regard the aim of education to be the fitting
of the student to the needs of his actual life.
It requires no great perspicacity to recognise
all this. What was required was simply the
courage to say it, a courage too great for the
generality even of men of calibre, for the influence of the Universities is so great as to throw
a glamour of reputation upon their follies themselves. That courage, however, the philosopher
finds in the calmness of a logical argument;
the Kaiser in the need of assertion of his individual views. Consequently where his individual
views run counter to the ideas of a thinker, we
find this Reformer the most prejudiced of re-
actionaries. He refuses to tolerate Virchow as

Rector of the University of Berlin; he "snubs"
a committee of artists by reversing their award;
he talks at large a crude theology worthy of
Attila; he insults the burgomasters of Berlin
for refraining from laying their hands upon the
liberal newspapers, reminding one of the Teutonic
Count that Carlyle thought obsolete enough to
laugh at in "Sartor Resartus" ("das ausrottende
journalistik"); and even in the very matter of
the reform of the curriculum of the gymnasium
he is desirous of minimising the classics in order
to teach the history, not so much of the German
people as of the Hohenzollern House; and he
directs that French history shall be taught only
from the point of view of the Revolution being
regarded as a crime against God and man.

The Kaiser has his hand on the lever of a
colossal machine, and his every act and his every
opinion are of importance with regard to its
material effects. It does not follow that it is
intrinsically of value in indicating upon his part
either energy or depth of thought, or even power
in developing his own plans. The Kaiser rides out
into the country and apropos of some chimney-
stacks delivers a lecture upon the nation's in-
dustries. But these discourses are not valuable
contributions to economics. His interest in
detail is said to be remarkable; but that is not

the sign of a powerful mind—on the contrary—
unless the detail be the filling up of the lines of
a general scheme of work. The appetite for
detail is not even the best characteristic of a
reporter.

The fact that there is no consecutive plan in
his habit of thinking or in his habit of plotting
is shown by the frequency with which he has
changed his tactics.

And similarly it is necessary to be eclectic to estimate the value of the Kaiser's physical energy. If
the miles of travel be the measure of energy, then
the Kaiser cannot compete with the veriest bag-
man. If athletic prowess be looked for, we cannot
find it in a man of the Kaiser's physique. If the
capacity of sustaining long vigils or of enduring
great toil under adverse conditions be looked on as
the criterion, when have we ever found an instance
of that in the life of the Kaiser? How then can
we interpret on this basis the prominent political
acts of his reign? The answer must be, first of
all, that we must search for the man beneath the
trappings, and endeavour to avoid the mystifica-
tions of the " mirage " of which we have spoken.
For a review of troops is magnified to the proportions of an Iliad, and a pleasure trip becomes
more wonderful than an Odyssey. And further
we must keep in mind that the external conse-

quences of the mental acts of autocrats often bear a very curious relation to the inspiring idea. A Kubla Khan decrees a " stately pleasure dome," though indeed the elevation and beauty of the architectural work may be far removed from the quality of his pleasures. An Ivan of Russia ordains a St. Isaac, though a worshipper neither of the beneficent nor of the sublime. A wonder of the world arises to gratify the whim of a monster. A poor mad King of Bavaria in the midst of a strange extravagance of ideas has one fine inspiration that makes Munich a centre of art. An obstinate and deluded Charles I paves the way to a Commonwealth. An obstinate and well-meaning George III insists upon vindicating certain of his prerogatives by that " shooting down in heaps" that led at length to the Independence of America. A weak and well-meaning Louis XVI is swallowed up in the storm of the Revolution. The Kaiser overturns a Bismarck by the use of that instrument of tyranny that the Iron Chancellor himself had so elaborately built up.

He proclaims himself a child of the Newer Time. He receives the delegates of the Westphalian strikers, and threatens slaughter should they venture to oppose his will. He presides at an International Labour Congress. We are kept *au courant* with his journeys, his voyages of pleasure, with the minute details of his vestments, the details of his eating and drinking, and we are always mystified respecting the details of his health. We hear of him directing theatres, encouraging anti-socialistic plays, pronouncing— nay, "his speech was a thunderbolt" (*vide* "Supreme type") on education, posing as a War-Lord, and declaring himself to be the Preserver of Peace. Consider the amount of valid, effective intellectual energy involved in these displays. He speaks : Let there be a Labour Conference, "Thousands at his bidding speed." He smiles patronisingly on M. Jules Simon, and forthwith he takes high rank as a Political Economist and Friend of Man. He institutes a great drama, "The New Master," and the Teutonic Talmas cannot fail to discover their Napoleon. What then is the reasonable value of this man's opinion upon the Labour Question, upon Education, upon Religion ?

What assistance would his mind be able to render the diligent student, whose concern is not with the glamour and the "baaing vanities" of Royalty, but who is bent on seeking a cogent exposition of his subject ? Has the Kaiser made a profound study of these problems ? Has he considered down through all their perplexing details the consequences of proposed acts of legislation ? Or do not these explosive outbursts ("his speech was a thunderbolt"), with all their theatrical situations and sensational fireworks, savour less of the thinker than of the Roman Emperors who succeeded Augustus?

The argument need not be over-ridden. The Kaiser's intellect is of the order incoherent, active but desultory, and only remarkable because armed with authority. The best service of such a mind, as well illustrated, for example, by Napoleon III, is in an executive capacity. And here, it must be said, is an undoubted strong point of Kaiser Wilhelm II. He has the advantage of being surrounded by men of great knowledge and sagacity, but this advantage is in no small measure due to his own acumen in selecting his advisers, and also to a certain much-to-be-respected quality in his tastes and a masculine dignity well befitting the youthful Head of his House. Truly the best function of an executive is to carry out the suggestions of the men of understanding ; and logically we cannot but be convinced that its nearest approach to excellence in a Constitutional monarch consists in becoming as automatic as possible. The best characteristic of a monarch is to be a nonentity.

The moral qualities, or rather the displays of conduct of a man, are in the main fairly to be

inferred by estimating both his emotional characteristics and his intellectual power and range taken
in conjunction with the *milieu* of his activities.
The emotional qualities again are to a considerable
extent practical corollaries from his physical constitution ; the impulses, however, being continually
reacted upon by the stimulations and restraints
of the surroundings. Therefore all manner of
considerations must be taken into account in
interpreting an emotional display. It is not,
for example, the powerful character that exhibits itself in violence, nor in these latter days
would an epileptic fit be taken as a sign either
of divine possession or of the superabundance of
animal vigour and health. Accordingly we are
not surprised to find that Michelet, in a fine
criticism of Marat, points out the delicacy, the
over-strung sensitiveness, the womanish nature of
that individual. That is the true type for a Reign
of Terror. Robespierre was a man certainly of
tougher clay, of more control, than Marat, yet
withal lacking in the emotional powers of a great
leader. Pressed hard he uses the lethal weapons
that a Mirabeau or a Napoleon would have for-
borne to bring into the conflict. The Kaiser's
displacement of Bismarck must also be regarded
in this light, for it will hardly be said that the
strong man was overthrown by a stronger man.

The edge of vanity and ambition was turned against the imperious statesman who had made Kaisers possible. The weapon was to hand. To strike was to cast off an incubus grown intolerable. The old lion was thrown down, and the asses rushed in to kick him ; and the fate of Bismarck is a satire upon the whole of the Blood and Iron work of his strenuous life. The minions of the Chancellor have found a new idol, and their adulation is bolstered up in language savouring often of flat blasphemy. It is in this environment that it is necessary to consider the Kaiser's temperament. His natural courage has been fostered by the habit of command and the delight in the exercise of power. The commander of great troops rejoices therein like Briareus of old rejoicing in the strength of his limbs. But it must not be forgotten that this military hero has not yet fleshed his maiden sword ; and courage, judgment, decision, resolution, depend on the repeated experiments and tentatives that serve to map out for a man his limits. The fearless sailor would be aghast at taking a five-barred gate. The brilliant Little Corporal wavered and blenched before the clamours of the Five Hundred ; it remained for the Abbé Sieyès to urge him on. Yet though we speak of strength of will, decision, courage, as being greatly dependent on a knowledge of the field, there still remains to be taken into account the fundamental difference of fibre that makes one man bold and successful where another halts and trembles. Kaiser Wilhelm II gives one the impression of a man resolute to meet danger. And if there be exceeding arrogance, the personal note being always dominant, it is nothing more than we must, of course, expect to find. Maudsley tells us that the child is the true egoist, but he would doubtless consent to join with the child the autocrat. Between these limits the personal idiosyncrasies are continually being pressed on and tested by the weight of opinion and the necessity of conformity. Under these circumstances self-assertion may, it is true, be the characteristic of a powerful and superior nature, and may fairly well win out its vindication. But the child and the imbecile, on the other hand, are egoistic by reason of their limited objective world, and the autocrat is egoistic because that objective world is not made sufficiently realisable to him in restraint. The danger in this latter case is lunacy; and the history of former empires furnishes the sad and convincing commentary. The Kaiser would appear to think that Europe exists only to fill in the pages of his biography—a delusion, it may be said, easily paralleled elsewhere, and hurtful only when escaping the bounds of necessary beneficent control. In the case of a young Kaiser puffed up by the idea of military glory and commanding four millions of doughty warriors, a situation very interesting to Europe may suddenly be created.

The Kaiser is the modern Teutonic representative of the Louis XIV tradition—*l'état c'est moi*—a tradition that, joined with laxity of purpose in the case of Louis XVI, and with rigidity of temper in the case of Charles I, proved disastrous to its believers. But it is in this atmosphere that the Kaiser must be contemplated.

The *Roi Soleil* marched booted and spurred into his Parliament, and set Europe ablaze while toying with his *mignonnes* at Versailles ; the Kaiser affects more serious coquetry, but the motive force is the same in both.

The Kaiser, withal, in common with Louis XIV, in common with the *parvenu* Napoleon Bonaparte, in common with Cæsar, with Tamerlane, with Charlemagne, has that note of the ruler— the sense of authority, power, governance, which is after all perhaps the most distinctively masculine of qualities—that which made Agamemnon and not Achilles leader, Jupiter and not Apollo or Vulcan supreme. This quality is fundamental, characteristic, impregnable. And consistently with this idea the Kaiser, like Charles I and the

Roi Soleil again, has built up a little scheme of theocracy to suit his conditions—God, the Kaiser, the German nobility, the people; there is the Hierarchy. And we find again the same "infantile familiar clasp of things divine." Louis XIV averred that the *Bon Dieu* would think twice before interfering with a man of his condition. The Kaiser assures his soldiers that their old ally of Rossbach will step in without fail to the strains of the *Die Wacht am Rhein*.

Apart, however, from such a culmination to our civilisation, it is pleasing meanwhile to note that the Kaiser in his moral conduct is temperate, but not ascetic. He eats and drinks moderately, and is much less devoted than is usual in the "highest circles" to the elaborate cult of the stomach. Happily married, and the father of several promising youngsters, it is worthy of especial commendation that he has abandoned the vices of his early manhood, and though supreme in station lives decently. He eschews the imbecilities of the gaming table, and interests himself in the conversation of capable men. Further, one who has been blessed with the happiness of domestic life, and who has been made familiar with physical pain and mental anguish, has necessarily been led to sympathetic feelings. Accordingly we find the Kaiser well-meaning towards all sorts and

conditions of men, except those, to be sure, who
are in any way opposed to him. He pities the
poor, and fain would mitigate their sufferings.
His view of society being that of an elaborate
hierarchy of impassable grades, himself the one
absolute ; within this scheme it would gratify
him to see his household well appointed. He
welcomes all who are bent on assisting him ; the
disobedient he threatens to shatter in pieces. . . .

But before concluding it may be well to contemplate the obverse side of the picture, for the
adulation of those who discourse of the Kaiser
in dithyrambs is paralleled by the cynical detrac-
tion of his enemies ; and between what Diogenes
of old called the most dangerous of beasts—the
flatterer, the tame beast ; the slanderer, the wild
beast—it is possible that this over-zealous young
man may come to a very bad end. However,
shortly after the Kaiser's triumphal progress through
London, and while on his famous cruise on the
Hohenzollern, it was reported that he had injured his knee. Thereupon a Parisian journal of
second-rate importance, *l'Eclair*, served up to its
readers a sensational account of the misadventure,
written not without a humorous appreciation
of its own preposterous performance, but otherwise worthy even of our own "supreme type of
the most vigorous type." Therein was recorded

that the Kaiser had appeared on the deck of his vessel wearing a white chasuble. Setting up two altars, he began by reading the most warlike passages from the Old and New Testaments. Afterwards he orated to the sailors, at considerable length, on the duties of a sovereign and the duties of his subjects. He then descended to his cabin. Soon he reappeared in the uniform of an admiral, and commanded the captain to go below. The captain ventured to suggest danger ahead, but was forced to comply, the Kaiser declaring that God would aid him. The second officer, however, refused to leave his post, perceiving that his Imperial master, though much in need of aid, was rather in the condition of those whom the Gods have resolved to destroy, viz., stark mad. Thereupon ensued a dreadful struggle, ending in the Kaiser fracturing his knee-cap, and being confined to a padded room till the paroxysm of mania had passed away.

It is hardly necessary to be gravely assured that the story was a *canard*. It was monstrous and incredible on the face of it. It had as much sense of reality as Gulliver's elaborate descriptions of the Liliputians. But now that very phrase is suggestive.

For can it be that the witty rascal of a Frenchman had taken a leaf from the immortal volume of Swift? Can it be that as Swift delineates in miniature our modern world, *l'Eclair* has but reduced the proportions of an episode? Truly the strangest follies, if they be but magnified enough, loom up or boom up towards incomprehensible sublimity. The mind which seizes the absurdity of Kaiser Wilhelm navigating a ship regards him with complacency directing the course of a nation. The mind which recoils with horror at a disaster at sea and the drowning of a ship's crew rejoices mightily in the prospect of European war and the slaughter of hundreds of thousands of men. The white chasuble is but a modest vestment to bestow upon a Summus Episcopus. The sermons from the Old Testament are not ill-befitting a War-Lord. And fortunate would it be if but the *dénouement* of this reign were to take place before the actual disasters that it seems to portend. . . . Bewildering chaos of human life! Gargantua's boisterous laughter is heard through all our tragedies. Our spiritual foes range from Lucifer to Punchinello.

Finally, let us regard the conditions within which the whole problem is confined. The conditions of the wellbeing of a people are broadly based upon the relation of population to the productivity of the country, and the facilities of exchange. The functions of the best legislature would therefore be to remove in as far as possible the restraints, internal and external, to the exercise of those powers that subserve the gathering of all excellent produce and its due distribution. Of all those causes that tend to multiply restraints, destroy productivity, and embarrass exchange, war is the most disastrous. If but these cardinal principles be clearly appreciated, it will appear on the one hand that a wise Kaiser can do comparatively little for his people, for the simple reason that the conditions are almost entirely beyond his scope, and his best service would be but to destroy the elaborate machinery of his own power ; but on the other hand it is evident that a foolish Kaiser can bring "woes unnumbered" upon his land. It is but the old satire again of King Log and King Stork. The "Gods are just," and not only of our "pleasant vices," but also of our cowardice and folly make "instruments to scourge us."

JOHN BURNS

John Burns is the Mirabeau of the British proletariat, and Mirabeau's description of his own personal appearance, "a tiger pitted with the small-pox," would be little overstrained in application to John Burns. Whoever has seen him in moments of suppressed passion would be struck by this—the low, flat forehead, the dark and grizzled or brindled hair drawn back, the short tawny beard, the nostrils quivering with the deep inspirations of breath, the eye flaming, jetting out flashes—the man intent and fierce.

John Burns is of middle height, well endowed physically, strong, tough and muscular without being big or burly or even athletic in shape. His constitution is adapted to his life of prodigious physical energy, wear and tear, violent commotion, sleepless nights, and all the hard campaign of London strikes. His temperament is in the main sanguine, though his physique is worn by a life of toil at high pressure, and the whole aspect of the man is that of one harassed, but also to

some extent refined, by continual difficult encoun-
ters and frequent occasions of nervous stress and
strain. His mental energy is remarkable, but it
belongs to that kind in which mental application
owes much assistance to the endurance of the
physical powers. He is neither a many-sided
man, nor of a complex intellectual type, nor
inclined to, nor perhaps capable of appreciation
of, high intellectual work. On a much lower level
we must expect, naturally enough, to gauge the
intellect of John Burns. He is like the man who
sees the screw of a steamship, and cries out that
now at last he has beheld unmistakably the
motive force of it all. The printer and the book-
binder are the makers of books. That is evident.
The hodman is the visible builder.

To be sure he can lift his vision above this, but
there is conflict on the way ; for the publisher,
for instance, and the architect see clearly enough
that it is only to accomplish *their* designs that the
proteges of Burns are called into existence ; and
so in the estimation of the requisite degree of
oppression their elastic consciences are adjusted
only by the resistance from below. Accordingly
the limitations as well as, in this regard, the uses
of our Tribune are determined by the somewhat
base and unenlightened but very practical position
of his opponents. He takes the measure of what

he can see, and plunges into the middle of things
and smites vigorously wherever he finds a good
point of attack, endeavouring to make hisinfluence
felt, not only by his own activity, but by his encouragement to others.   But, naturally, his intellectual structure, though full of good service in
its range, is somewhat truncated.   Even within
his own sphere his mind, though healthy and
rational, is not highly circumspect, and in a still
less degree analytical.   He says :   All men are
born equal ; privilege is tyranny.   He says :   We
must throw away the useless scabbard of Trades
Unionism, and take up the bright and shining
sword of Legislation—for that seems to him the
best means of slaying free competition.   He does
not stop to consider in a large scope the question
of free competition, nor the tyrannies of his own
proposed legislation.   His idea of social intercourse is a sort of universal brotherhood, yet
he beholds his own little community torn by a
hundred jealousies and the discords of personal
vanities, passions by no means scourged out of
himself ; his ideal of society at large is a stu-
pendous inconceivable structure of Socialism,
monstrous in design, contradictory in operation,
and, indeed, with respect to all practicability,
farcical.

By no means is this contradictory to the statement that John Burns has plenty of intellectual activity. Belief does not depend on reasoning, except in matters removed from passion. Belief is more often the obscure expression of some great emotional want. The examples are every-where around us—the scientific man, finding no foothold in the religions which have comforted others, whirls into the extravagance of Spiri-tualism ; the pious follower of Christ is still content to believe we live in a Christian age, beholding millions armed for mutual slaughter, and meeting on every hand the preposterous instances and arguments of the Churches ; and those again who have beheld our modern civilisa-tion built up by the workers, the great inventors, the heroes of literature, the champions of liberty, turn aside to the worship of the Golden Calf.

Myriad are the examples of our human errors ; yet behold even in the pursuit of follies the ant-like activity of the man. For in this human life it would seem that it is not as though we worked out a cogent problem and held up a finger for the intercession of Providence. Our fabrics tumble into chaos, and the world has not swerved from its course. Brutus cries out that he has pursued virtue throughout life and finds it at length a shadow. Yes, but dost thou presume to measure the whole scheme of things by thy standards of

virtue? . . . The anchorite exclaims in anguish :
I have lived chaste in body and soul, and go now
to the grave unblest, unrewarded by any guerdon.
But to be chaste, does that sum up the whole end
and purport of man ? . . . Will godliness of mind
save you in the shipwreck, where the swimmer
only is able to strike out lustily to land ?   Will a
sweet and persuasive manner of speech avail that
a house built on the sand may not be swept away
in the storm ?   Or will the most speculative and
metaphysical mind be of much service in a contest
with navvies or dockers ?

These complaints are really the offspring of
pessimism, for by the complexity of our difficulties so has the complexity of our own faculties been evoked, and so are we linked each to
each.   The biceps muscle will do the work of the
biceps and that only, nor will at any time an exalted
perception of musical harmonies supply the place
of that particular factor in culture. . . . Truisms
doubtless, but the principle here involved is in
general sedulously banished from the mind.   Culture, morality, education, must be regarded with
reference to the whole scope and purport of a life
within its environment.   Consecutive reasoning
forms but a small part of the plan even of a man's
intellectual life ; each is a complex being thrown
into a whirl of like atomies, each with its narrow

little "free-path"; and within his corner, struggling in the storm, the individual strives here and there to make his faculties tell, and to gratify the more imperative of the demands of his emotional nature. And so it may happen that John Burns, doing some good and attempting much that may really be productive of evil, and heating his brain with ideas that would be intolerable were they not utterly futile, may yet stand on as high an intellectual level as many who fill the dubious pages of history.

John Burns has in great proportion that kind of mental energy that subserves tenacity of purpose, endurance, resources. He is in all moods full of pluck, dashing at a charge, stubborn in resistance. He has travelled a good deal, searching knowledge everywhere, that kind of knowledge that has a bearing on the practical duties of life, or at least those aspects of life that enter in the purview of his own political economy. Few men have a wider knowledge of trades, of the conditions of the lower forms of industry, of workmen, and of the details of their life. He is a considerable reader, and has grappled with Herbert Spencer, though not very intelligently. It is sad but not wholly without amusement to hear him "pitching into" the philosopher.

His intellectual training has lacked a proper

foundation. He seems to have no clear intellectual outlook, but is content to flounder interminably in the floods of false solutions poured forth in Socialistic literature. Anything he cannot understand he rejects in the bulk, refraining not at all from denouncing his intellectual opponents in rhetorical strains to the open-mouthed wonder of the proletariat—"'e guv it 'ot to 'Uxley."

So too with the morality of our tribune. He has neither the time nor the temperament for patient, explicative thought in matters of belief or exquisite points of casuistry. Simple and direct in character, earnest and, at bottom, honest and healthy, it is a natural feeling in him to hate degeneracy and wrongdoing, and particularly the "sweating" of the poor. He is content with dogma and plain doctrine. He requires settled positions there, and he does not go far afield. John Burns, not renouncing the hatred of the rich, loves the poor. He has shared their toils and endured their oppressions, and felt their vague aspirations. He has raised himself above the limits of their life, and has remained true to his old associates. He is a lion amongst them, and he is their leader. It is a great emotional world, that of John Burns— the storms, the baffled purposes ; the hopes and fears of which he feels the very pulse ; the hard battling, the hot affections of a great people. It is at the head of his proletariats that John Burns particularly shines. His presence is "magnetic." His vehemence is infectious. His courage and his faith rouse his people to enthusiasm. They shout their responses hoarsely, and each man and each woman tries to get the closer to him in spirit by shouting the more loudly. He carries them away in a sort of strong emotional wave.

His orations, however, though passionate, are even in their barbarous metaphors still based on the practical, and leave no doubt as to their purpose :—

" All right, men. We're starting from Poverty Corner —(murmurs)—but we've got two good old horses at the pole, and one of 'em is called—Trades Unionism, and the other is called Strike—(wild cheers)—and if we stick together, men, we'll drive along through Oppression Street, and out of Starvation Lane, and we won't pull up till we've passed through the Gate called Twelve Hours a Day ! (Enthusiasm.)"

Or again :—

" What have the aristocracy done for us ? Are they any better than us? ('No !') Are they any better in education ? ('No ! no !') Better in moral character? (Loud shouts of ' No !') Better in pluck—(contempt)— or good for the country? (Vehement cries, ' No ! no ! no !') I tell you what it is, men. They're the drones of the community, and live by demoralising your wives and your daughters, and exploiting the labours of the British proletariat !   (Sensation, turbulence.) "

So John Burns fills the ears of the people with his big, shouting voice. And counting the heads of his followers he overrates the power of that undisciplined and ill-provided host. His movement grows, but he takes but insufficient account of the huge-organised and strongly in-trenched forces of his enemies. He sees but the local results of his purposes, and neither greatly speculates upon, nor is inclined to heed, the effect on inter-related spheres. Movements of this kind, however, have produced revolutions elsewhere, and John Burns is just the man who, in a more excitable community, might have figured in the early stages of a revolution, a man able to work like ten, a believer in his purpose, ambitious and vain, it is true—but that drives him on ; free from corruption, a man trusted by his followers ; a Tribune of the People on forty shillings a week. In England a revolution he would hardly consider feasible, nor in any respect advisable ; not indeed, and this reason holds the others, necessary. He has a better instrument. And so too have those who fear violent and irrepressible tumults from his agitations. There are many reasons why John Burns should have a seat in Parliament.

This "document," down to the last sentence, was written before John Burns had become a Member of Parliament. The import of that sentence has been fully verified by John Burns's subsequent career. That career has been a renunciation of many of his former principles, and an undoing of much of his early work.

But, to be just, it should be questioned also, as to whether in much of this renunciation and undoing, Burns has not acted, if not with candour and nobility, at least with shrewdness and common sense. No doubt as a red-hot Socialist John Burns at the beginning of his career was perfectly sincere, sincere partly because of the limitations of his knowledge and the insufficiency of his reflections. But even while sincere he was accustomed to utter a good deal of what must have sounded even to himself in calmer moments as bombast and bunkum. And, moreover, as invariably happens when a man is a working member of an organisation, he was compelled to approve of policies and tactics in the programme of the Social Democratic Federation, which his practical business aptitude must occasionally have condemned as ridiculous.

With John Burns's entrance into Parliament begins a period of education, not a little unexpected and surprising to himself. He discovers in the first place how little he can actually do; how poor a weapon is this "bright and shining sword" that cut such a fine figure in the peroration of a Hyde Park speech. He discovers also that the structure of society is very different to that of his early imaginations; that the broad image of a working class supporting on its shoulders a community of drones — "bloated capitalists," "gilded popinjays," and the rest — is absurdly untrue. He begins to explore in a thousand unexpected fashions the subtle structure of our civilisation; he begins to discover the profound import of phrases that before were mere rough indications—"higher education," "science," "division of labour," " interdependence of parts," "organisation of society," "complexity of type," "function," and the rest. Even "culture," even "art," are words that give him intimations of deep and marvellous meanings; nay, he discovers that there are privileges almost impossible to eradicate even—*infandum*—in "birth."

He discovers that Society is exceedingly complex because it has developed according to successive needs; and that where it is faulty is simply in the lingering of the relics of old organs and functions that have served their turn, or in the obstacles set to the introduction of new beneficial agencies. He discovers that above the

manual labourer are classes of intellectual workers
in whose hands is entrusted tacitly the very
palladium of our civilisation—the scientific men,
the professional men, the artists, the thinkers,
the promoters of great enterprises. He perceives
that the work of these is often thrown amid
circumstances not less severe, and certainly demanding the concurrence of a hundred times
rarer qualities, than that of the mere labourer.
And he finds that it is often by the development
of these classes that the work of the labourer is
provided at all. He discovers that apart from
factitious organisations with which he has been
associated, and to which he has restricted the very
term organisation, there exists a tacit organisation
of Society, far more complex, far better tested,
and far more durable than any artificial combinations. And he begins to realise that in the
complexity of Society the vast formless power of
the masses is not so terrible as that of the
successive grades that really severally hold the
"people" in their hands. He finds that his
agitations and demonstrations are like the waves
of the sea beating themselves in futile fury against
an immovable breakwater.

And then too in Parliamentary action he
discovers that a mere voice, even an eloquent
voice, has little power except as representative of

a movement, a power outside ; and that of the
six hundred or so grave and reverend seigneurs,
dull and uninspired as they may be for the most
part, the majority are representatives, each of
some special interest, and that the test they demand of the validity of any theory is the actual
working out of that theory in practical life.   They
demand even that it shall be weighed in money
value ; in sounding gold.

And hurtling against this multitude·of obstruc-
tions, hardly visible before, this *vis inertiæ* of a
sober, well - settled, conservative nation, John
Burns finds how helpless have been most of his
own projects, how vastly more telling, more
practical, and even, for the most part, more just,
is this silent standard of values, and how viewy,
frothy, and empty have been most of his own
flamboyant rhetorical efforts.

He discovers that the best meaning even of
Republicanism is rather that of the Republicanism of Rome, or of Greece, or of contemporary France; that in fact the Republicanism of
the purest minded enthusiasts and patriots, of
the Mazzinis and the Castelars, must preserve the
hierarchies of powers, even though the principle
that determines the *personnel* that fills them
be changed; that in fact after the upheaval of
the old *régime* in France the only stable constitu-

tion must perforce imitate in great part the ancient structure.

John Burns, likewise, though not perhaps setting forth the matter in a definite exposition, has been brought to see that even the despised Herbert Spencer has not always talked reactionary nonsense, that in fact his own experiences have led him to appreciate the force of Spencer's Principle of Evolution—the development from an amorphous, indefinite, and simple structure to a highly complex structure extremely differentiated in function, yet all bound organically together.

In the course of these experiences John Burns has turned away from much of his early teaching and has quarrelled with many of his former colleagues. Seeing clearly the folly of much of their programme, he has too much common sense, and, even in the midst of his inconsistencies and intrigues and wrigglings, too much honesty, to return into the old camp. His old colleagues have attacked him with acrimony; he has replied with violence and extravagance. The position of a popular idol he has found very difficult to maintain, because a mob has the mind of a child. He had promised it the moon; it clamours for the moon; and it is little pleased when he tells it, with asperity, that the moon is unattainable.

Jealousy, vanity, the combative spirit, the

necessity of securing himself if only to further his ideas, are all motives that have pulled him hither and thither in his course, and the simplicity of stump oratory and agitation of the Tribune has given place to the more complex wire-pulling and intrigue of the political Boss. The great but rather bombastic Socialist has developed into the practical but not quite ingenuous Liberal.

Happy is England to-day in this respect, for example, that every movement for social advance and the amelioration of the condition of the people, even if delayed and thwarted at first, may be sure of attracting at length to its standards unselfish and zealous advocates, and generous helpers drawn from every class in the community.

Unhappy again is England in that these social stirrings and strenuous endeavours towards a new state of things are brought into existence by fearful and widespread miseries and almost desperate maladjustments, and that most of the schemes of improvement, the outcome maybe of noble aspirations, are ill-conceived, ill-reasoned, hopeless of feasibility, and even self-defeating.

But in order to throw a glimpse upon the environment of which we have to treat, it will help us at the outset to consider one cardinal position. Our great social structure grows, adapting itself according to contingencies, combining opposing factors, curtailing, expanding, developing itself, not upon any provident *rationale* of its members, but with infinitely more complexity and, so to speak, infinitely more intelligence than the wisest and the most complex of its individuals. It is true that the most unthoughtful and simple of Socialists is ready at a moment's notice, not merely to give a better shaping to the whole scheme and every detail of the structure, but out of hand and *a priori* to give us an entirely new one. There is no need, however, in order to dissuade from undue hopes in these ready-made Utopias, to make a very strenuous appeal to men whose brains are in an ordinary way considerate ; for even in every commercial enterprise that has attained any noticeable development, whether it be the railway system, or the banking system, or the manufacture of soap or blacking, one cannot but be struck with the sort of inevitableness of extension and complexity, utterly incapable of being foreseen even by the most intelligent of the originators, and bearing indeed to the germinal idea the same relation that an oak does to an acorn. The problem of Society, however, containing as it does these and a million other diverse elements, is immeasurably more complex ; and this complexity is rendered intricate even to the degree of bewildering confusion, by the fact that there are to be discovered in its development no clear authoritatively expressed standards, no defined or in any respect decisive purposes, still less any single intelligible aim.

Dealing with only one aspect of this strange organism, which the sum total of all our little intelligences does not contribute to make conscious, we find that the conditions of individual life—let us say, to come down to a point, the rates of wages, for example—are determined in the main by competition, and the question of competition again hinges upon the larger problem of population. Then, bearing in mind the *tendency* of population continually to increase, we shall see, and with the greater clearness in the lower grades of society, that the question is finally one of maintenance of one's position, in unending contest, above a certain level under which existence is no longer possible—what we may call the death-level.

This death-level is always fluctuating and uncertain with respect to an entire class, and still more so in the individual case, and may be influenced ultimately and through a long consecutive series by a failure of wheat in Russia or by a bad season for wool in Queensland, and, indeed, by a thousand causes of direct and indirect incidence. The workman who has provided for his family fairly well for years, is suddenly called to book on account of contingencies completely out of the scope of his ideas, and finds himself and his family menaced with extinction. The problem is not at all definitely worked out and ticked off to his understanding. Poverty and helplessness deprive him of the few little good things that made life supportable, and of the power of making any effectual resistance to disease : influenza, diphtheria, typhoid fever, pneumonia, or what not of diseases arising from not irremovable conditions, do their work.

"Hell is a city much like London," Shelley said ; but eliminating the superfluous supernatural "spook," and regarding Hell as a place of punishment of ourselves and punishment of our children for our sins of commission and omission ; intellectual, moral, and physical shortcomings ; and especially for the definite crime or "tort" of poverty ; then Hell is actually in London, less æsthetically grand, but hardly less in misery than Dante's. Beneath the death-line, wherever it be, and with its agencies invisible beneath the show of things, that underground London is Hell.

And it is in this *milieu* that we have to consider the thousand efforts and movements for the salvation of the people from the last depths of despair ; but we are afraid that if ever Macaulay's New Zealander stalk through the ruins of our exquisite civilisation, he will find amongst the shades of those who have departed a solitary thinker here and there to a legion of what we may call "enthusiasts"; but the thinker by no means their leader. Nor is it too presumptuous so to express oneself, for the various movements themselves are antagonistic or inconsistent one with the other, and not a few indeed, as we have said, self-contradictory.

If one turn to the Socialists, with the most burning and very best desire of being of their goodly company, he finds that amongst the Socialists themselves there are a hundred fine but never-to-be-healed divisions all disputing as vehemently, or perhaps—according to the *odium theologicum* —more vehemently than if their ideas were in the least feasible or capable of inception.

Here for instance is one—whether Marxist or Possibilist one knows not, Impossibilist doubtless—who with perfervid utterance and coruscating eye would persuade us to be all equal in talent, in education, and in privilege, and, himself directing the rather complicated machinery, would make elaborate provision for interfering with the minutest details of each of his "equals'" affairs—even the milkman being "municipal," and of course the "poet" and the "philosopher" also —and our Socialist would order even the texture of our souls and the colouring of our thoughts.

However, as long as the earth is inhabited by our present erring but aspiring little selves or our descendants, we fear that this community will never rear its simple but sublime plateau. Again we find a " Fabian " who has arranged everything according to the little clockwork of his own brain, but, being too elaborate in culture and diffuse in speculation, and having no great initial impetus, pursues for ever the policy of delay, and in the end paves our Hell with nothing better, but luckily nothing worse, than his own good intentions. Or again, another of the same circumstantial sect, an irresponsible Irishman perhaps, though in favour in a general way of universal brotherhood and "all sorts of things like that," is at bottom constitutionally disposed to let, in the concise formula of the Far West constitution, "every man do as he dam please." Or again, amidst a hundred remarkable charters and schemes we cannot avoid hearing of one, that of the Salvation Army, a scheme which is zealous and alive, but which after all, like a war-dance of North American Indians, " proves nothing," and perhaps leaves its zealots weaker in the end than at first. We refer not at all to the religious exercises of these militant champions of the doctrine of non-resistance, but to the definite social scheme of General Booth. In project, that can never be anything better than a treatment of symptoms and consequences of a social disease of which the principle is left completely untouched. It is but on a par with all those schemes of tentative relief, whether by virtue of Government Poor Laws or by private benevolence, of which the fundamental fallacy has been shown, and of which the unlooked-for sad results have been practically verified, times without number. It is in fact but the depression of the death level by adventitious conditions. The toiler, not perhaps the individual but the class, is by the unchecked operation of the processes which have told against him hitherto soon forced again to that level, and finds himself more hopelessly dependent than before. The tendency is in fact for ever to drive the workman towards the fluctuating line of death ; and there can be no hope of a surcease from that operation even by permanent, much less by temporary and merely local adjustments of the level, nor indeed is there hope even in divine renunciations and self-sacrifice above. The question, apart from individual cases, is simply one of social statics; and the settlement of the foundations of our Society must be determined by the resistance from *below*.

We will not delay by referring to any other plans or movements, even though some may appear to be wider in scope than that which now immediately concerns us; nor will we refer to the vexed questions of parties and politics. One may have desired simply to take a glance at the environment, and without committing one's self to faith in anything more than local good effects of the trades unions. One might expect to meet with, if less enthusiasm than in any form of socialistic scheme, yet on the whole more valid grounds of assurance in looking to a movement which has grown up step by step, always in touch with the stern guidance of experience, and which has developed from the spasmodic unions of classes of men for temporary purposes into permanent systems of union with elaborate organisations.

The trades unions have shown the depth, the genuineness, and the vitality of their movement by persistently setting forth a resolute and fairly consistent policy, and by bringing to the front at each stage of increasing complexity the men best fitted to control the powerful but difficult machine. And of these modern tribunes of the people none is perhaps more worthy of study than the subject of our sketch ; and we will do our best therefore to arrive at a fair estimation of his character.

Tom Mann is of medium height, muscular, well packed up, and athletic. The head neither large nor small, well poised and well shaped, fits into the symmetry and balance of the general frame.

The first and the last impression one has of Tom
Mann might be fairly enough contained even in
that brief description. He is "ship-shape," taut,
trim, and handsome, built to stand rough weather.
To differentiate, however, the individual from the
type, it must be said in detail that his hair is dark,
usually closely cropped, and the forehead is neither
high nor broad nor marked with the lines of deep
thought. There is nothing of luminous insight,
nor of divine afflatus, nor genius, nor even of
great enthusiasm about Tom Mann. He is a
workman-like, hard-headed leader of the trades
unionists. He would be accounted a good man
in any part of the world and at any time—amongst
Kaffirs or Maoris, if we can imagine his fate to
have been so cast, or in Rome in the sturdy days
of old. Cromwell would have been gravely satisfied with a sound fellow of that stamp for captain;
John Smith, the founder of Virginia, would have
found him the trustiest of henchmen; Danton
might have slapped him on the shoulder and
made him a deputy in the provinces.

Yet Tom Mann has been born right into his
proper time. His talents fill the measure of his
work, and none runs to waste. His countenance,
though not highly intellectual, shows at once the
"live man," intelligent and purposeful. The eye,
under the dark eyebrows, is quick, direct, and

undeniably candid. The countenance is regular in type, well proportioned, with straight well-cut nose. His complexion is pale, as of a man working hard, but clear enough, as of a man temperate in living. The face is lean, by no means sharp or haggard, but firm, muscular, and a good "study."

His dress may without impropriety be noticed, for dress we are inclined to think stands in pretty much the same relation to personal appearance as habit does to character; and that it is not at all a trivial matter can nowhere be better seen than in those who disport on their persons the banners of unconventionality. In many of the more intellectual party of the "forward movement," as well as in those whose striving is mainly directed to the "higher culture," the garment, if it do not make the man, yet seems indeed not seldom to be the chief point of his total demonstration. Here is one who would make all men brothers in "all wool," and quite unnecessarily thick boots; and there again is one who makes for "sweetness and light" in a flamingo scarf and a billycock hat.

Tom Mann has none of these vagaries. He is unostentatiously and decently clad in good strong material, well made, and well fitting. He is neither spick and span, nor neat, nor slovenly, but wears his clothes with the style of a man who would look well in kilts, or in knee-breeches, in a slouch hat or a helmet, but by no means builds his reputation on the distinctive cut of his attire.

It is out of a different environment that Tom Mann takes his rise. He is a good honest man of the people. He has seen their miseries. He has seen the heroic struggles and known the heroic souls that one may find among the poor; the devotion, the patience, the good cheer; and withal he has seen the day when the tired hands can work no more, when the sturdy limbs that might have borne an ox can only totter to the workhouse door, and the cold cup of charity is the reward for half-a-century of toil. He has seen the mother, whose life has been a trial of fortitude and self-sacrifice, herself in the end wholly sacrificed, starving in this city where the waste of the rich man's table would make happy a hundred homes; where luxury and vice and the whole round of sensual pleasures are to many of the most privileged the sole assiduous business of life; where the worker is ground down to the bare possibilities of toil and existence; where the young boy must leave his home to search for work, never to be seen perchance again; where the factory girl drudges like a galley slave, flogged to her tasks at the keen edge of hunger and despair; and where the wages of prostitution must eke out the meagre dole of industry.

There is no need to enlarge or to insist on these details. What here is read coldly Mann has lived in, feeling the horror of it, and the shame of it, and the wrong of it cutting into his heart, and that not once or now and then in the way of a new emotion, but day by day, and with the stern impacts of a reality to be faced.

For the poor do not knock under easily. They fight a desperate battle, a battle of huge passions —courage, fortitude, the promptings of love and self-sacrifice that wring the heart even of the stranger, the sharp unknown sufferings, the wild upheavals of fiercer riots. Therein is the stress and hard exercise of experience to train a man of good fibre ; and he who has grown up beholding all this well might ask : Who can call that nation great where wealth is wrung out of the flesh and the souls of our fellowmen ? . . . The degradation of the poor, the grinding heel of the slave-driver —these are in the march of commercial enterprise ; but the raising of the people out of the slough of despair—shall that be but the occasion for derision and insult ? . . . These people are but fighting for the common rights of man, for subsistence, for shelter, for a home if possible, for the comfort of their children. These people are low, say their enemies, vicious. Many are. Doubtless it is difficult to live in a putrid swamp and escape for ever the infection of malaria. Give them hope, and an outlook. . . . Cast one's eye upward, and at the summit of all this huge machine that crushes them down—do we always find the examples of greatness and high character and classic ideals and purer life ?

Tom Mann may have regarded these things with a steady eye, and beheld on the one hand misery almost beyond human suffering, and on the other, not unknown, the insolent and hideous shapes of sensuality. But a strong man has hope in the work that his right hand is doing. So Mann has girt himself up for a tough fight.

Mann on the platform is like a captain leading on his soldiers to storm a redoubt. The words themselves are but an inferior part of that oratory. He grapples with their minds. He drives home his points, going straight to the mark, and carries his men with him onward. The muscular form is strung up, vigour in every movement and stroke, in every attitude resolution and pluck ; the veins swell on his head and on his neck, the eyes are like live coals, the voice rises and breaks at times even into a sharp yelp. He is in full cry, and

tireless as a foxhound on the scent runs out his
course :—

"Remember that this strike is only a link in the
chain. When I think of what you have come here to
fight for I am surprised at the moderation of your
demands; I feel ashamed to stand before you to support you in such a contest—a struggle for twelve hours
a day! But we have organised you for this strike, and
that organisation must not be allowed to fall to pieces.
You must make that organisation stronger, you must
make it permanent! You must consolidate your trades
union and join in with the general body of trades
unionists! This twelve hours a day is only a stepping
stone, and this strike is only a part of the general
movement, and we must not stop till we have welded
together the whole force of the trades unionists and
can show a solid front to the men who want to
crush us."

That is Mann's project. Each Trade Union is
a serviceable regiment, but an army must be built
by the combination of them all. Mutual help and
protection, a fair wage for the labourer, opportunity of intercourse and instruction, these are the
provinces to be conquered. The standard of the
people must be raised. It is a campaign as extensive, a struggle as desperate, as any recorded in
the annals of our race. It needs a hardier courage
than the fiercely waged conflicts of the battlefield ;
for there the panoply of war, the immense visible

force of armies in motion, the roar of the cannon, the tumult, the infectious excitement, the "rapture of the strife," all overwhelm the mind, and whip even the coward up to desperate deeds.

But the striker has a tougher task. Hour by hour and day after day he feels the pangs of hunger. His strength is failing, starvation stares him in the face, his children cry for bread, his wife droops in silence, and death is in the house. It needs plenty of "steel" to look upon all this with steady eye, and still give the word for holding on—the unflinching "bulldog-resistance"; but Mann belongs to that good breed of generals who can march with their men, bivouac with them, do without brandy, and eat no better brown bread.

He is at his best during the crisis of a strike. He is all activity. Passing from post to post, keeping a sharp look out for all that is happening, cheery, resolute, unsparing of himself, snatching brief opportunities of sleep, then alert and about again, orating, reasoning, persuading, exhorting. This is wearing work, and would quickly kill an ordinary individual ; but Mann is able to do it well, and come out again but little hurt.

So we meet at every turn the features of a man well balanced, tough, and active, working at a great work. His intellectual qualities are just of the kind to be most serviceable to his purpose.

To be sure he is in many respects lamentably restricted. Worlds of literature, art, and science are dark to him. He knows no more of Homer's Greece than of Dante's Hell, and his opinion is not to be sought on the virtuosity of Hobbema or the peculiar excellence of the coloring of Velasquez, or even upon the fine points of universalistic or psychological Hedonism. For "metaphysical sadness" he probably has as little sympathy as good old Samuel Johnson himself, and for the same understandable reason—he has seen too much of the more tangible aspects of grief.

Hence some of those more exquisite trances of Pessimism, which are by the intellectually luxurious much sought after—partly as enabling them to look down upon their neighbours—must naturally be out of the reach of Tom Mann.

All this we say of him not in the way of reproach, but simply with the endeavour to define him, and perhaps it may be discovered to be not entirely without point. For in the forward movement are many men whom even their enemies acknowledge to be highly intellectual. There are many who can talk as glibly of Plato as of Petrarch or Ibsen, who are packed full of the lore of history, and who are not merely immersed, but even fairly submerged, in all the philosophies from Thales to Kant and Henry George. Yet in intellectual grasp, even in valid intellectual energy, in knowledge of the actual present conditions, in judgment of men and of movements, to say nothing of sense of proportion, working power, pluck and grip, one feels, with that certain sadness associated with metaphysics, that many of these *doctrinaires* are considerably the inferiors of Mann.

The fates forfend that we should make the application too general, or seem in any way to disparage the value of genuine theory, for that is simply the luminous guide, or in another aspect the apt commentary upon practice ; and further it is the deficiency of reading, and the lack of opportunity for patient, persistent thought, that will prevent Tom Mann ever throwing much light on problems such as those of Free Trade and Protection, which, though infringing on his own particular domain, yet have causative processes and incidents of which from a narrow standpoint it is impossible to foresee the result.

There is no need to insist on this. It is simply necessary to refer to Tom Mann's education and field of action to show that there must be a hundred worlds of intellectual work, all in the "forward movement," of which he can form no clear conception, still less appreciation. His mental energy has been well employed in a re-stricted area, and he knows, as sportsmen say, every inch of that country. But, without any inherent badness of heart, and simply from lack of instruction, he is apt to despise the *doctrinaire*, and the man of abstruse studies.

John Stuart Mill or Herbert Spencer might set forth a general position that summed up the whole scope of his exertions, but their words would possibly be out of the ken of Tom Mann. Did he find them ignorant of some inessential details, the "professor" element would have a hard time of it at the hands of Tom Mann, and more par-ticularly of the friends of Tom Mann. His own command of details he sees to be very important to himself. Thus, for example, he would grant that even to fulminate against a dock company which has worked a man seventeen hours a day may be a good thing to do as well as the sign of a well-meaning character ; but that is to him after all only the smoke of the carbine.

Mann searches out the whole case, and knows the docker's name, and discovers in what par-ticular corner of St. George's-in-the-East you can put your finger on him when you want him, and how to make use of this point to beat up fresh recruits.

His grasp of details, facts and figures, is not to

be beaten.   His information is always ready.   He is never befogged.

Look at him at the Labour Commission.   He is alive to every point.   The shipowner and director would like to make picketing illegal.   Mann follows him up on his own argument, and in a few smart thrusts point after point brings him quickly to a helpless standstill.   The docker's position he seizes on at once, and by a trenchant stroke frees it from confusion and sets it out, emphatic and definite.

His intellectual faculty is strong and clear within his own limit.   He observes proportion and perspective, and leaves quibbling to the pedant.   He asks, what becomes of the docker injured at his dangerous work ?

Have not the trades unions improved the wages of the men ?

Is the half-time system favourable to the schooling of the children ?

Facts, material points—that is the ore he is in search of.   True, he is a partisan, and avowedly so.   The consolidation of the Union, the combination of Union with Union, the solid phalanx which will at length force the lash from the hand of the slave-driver—that is his work.

It is a great work, and Mann is a good citizen. The more intelligent among his enemies can

hardly fail to recognise that. It is true that he
fights vigorously the cause of the people whom
they have so long successfully "exploited," but
he is also a tower of strength between the rulers
and the blind passions of the mob ; he is an
interpreter to whom they can address words of
argument and good sense, who can intelligently
represent to them the crying hardships of his
men, and give an articulate voice to what otherwise might be menacing and irresponsible demands.

I⊤ behoves us to take Mr. Balfour with the utmost seriousness. He is the chief figure of the Conservative party, and around his name have been heaped the titles not merely of genius, but of chivalry, magnanimity, and of all the greater virtues and all the lesser virtues, so that indeed he has been set forth on the one hand as a Richelieu in statecraft and on the other as a King Arthur in heroism. But then again we have another reason for being serious, for, as may be traced in the histories of all languages and peoples, there is no more certain sign of degeneracy than a tendency to superlatives and the extravagant laudation of mediocre things ; and knowing of that tendency elsewhere, and having already had experience of the "tumid and vapid" —for we are constrained to come to these very words again—displays of the gazettes, let us, if only for the very truth's sake and the love of the fresh air and a glimpse of the blue sky, purge our eyes of false vapours and cleanse our souls from that prevalent, insidious, thrice-accursed disease —cant. And even if our pictures thereupon appear unfamiliar, yet we may be not without hope that gradually they may make their impression in their own sober but tenacious colours.

And first let us seek out the man in his most interesting *milieu*, the House of Commons; and approaching that great institution with appropriate respect, either vague and ill-defined but massy, or complex and well-drawn-out and pointed with a thousand brilliant examples, according as our knowledge is scanty or voluminous of the doubtful lore called history, let us then dispose ourselves to listen to the debate. Suppose Mr. Gladstone to be absent, and the Irish party, of course, leaderless, then a great trial awaits our veneration, for as we rub our eyes and yawn we may have a recollection of its having been whispered that this is the arena of the men of ability, and that compared with it the House of Lords is but respectably stupid and dull. One wonders. For speaker after speaker has arisen, and has striven even at the exigency of the most ridiculous gestures to eke out a little of very poor sophistry, a half-hearted driving at false issues, or a stammering upon antiquated pass-words of special pleading. There is, in general, a lack even of a straightforward articulate expression for simple ideas;

and the speakers, while not particularly advancing
the argument, could never be suspected of orating
as the French members ostensibly do "to show
ability." And as each successive wight sits down
after having got up, even our great original stock
of reverence is powerless, yes, in spite of ourselves, to prevent the words resurging, again and
again, with which old Samuel Johnson used to
stigmatise those who did not agree with him :—
Barren rascals, barren rascals.

Then after a time Tim Healy pops up, and we
prick up our ears in expectancy ; for the Irish
have a reputation, conceded by their enemies, for
rhetoric at least, and something of wit, and Tim
Healy is believed to be the astutest and cleverest
tactician of them all. But Tim Healy is simply
droning on at present with no very agreeable
voice, in attitude cramped and unmanly, making
vexatious little points in a style unworthy even of
a well-mannered schoolboy ; and, following up
not very closely the drift of an argument futile
at best, is endeavouring apparently to "draw"
Mr. Balfour. Then, after a time, John Morley
arises, direct, business-like enough, and well contained, with his precise voice and the suggestion
of academic investiture, and his excellent matter,
and his neat and ineffective manner—a piece of
correct but forceless sparring play, a hit, really a

palpable hit ; and it is an instructive study—his style exhibiting the form of the good second-rate man.   There is no *devil* in John Morley, but, or perhaps therefore, he sits down fairly contented. Then Mr. Balfour elevates himself, and we are ready to forget all disappointments in the desperate interest of, for once, seeing a man really of genius.

We have some vague notion that he will ride over us as though at a cavalry charge, carrying our outer entrenchments of reserve, then the whole structure of our antagonisms, and finally, sweeping on unchecked to the inmost stronghold of the mind, lodge there for ever.   At least something of the sort one may have read before of genius, and Mr. Balfour has been bolstered up to a pitch somewhere about that height.   Mr. Balfour, however, in the flesh, or inasmuch as in him is, figures in a considerably tamer guise, and the elements of his genius are evidently more circumstantial.   His figure is tall, thin, weak-looking, ill-braced, ungraceful.   He leans a little forward and a little sideways, and this want of symmetry makes his figure, so ineffective at best, more ungainly.   His attitude is limp, his neck bent, one arm extended forward in an ungraceful gesture, the other hanging listless at the side, the head very unstatuesquely set on the neck, the

eyes peering, the lips a little retracted. Such is
Balfour as he speaks ; and as he speaks he warms
a little, or rather we should not say warms, he
gets excited, and he effervesces, but it is with the
effervescence of soda water. And as he pours, or
rather in a series of little efforts gushes out an
acidulated stream, his followers cheer, and he
turns half round in response ; and the long arm
that had hitherto been driving in his points in the
somewhat feeble and reiterated and always ungraceful gestures, now swings round as if to catch
on to that cheer, and he effervesces the more, and
drives home with more violent agitations : but his
gestures are one-sided, always ungraceful, too
rapid, stringy, and, though in intention forcible,
yet weak in effect ; and the while the attitude is
limp and unmanly.

Of the matter of Mr. Balfour's speeches, later
on ; but the manner gives one somewhat the
same feeling of discomfort as in looking at the
movements of an hysterical lady. Mr. Balfour
may be a genius, but he is not entirely a man.
The voice is thin, flat, heady, altogether lacking
in the sympathetic qualities of roundness and
verve, rather scratching the tympanum with its
squeezed-up notes, and irritating by its mincing
mannerisms, and with an occasional sort of pasty
reluctance in its languishing drawls. This is,

however, the shibboleth of the aristocrat ; it is
the voice of culture ; it is that most unmusical,
possibly, of all human utterance, the voice of that
Elegance of which Piccadilly stands for the Par-
thenon.   And when we speak of his voice being
"aristocratic," that indeed is strongly brought
home as a word to play upon ; for it is considered
sufficient to describe Mr. Balfour's figure, for
example, as being *aristocratic*, and Mr. Balfour's
manners as being *aristocratic*, and Mr. Balfour's
voice as being *aristocratic*, and Mr. Balfour's brains
as being *aristocratic*.   And it is implied that some
peculiar excellence must necessarily therein re-
side.   But this cast of mind is not unique, for
in every coterie and in every cult and in every
set of men, not merely their peculiar excellences
but even their peculiar deficiencies become esteemed in the circle as something to be particularly nursed up and petted ; and the Chinese
lady is proud of her deformed feet, and the
modern belle of her deformed waist, and the
London poetaster languishes over his "decadence," and the Rossettian school of painters
adore the peculiar expression of phthisis.   But as
documentators, though looking at these vagaries
with regret, we may desire on the one hand to
note the full value and the influence of the
shibboleths, and on the other to come down

through the trappings to the man, and rest upon
nature. Therefore we will, in speaking of grace
and of the "points" of a good figure, whether
it be of a man or of a woman, have in mind as
our standards the statues of Phidias; and in
speaking of great emotional qualities we may
also refer to as standards the best types that we
know, derived also perhaps from the antique;
but in discussing the intellect we will not refer
to the antique for our exemplars, but bring to
mind rather the thinkers who have helped to
build up our own interesting and intricate show.
All this is said, not to demand of poor erring
human beings even an approach to excellence in
all of these points, nor to apply the measure even
in the least degree with severity, but simply to
have an ultimate reference, a sure standard, and
so to help out definition.

And as Mr. Balfour advances, leaving the
House after making his speech, we note his aristocratic figure more nearly, and we are reminded
of the aphorism of an old prize-fighter: You
ought to measure a man only up to the shoulder;
anything above that's no good. That prize-fighter
would have said of Mr. Balfour, You must measure
that man above the shoulder, if everything in this
world is of use, for below that he certainly is
not worth the "sizing." For as he walks off

in company with a wooden and pompous and somewhat corpulent friend, Mr. Balfour's step has no energy, his frame is still not braced up, he is weak at the knee, and he saunters languidly, and with the supercilious look on his lips. He seems a little wearied, even worried, and truth to tell the languid gait, the supercilious look, do not appear altogether misplaced.

His countenance is certainly that of an excellent intellectual type. The forehead is large, and marked with the lines of a man who has done a good deal of more or less severe thinking, and the dome of the head is sufficiently well-shaped and expansive. The weak hair—for the impression of want of vigour is marked even there—is prematurely turning grey ; and the features have the appearance as if, having been strung up to the tension of keen and close thought, they were relaxing, tired, with the vitality drained off. Yet the mask of the face is of no bad original type. It gives one the impression that if there had been fire enough in the soul and vim in the blood, and hardness in muscles and nerves, it would have developed into a countenance handsome and resolute. But now Mr. Balfour's appearance suggests the man who has been debilitated, physically and morally, by the lack of a *régime* of good, natural exercise ; emasculated by a life of luxurious but not very wholesome surroundings. And so it is that a certain "bull-doggy" look, with the rather short but almost good nose, the steady and almost resolute eyes, the well-set but rather weak jaws, just glowers beneath the aspect of the precious but ineffective aristocratical product. The cheeks have lost their freshness, and are a little sunken ; but the mouth is the worst of his features. The lips are hard but not firm, with little kindness or sweetness, rather cruel, with the lines about the mouth drawn, in their slight, peculiar retraction, suggesting to one, in some way, a cat.

Such, then, is Mr. Balfour's physical appearance, and it must be confessed the type is not a very sympathetic one. It is that of the too-clever, nervous, sickly, superior boy, grown up to manhood's estate. And this is the great ruler who has governed the Irish because, as he asserts, they are not men enough to be entrusted even by an indulgent authority with the management of affairs that concern only themselves. If so— and it is not our present business to discuss politics further than is necessary for our description—then the Irish people are in general at some immeasurable distance below even their own genuine types ; for Dan O'Connell, for example, with his superabundant generous nature, his vigorous expansive intellect, his rich and rolling but also hard and telling oratory, his real and simple greatness stamped on all his acts and all his records, must surely be reckoned as having hailed from better, sounder, livelier stock than Mr. Balfour. Dan—we have taken him merely as an example for comparison—was a man, where-ever he stood, whenever he spoke. Mr. Balfour is only particularly precious in the gilded halls or in contingencies where a thousand conventional adjuncts serve to swell up his prestige.

However, as Mr. Balfour converses with his pompous and wooden friend, he exhibits a very kind and courteous demeanour, and gives one the idea of his being capable of effusion, though on the whole his style is meagre and flat and colourless. His manners are esteemed to be excellent by his friends and by most of his enemies, for again his whole style is aristo-cratic ; and there are people who are pleased even by an air of condescension in one of that class, if with the assumption of the peculiar and barrier-like superiority of caste there yet be in-fused a concessive and encouraging, "affable," manner. And, further, though there be only too many instances of vulgarity of body and of soul even in the "highest circles," and though there be examples without number of refined and sweet spirits in strata of society lower according to popular orthodox appreciations, yet we have the authority of Thackeray, a remarkably well-balanced man, to induce us to believe that in general manners are better cultivated, more liberal, less provincial, in the spheres in which Mr. Balfour is particularly at home.

Mr. Balfour's manner then is precisely what might have been anticipated from the previous descriptions—facile, polished, thin, neither hearty in expression nor sincere in intention ; sophisticated, a little nervous, a little finnicking, so affected according to his surroundings that all the disagreeable mannerisms we have noticed with respect to his voice have become second nature ; accomplished, "affable," "amiable," and irritating, particularly to his Irish opponents ; nay, stinging to the less dignified amongst them by its intangible supercilious regard ; interesting and fascinating and distinguished with a sort of east-wind-in-reserve to the pompous and aspiring vulgarian ; and easy and easily superior and satisfactory to his friends and supporters.

This is a considerable amount of attention to devote to mere manner, but it must be remembered that we are speaking of a man whose authority and prestige have been enormously aided and enhanced by the class from which

he springs ; and that that class, being beaten
in all the works of life which have contributed
to build up our civilisation, make, as is usual, we
repeat, in all sets and classes, a sort of religion,
a cult, of their rituals, and bolster up and pay a
deference, that would seem ridiculous were it not
by so many outsiders egregiously respected, to
mere conventionality, to talk of families, lineage,
blood, to etiquette, even to various little farces,
and luxuries, and vices, and all the fantastic
tricks which tickle our mortal eyes and ears even
though they make the angels weep, or laugh ;
and so we dwell on Mr. Balfour's lineage and
associations and manners. For though to avoid
a possible confusion of meaning we will not
speak of Mr. Balfour being of good blood, yet
continually the question of lineage and influence
and privilege will be again forced on us, if now
leaving his present condition we go back a
considerable number of years to study his first
performances about the time of his *début* into
political life ; for truly we find nothing therein
which could have hoped to have been fostered
were it not aided by peculiar adventitious surroundings.

The book on "Philosophic Doubt," for instance, is habitually spoken of, and with the
more certainty by those who never would, who

never could, read such a volume, as a work of remarkable ability. It is curious to consider this, for if there be a point of which the typical stolid first-man-you-meet in the Tory party would be likely to have at once a dark distrust and a contempt necessarily vague, but perhaps therefore more strong, that point would be something that savoured of metaphysics, psychology, speculation, anything indeed that suggested inquiry and thought into the constitution of things ; but especially he would have (for these matters might impinge on his own peculiar position) a rooted horror of *doubt*—and of Philosophic Doubt ! Yet when "a leader out of their own ranks," whom " the astonished and delighted Conservatives recognised with rapture that Providence had raised up for them," was known to have dabbled in philosophy, no matter how doubtful, his friends were inclined to make a virtue of his failing ; and gradually his reputation in this respect has grown amongst them by reason of the respect always dimly felt for all that is incomprehensible. One may be justified in reading the " Philosophic Doubt," in order to make a study of Mr. Balfour ; one would hardly be justified or, at any rate, rewarded in reading it to study philosophy. We do not mean to assert that it is false, for this is hardly the place to discuss such a point ; but we can assert that it is weak, meagre, nay, attenuated to a very distressing degree.

The argumentation is acute enough, certainly, the style is the approved dialectical, the order is consecutive, and the result dreary and barren. For Mr. Balfour in this particular book illustrates the difference between mere logic and thinking and reasoning. Had he had wider knowledge, had he been trained in a better school than in the somewhat—in respect to philosophy, what shall we say—hampered Cambridge ; had he but a cold portion of the deep analysis, the power, the grasp, of the great thinkers, he would have attacked the problem in a different fashion ; and, omitting his disquisitions on Kant and Schopenhauer and others of whom it is fashionable even for the ignorant to say a superficial word or two, he would have given us a less attenuated, narrow line of tedious schoolman's dialectic. He had shown himself acute, shrewd, quick to detect a fallacy in form, an amateur fond of casuistry and delicate points, but hypersensitive in touch, and in tone rather feeble, valetudinarian. To give extracts from this book would be an unnecessary bore, but it has been worth a particular reference because it is an academic product, a work that could never have emanated except from a university ; for it is in itself a sort of commentary on the schemes of dilettante speculation and sophisticated manners of logical "pretty" play, which have in general little more importance than so many chess games to the onward march of modern thought, but which are conserved, elaborated, and refined, and accentuated to an extraordinary degree by the conditions, always too rigid and artificial, of university culture. But the universities, though they have failed to produce a single great thinker—unless the mere fact of a man attending a university and then turning away from its teaching make him a product—yet are able to secure a *succès d'estime* for any work that bears in its style the impress of their own hall-mark. Hence again we see into the force of the terms which one may select to describe Mr. Balfour. For just as many an infant finds a chance of being reared solely because born under some tinge of purple, so many a work of art or of thinking which has enjoyed a reputation has escaped perishing from inanition simply by being permeated by the mannerisms of a school. Mr. Balfour's " Philosophic Doubt " is such a product. Its thin-beaten substance could be crushed into a nutshell.

The following extract from a speech, revised by the author, delivered to Conservative working

men, just about the " Philosophic Doubt" period,
will give an idea of Mr. Balfour's shillyshallying
manner, his inability to strike a nail on the
head :

" Gentlemen, you have greatly mistaken the drift of
my speech if you suppose my object has been merely to
show that the accusations of Mr. Gladstone against the
Government have no foundation.　His bitter and somewhat reckless criticism supplies (as, I think, I have
shown you) a very unsafe guide for judging the past;
but it may furnish a warning for the future, of which the
country will do well to take heed.　If it gives no trust-
worthy account of the present Government, we may find
in it clear indications of what the next one will be.　Mr.
Gladstone says that the Ministry now in office may be
judged by their actions, and that the country has ample
material for judging.　I agree with him ; and I also think
that in Mr. Gladstone's speeches the country has ample
material for estimating the qualities which we may expect
to find in their successors.　The question, gentlemen, for
you to decide is not simply whether you will continue
your allegiance to the Government against whom such
speeches have been made, but whether you will transfer
your allegiance to the party whose opinions and judgments such speeches embody."

And this is correct.　It is in accomplished style,
if we are inclined to attach weight to that most
distressing of styles, the style of the stylists.　But
it makes one yawn ; and though *ennui* be considered to mark the tone of superior circles, yet

it can hardly add to the instruction of working men, even of the Conservative ilk. A man who addressed them in this fashion at the age of thirty must have been lacking, not merely in a certain good tough quality of common sense, but in some of the essential qualities of a healthy human nature.

To be sure, Mr. Balfour has improved very much with the lapse of time, being trained to a little more mental athleticism in the course of experience ; but that the training was slow may be judged by some of his speeches, say, four or five years ago. A Rectorial Address at St. Andrew's University on the " Pleasures of Reading," delivered in 1887, is a study in this respect ; for if it be true that the English take their pleasures sadly, it would seem that there still remain of the Scotch those who would pour cold water in their soup lest even the gratification of its warmth be something too sinful. Carlyle used to say that he could read a page of Gibbon with a flash of the eye. If so, that was a great feat even for Carlyle's coruscating optical instrument, for Gibbon is full of matter ; but in reading Mr. Balfour's Rectorial Address one cries out in exasperation, Why cannot he grip this thin idea into one single grainy paragraph or two.

But we are coming to better work of Mr. Balfour's, and will delay but a moment to speak of his golf ; for Mr. Balfour is well advised, in respect to his physique, in playing golf, and it has done him much good ; and further, he has written for the Badminton series a charming little account of the humours of the game—a choice, genial little thing, with a good deal of quiet humour and an atmosphere even of good humour. It gives one a more favourable idea of the man than anything we have hitherto discussed.

The question of golf is not impertinent ; it is not even accidental. Rightly considered, golf is as much an integral part of Mr. Balfour's career as politics. For Mr. Balfour's best performances have invariably been done, not in the solid and serious work that appeals to ordinary men of capacity, but in those little side issues of interesting subjects into which he has entered half amusedly, half languidly, in search of enjoyment. In this regard certain of his "Essays and Addresses" are admirable. The reading of his biographical study of Berkeley, and his critical study of Handel, give an æsthetic satisfaction as distinct in literature as the flavour and bouquet of sparkling Rhenish Hock, "rich, generous, light," amongst wines.

He has been drawn to the study of Berkeley by virtue of a mind continually attracted to fine philosophical questions, continually delighted with the luminous *aperçus* that a phrase might show to his intelligent apprehension, yet content rather to please his taste with the delicate *morceaux* than to devour and digest the staple dish. Lacking the dynamic energy to obtain the full advantage of his highly polished intellectual instrument, he has contented himself with dilettante displays that illustrate its subtlety.

His appreciation of Handel has the rare, subtle quality of his appreciation of Berkeley. He is the highly trained amateur of sophisticated pleasures. He is the dilettante of culture; and Mr. Balfour's politics must be regarded from the same standpoint. He is seldom serious in politics, except in view of his intellectual satisfactions. He is perhaps never serious in his writings and speeches, except in occasional passages of self-revelation in his later productions, where he gives glimpses of depths that contain the evidence of a peculiar genius, of the detachment from the passions of the ordinary run of humanity that indicate a quite exceptional and singularly interesting, if not altogether admirable or attractive personality. His motives, his interests, his ideals lie as remote and secluded from those of the ordinary Tory as do the characters of the angel Gabriel or Lucifer. He would find more congenial—and he even finds some part of his own nature in each—Epicurus, La Rochefoucauld, Schopenhauer, or Swift.

The effete sap of his race has overblown into this brilliant but maladive flower. Half amused, half reluctant he has been drawn gradually into the stream of national politics; his clear intellect has worked amongst them; until at length, casting a look behind him and finding how much of his life has been absorbed in the interests of humanity, he has at times persuaded himself that he is serious, and has cried aloud after the manner, though hardly with the confidence, of a Correggio, "*Anchio son pittore!*"

However, it is in his Irish policy that Mr. Balfour has won his chief laurels. And on the whole it would seem that, from his own point of view and that of his party, his policy was very well adjudged. It was the best of all the feasible plans which that party could venture to adopt. It was not merely as good as could have been expected of Mr. Balfour, it was undeniably better. He seems to have "pulled himself together" for his task, and to have shaken up the original tougher character that a luxurious training, or lack of training, had done much to enervate.

But avoiding in reference to Mr. Balfour the preposterous epithets of high-souled, of genius, of King Arthur (for not all the fabulous puffing

could make the bull-frog a bull, and not all the
cant of the journals can make Mr. Balfour a
hero or even a great man amongst men), let us
see what he has actually done. He coerced
Ireland. He treated the people with that kind
of violence which we had reason to refer to
before as the sign of a weak, emotional nature.
But the consequence could hardly have been
all that he hoped. He injured the health of a
few of the members ; killed, as the Irish believe,
or asserted at least, two or three ; and in the
end was confronted with the spectacle of a people
—lawless, according to Mr. Balfour, incapable of
self-government, or of stable self-control—united
into a solid phalanx that could compel their
interests to be made the one great concern of
British Government, and held in discipline under
the leadership of a man without a shred of
constitutional authority, and who, after surviving
the open attacks and the thousand-and-one am-
buscades of the party of Mr. Balfour, yet continually gained strength, and was hailed at length
with a veritable enthusiasm as a hero by a great
proportion (the Liberals would have said a majority) of the English people, whose Government
had put forth its strength, more than its legitimate
strength, to drive him into a corner and crush
him. We will only refer to Mr. Parnell's fall

to say that it could hardly be supposed to have been due to Mr. Balfour. Nevertheless, it is simply on the strength of the consequences of that fall that Mr. Balfour's friends are able to congratulate him on the success of his policy in Ireland.

But though a coercion policy should hardly expect to be bolstered up mainly in virtue of a divorce court decision, yet in the long contest through which Mr. Balfour—certainly with all the advantage of fighting behind entrenchments —defended his policy, the Tory statesman's own personal powers improved greatly. His intellectual thews and sinews strengthened. Continually in the society of, or in contact with, men of importance, either as friends or opponents, his knowledge of affairs filled up with detail much that he had lacked in his formula of a mind ; and his grasp, his directness, his capacity for valid work, greatly increased. And in his later Irish policy there were two or three quite masterly strokes. For whereas many of the Irishmen themselves and many of their English supporters have been packing themselves with tomes upon tomes of what was practically, a couple of centuries ago, dead learning ; and whereas the whole wide world, both ancient and modern, has been searched for ridiculous "parallels," Mr. Balfour had actually by a great inspiration visited

Ireland himself, and travelled about a little to
see how the land lay. It is true that this was
after years of his famous administration ; and
it is true that the trip was no more extensive and
arduous than he could take in company with
his sister ; but still it was *something ;* nay, compared with what had ever been done before by
an English statesman to study Ireland, it must
be thought really a great thing. And that trip
bore good fruit, and Mr. Balfour, finding after
the fall of Parnell a great demoralisation in the
different divisions of the Irish parties, and observ-
ing too a good deal of uncertainty about the
attitude of the various English Liberal parties,
once more brought in a great stroke at the right
moment, viz., his pressing of the Irish Local
Government Bill. He has so adroitly changed
his tactics, not only with respect to Ireland but
also with respect to the issues in English affairs,
that many of his well-judged schemes might have
been supposed to have emanated from the Liberal
camp—and probably did.

For Mr. Balfour is becoming terribly astute,
and whereas previously really ruining himself
and his party by what they most applauded—
his rigidity and his cynical want of concern—he
is now much more likely to be dangerous to
his opponents by his more workman-like, his

more expansive, more sympathetic, and, whether
sincere or not, more liberal advances and projects.
And further, Mr. Balfour's platform oratory has
become much more effective.

To be sure, even to this day he expresses himself in forms in which perhaps few mortal brains
could ever think, and still fewer of his auditors
intelligently follow ; but he puts more point into
his utterance ; he hits sometimes fairly hard ; he
throws in a little colour ; the " pawky " humour of
the Scotchman has become a little freer ; he makes
a more direct effort at being popular ; and, though
tortuous in manner, is obligingly superficial in
matter ; and, finally, he has learnt two or three
other forms of cant besides his natural cant of the
superior person and his easily acquired academic
cant, and he does not disdain the most banal, the
rankest clap-trap.   In other words, Mr. Balfour
is doing his level best to keep himself and his
colleagues in office.   The following consecutive
extract from a recent speech will serve to illustrate
most of the points referred to.   It is a characteristic example, and worthy of study :—

"I recollect well enough that when, with the common
consent of both parties, the last Reform Bill was passed,
before then and ever since then, we have had it thrown
most unjustly in our teeth that we were the party that
refused to trust the people.   Those gentlemen do

indeed trust the people, but they have their own way of doing it. They trust the people in the same way that a quack trusts the mob in front of him to swallow the universal medicine which he offers them. (Laughter and cheers.) I, too, trust the people—(cheers)—but I hope in a very different spirit and for very different objects. (Cheers.) When the agricultural labourer was called on to share more directly with his fellow-country-men the privileges and responsibilities of governing an empire, I certainly never contemplated that those who attempted to gain his favour would confine themselves to the lowest arts of demagogy, and would sink to the depths indicated by the pamphlets which I have read to you. They have been called upon to share the government of an empire; appeal to them on a broader basis than the sordid, contemptible motives held out to them in such documents as those. (Cheers.) They share with us these great responsibilities, they share with us these great privileges, and my belief is that if those who attempt to gain their favours will indeed treat them as beings of the same flesh and blood as themselves, animated by the same patriotism, animated by the same desire for the greatness of their country at large, and for the welfare of every class of which that country is com-posed—(cheers)—they will not find them the sordid beings which apparently the Radical agitators think they are, but that they are as capable of responding to the appeal made to them as you, gentlemen, or any of the inhabitants of the great towns, who appear to be more and more coming round to the great Conservative and Unionist principles, on which alone, I believe, can be based the future happiness and the future glory of the empire. (Loud and prolonged cheering.)"

That speech is really choice, a perfect little epitome of latter-day Balfourism ; and to the reader of this sketch there would be a feeling of disappointment if it did not come apt as a corollary to what has been indicated as the rise and progress of Mr. Balfour.

It is of no great service to pursue the consideration further into Mr. Balfour's qualities, his so-called high-souledness, his courage, his chivalry, his heroism, or demigodism ; in the mere transcription of these epithets there appears to reasonable minds an effective enough comment ; but even at the best such qualities would be but derivative, and to treat of character in that way (apart from the fulsomeness of its present application) is but the evidence of a superficial mind. A point may be gained, however, by a comparison of Mr. Balfour with a notable predecessor of his, the redoubtable " Dizzy "—that brilliant individual who in his heart detested and despised the Bœotian party that he led. Disraeli could not have written the " Defence of Philosophic Doubt," but his capable mind could have at one effort spanned over all that was in the position, and then have decided not to touch it. The courage of Disraeli was that of the adventurous player at a game in which the nation was the plaything. He recked little for all he could lose, but in a bold cast a prize worth grasping might be won. Again, Mr. Balfour could not have written Disraeli's novels, with their overweening vanity insensible to contempt, their brilliancy, their spangles, and their theatrical glare, and withal their audacity, and their passion, and their magic. Mr. Balfour, secure in his aristocratical prestige, has no occasion for theatre or posings. His mind is too flat for Dizzy's cleverness and wit and adventure, and his emotions too acidulated for the swooping audacity, the enjoyment of the mere playing a game, of the " superlative conjurer."

Mr. Balfour, then, hails from a class whose power gives him at the outset unmeasured advantages. His continual associations have been those of what is called culture. It is true that, referring again to great examples, whether in art we steep our minds in the appreciation of the ideals of the Greeks, the simplicity and the greatness of the works, say, of Phidias ; or in the world of literature seek out the sources whence have emanated the noblest examples of all that the world has found true, great in spirit, heart-stirring, and irresistibly admirable ; or whether in the march of thought, either in all that contributes to material advancement or in all that leads on and develops the intellect of man ; it is true that regarding these things we find much in the so-called higher circles that are mere elaborate ineptitudes, or worse, rather than culture. Yet that class is so affluent and, it cannot be denied, so secure of adulation, that even on its deformities it is able to set the seal of approbation ; and frequently enough these deformities are all that the vulgar who aspire to enter its ranks are able to hold up as their paragons. And it is in this *milieu* that Mr. Balfour, as a young man debilitated by its unwholesome conditions, could yet prosper with his lack of virility. The enervated appearance was aristocratic, the thin unmusical voice was the product of "culture," the soul without colour, without warmth, meagre and sickly—that was superior.

Then we have to consider a period of fighting, at first feeble enough, then with encouragement, exercise, trial, gradually stronger and stronger ; until now, as believed by all parties, Mr. Balfour is the best fighting man on his side. He is fighting for his own hand, or at best for the interests of his class ; and though one hears the cant of his patriotism, and his concern for the future happiness and glory of the Empire, and all the rest of the good old phraseology of the political game, yet after all by patriotism he means the holding on to the privileges his own people have gained, whether by fair means or foul ; and by the Empire, its glory, its happiness, he means his own party, supported of course in a very "responsible" way by Hodge, Nokes, and Smith. Nevertheless, even in the development of himself, in his wider knowledge, his greater strength, Mr. Balfour has become much more sympathetic to others. And so far all is well; but it must not be forgotten that Mr. Balfour has not yet known adversity, that steady analyst that may strip off his conceits and, in turn, the less vital of his interests and aims, and in the process make known to him a new sort of psychology. For if any one in the semblance of a good man is to arise in the future to bear on the flag of progress, it may lie in his way to drive Mr. Balfour in a hot, close, decisive fight, and then Mr. Balfour will at the very pinch be found wanting. He will give way suddenly somewhere, and the flaw will be found to have been an essential part of his constitution. And in the summing up of history after the fuming and the fret and the passions of temporary politics have passed away, and matters have been reduced to a truer perspective, Mr. Balfour will be remembered not for his politics at all, but for a few choice writings, a few genial and airy fancies, the glimpse at the terrible philosophies of the constitutionally timorous man, and the delicate tastes that have made him the Dilettante of Culture.

JOSEPH CHAMBERLAIN

Mr. Chamberlain is not one of our most attractive types ; he lacks fascination ; but though we have, we confess, little hope of his adorning our tale, he may nevertheless serve to point a greatly excellent moral. For to the diligent student of human nature the study of his career may give occasion for many wise after-thoughts and sage reflections upon the chances and opportunities and talents that in these latter days are most likely to aid a man to rise to eminence in the councils of the Nation, and even in the esteem of those whom, at the outset of his career, he attacked, not only as his own bitter opponents, but as enemies to the Commonwealth at large. For indeed it has been a remarkable fate by which the rising hope of the Radicals, the reformer, the still strong man, the friend of the people, the Republican of yore, should have at last become the champion of the Peers, the sheet anchor of the Constitution, the oracle of Duchesses, the thorn in the side of the Liberals.

But in no fashion can the versatility of Mr. Chamberlain's character and the energy with which he is able to adapt himself to new circumstances be better exhibited than by extracts from his own very neatly couched oratory. In the year 1884 Mr. Chamberlain was valiant enough to say :

" The chronicles of the House of Lords are one long record of concessions delayed until they have lost their grace, of rights denied until extorted from their fears. It has been a history of one long contest between the representatives of privilege and the representatives of popular rights, and during this time the Lords have perverted, delayed, and denied justice until at last they gave grudgingly and churlishly what they could no longer withhold."

All this is pretty severe invective, but to the heavy infantry charges, Mr. Chamberlain is able to add the display of light cavalry attacks, and to fall upon the ranks of the enemy armed with those epigrams and phrases that have all the spontaneity and aptness resulting from hard preparation. The House of Lords, he tells his hearers, is a " club of Tory landlords, which in its gilded chamber has disposed of the welfare of the people with almost exclusive regard to the interests of a class." And, again, they are a " miserable minority of individuals." But perhaps

the acme of sarcasm is reached where the great Caucus-compeller of Birmingham speaks of them as "interesting ruins."

These interesting ruins, however, are evidently more tenacious of life than Mr. Chamberlain has been of convictions. For would it be believed that it is the doughty Radical of '86 who assures us that,

"although the House of Peers is a good deal threatened now-a-days, in all probability it will outlast most of us, and will remain for several generations to come a picturesque and a stately, if not a supremely important, part of the British constitution. (Hear, hear.)"

And not only are the Peers likely to endure to a somewhat indefinite future, but it is interesting meanwhile to find in one of Mr. Chamberlain's speeches a tribute to "the liberality in its best sense—(hear, hear)—of the policy of the Government. (Cheers.)"

A change has certainly come o'er the spirit of his dream, a change little anticipated by his auditors in gallant little Wales who heard him declare not very many years ago, with all that vehemence which is rightly regarded, for platform success, as a good deal more requisite than sincerity or logic—"We cannot," he exclaimed in terms of withering scorn, but possibly more in sorrow than in anger, "we cannot turn and twist and change our opinions and put forward new ones every full moon as the Tories do."

Now, down to the words "every full moon" we may readily grant the perfect truth of this observation, for Mr. Chamberlain at least required for the process of twisting and turning not merely a longer period than a lunar month, but also a pretty fair certainty of good prospects ahead ; but the phrase "as the Tories do" is certainly difficult to reconcile with the later utterances of our stalwart, even though "our way has been made smooth for us by the personal influence of Lord Salisbury—(cheers)—and by the patriotism of his friends."

Such are the words of Joseph, who having been born in London in 1836, and having distinguished himself by much sharp business capability in the hardware trade at Birmingham, became Mayor of that city in 1873, and won all sorts of good opinions from his commercial friends by his "expeditious despatch of business." It is the more necessary to advert to these earlier beginnings of a provincial reputation, because commercial aptitude and success, commercial standards of all kinds, are frequently insisted on by Mr. Chamberlain as the true tests of greatness; and, finding that the aspirations towards liberty of an imaginative people are not at all to be assessed in a ledger, Mr. Chamberlain proceeds to crush their representatives and at the same time to insinuate, as it were, the lustre of his own particular achievements.

"But, gentlemen, one wants to know whether these men of words are also men of action—whether they have been successful in the conduct of their own business. Have they come to Parliament from a successful prosecution of great enterprises, either public or private? Have they deserved well of their fellow-citizens by the services they have rendered on local boards and in connection with the municipal institutions which Ireland possesses?"

It will not be necessary to explain that all the qualifications here indicated as being necessary to the equipment of a statesman Mr. Chamberlain possesses to an eminent degree; and in fact if we were to hear him discourse at length on the topic as to all that a constitutional leader of men ought to be, we should be tempted to ask, travestying the *riposte* given to Mirabeau,—And must he also be furnished with an eye-glass?

However, we left Mr. Chamberlain as Mayor, and while we cannot forbear a smile at Mr. Sexton's little epigram that the hon. gentleman was intended by Providence to be a Mayor, yet we know that not only the highest places of Birmingham, but the highest places of the Empire, are well within the purview of those respectable mediocrities of whom Mr. Chamberlain has reason to consider himself one of the most brilliant examples. Accordingly, at the reasonable age of forty Mr. Chamberlain is found as an ornament to the great House at Westminster; and four years later, in 1880, he is President of the Board of Trade with a seat in the Cabinet.

Mr. Chamberlain distinguished himself by his administrative ability, and also by encountering disaster with his Merchant Shipping Bill; for it is the peculiar virtue of the much-belauded British Constitution that there are a hundred ways by which the House may be prevented from carrying its own will into effect, to say nothing whatever of the desires of the bulk of the Nation; and in the last resort there is the barrier of that House of Lords of which Mr. Chamberlain was once so rancorous an enemy, and with which he now delights to display so amiable a coquetry. But at the time of which we are speaking Mr. Chamberlain, in spite of a good deal of personal unpopularity even with his own colleagues, was much more the partisan of the Commons:—

"I venture to say that the Parliament at Westminster is the best tribunal to which you can possibly appeal.

H

It is a democratic Parliament. That is to say, it is a Parliament which represents proportionately the strength and opinions of the people. It is a Parliament which has sympathy more than any other Parliament of the present century with all just and reasonable claims; and it is a Parliament in which no class and no vested interest would be able to silence any fair demand."

These are brave words, and bespeak the rising man. And even now Mr. Chamberlain is able to speak of the House that has witnessed the shipwreck of the ambition of his life as "the greatest of representative assemblies," and, while considering that the present House of Commons compares not unfavourably with its predecessors, takes occasion to praise its "marvellous common-sense" and "broad-minded toleration" in general. . . . When, however, Mr. Chamberlain relates of "a grave debate nearly brought to a standstill while the crowded benches on both sides pursued with infinite interest the movements of a cock-roach across the floor of the House," we rub our eyes; for really if the *infinite* interest be not exaggerated, how are we to reconcile this scene in its entirety with Mr. Chamberlain's other superlative phrase, the "marvellous common-sense" of the House? Or is it that he wished to illustrate that "broad-minded toleration" of which he was speaking? or is it, again, that Mr.

Chamberlain, in order to set his own position in the most favourable aspect, is bent upon disparaging by insinuation the House where his plans have miscarried, just as, on the other hand, he has little scruple about flattering the party which he had formerly so bitterly denounced?

But what, after all, is the style of this man, once the bulwark of democrats, now the buttress of Peers? For we hold that a man can be seen only as through a glass darkly—he is a mere effigy, a lay figure—if description stop with the record of his acts. Ah! how we could have listened down to the minutest item, even to the tips of the finger-nails, to one who had seen and could discourse of John Keats. How we could have plundered even the very rags and unconsidered trifles of the man who had beheld, possibly heard a word of, Napoleon! But go to the strangers' gallery of the House of Commons, and you will find that half the visitors stare at the House blankly, not knowing Morley from Redmond; never enquiring. Meet a man in Central Africa who has seen Gladstone or Parnell. Ask him for a description of one of them, and set your ears for the eager words to be poured into them during the rest of the night. He will tell you that such and such is an "ordinary looking man," and being hotly pressed will yield up the opinion that he is a "funny looking man!" and very little more can you ordinarily get.

Therefore, without compunction, but with scrupulous care, are these documents set down. On entering the House at a favourable moment one may behold on the front Opposition bench, in the seat nearest the gangway, a gentlemanly looking figure, a somewhat bare and unsympathetic countenance, with the outline of which photographs have made us familiar, but the expression of which no photograph could ever reproduce ; for that expression is not, as one should say, smug, and not exactly suggesting the astute, but rather inscrutably, and, because so inscrutably, not without a tinge of suspicion of being absurdly—diplomatic. It is as though Mr. Chamberlain were aiming at being impassive, but falling short by a shade of the necessary dignity and *aplomb*, has done himself an injustice in seeming rather wooden. The features are regular, but not classical nor fine, the forehead ample but uneloquent, and surmounted by the carefully brushed hair of drab colour. The eye is direct, but hard and shallow, and endowed with the lustre of a pebble. The right eye wears an eyeglass. It is an uninteresting, a disappointing countenance. One finds there no suggestion of those fascinating traits that proclaim a true leader of the people, no generous impulses, no warm and purple feelings, no bold dynamic impetus of noble passion, no exquisitely tender or softly luminous expressions, none of the radiant glances, the indefinable atmosphere, the deep regard, the steadfast lights, that tell of genius. But stop: this manner seems absurd, for we have been led away for a moment by the epithets of "marvellous," "greatest of assemblies," "divine missions," and what not of phrases that the most uninspired of journalists (*vide* Mr. Stead) delight to flourish about ; and for the moment it seemed not unreasonable to expect to find in such environments at least a certain excellence of type. A glance round at the House of Commons dispels these illusions.

Mr. Chamberlain is speaking, let us say. He stands erect. His attire is faultless. His figure is eminently serviceable. He is fairly tall, not stout, nor thin, nor athletic in build, but of a physique perhaps best of all adapted to the dull wear and tear, the boredom, the tedious business of the House. However, the House listens to Mr. Chamberlain, and two or three seats off John Morley is regarding him with a peculiar expression ; a half quizzical interest, in which regret, sorrow, distrust, and yet admiration, are mingled. And admiration could hardly be entirely withheld, for Mr. Chamberlain has readiness, acuteness, lucidity of expression, and what is called, in short, admirable debating power. Of eloquence, eloquence that stirs the blood and appeals to the finer passions of the soul, Mr. Chamberlain has none, nor can we imagine that he would esteem such a gift in another. He is a commercial man, and his manner is, if not distinguished, yet gentlemanly, "distinctly gentlemanly," for that phrase puts a finer edge to the meaning. And his voice is a treasure : cultivated, well contained, mellow. Mr. T. P. O'Connor opines that it would make the fortune of a lady doctor ; but that is not quite to the point. It is a voice adapted to the Commons ; in fact, as John Morley once remarked at the time they were friends, the best voice in the House. For though mellow, it is yet—if such a thing can be understood—hard and precise, and not at all sympathetic. There is in the whole manner a suggestion of that epistolary style affected by men of business — polished, urbane, served up with exaggerated politeness, but with the hard standards of trade and self-interest behind.

To speak of Mr. Chamberlain's political morality to those who have read his speeches, past and present, would be simply absurd. Rather it behoves us to deal with the question as to how such a practical man could have left Mr. Gladstone. Certainly Mr. Gladstone had not treated him particularly well, for after five years' service in the Cabinet as President of the Board of Trade, Mr. Chamberlain found himself in '86—he, the great Chamberlain—not the second in the Empire, but somewhat lower in grade than before. Mr. Chamberlain in 1886 figured to the world, not as the Premier presumptive, but as President of the Local Government Board.

The rupture followed soon after, and it is only just to Mr. Chamberlain to say that he himself has assured us, or rather the Tory friends to whom he delights to orate, that "it is not for a mere personal or private question that one can repudiate one's old leaders." It was in fact nothing short of "the existence, or at least the security of the Empire" that caused the Birmingham lapse. And—

"Even after the rupture had taken place there were many of us—I was one of them—who hoped that it would be only temporary, who believed that the Gladstonians would speedily abandon the path upon which we know, and they had good cause for knowing, they had most reluctantly entered, and we looked forward, therefore, to a speedy reunion."

So, when Mr. Chamberlain left the fold expecting the best part of the Gladstonian flock to follow so capable a leader, what must have been his feelings when he stopped to count heads? . . . And through what mental vicissitudes must he have passed before being led into the gates of the Tories. But at least the Empire existed, and Mr. Jesse Collings was faithful.

But if the discussion of Mr. Chamberlain's political morality gives but little scope for expansion, yet after all, it may be said, it is his intellectual power that gives him his eminence. Certainly there are not wanting those (Mr. T. P. O'Connor again) who dub him a "political baby," and insist that "the man is a fool." Well, there are fools and fools, but on the broad meaning of the term the majority are inclined to think that it is not among fools that Mr. Chamberlain finds his appropriate place. In tracing his career one cannot but gain respect for the range of practical subjects with which he has more or less efficiently dealt. His administrative ability has always been of the very first class. His success in his private business has given him a justifiable pride. Mr. Chamberlain's power in debate is likewise acknowledged ; and during these latter years, there are signs of striving for "culture."

And then with respect to the famous debating

power, let us look at the matter more closely, in order to discover wherein this power of his peculiarly dwells. Mr. Chamberlain, for instance, has frequently had occasion of late to criticise the Newcastle Programme, and, if one may judge from the responses of his audience, with remarkable success :—

"It is not a serious programme. (Laughter and cheers.) It is a programme that would crumble to pieces from its own weight and cumbrousness. How shall I describe it to you? I should like to define it scientifically, and I am inclined to take my definition from the science of geology. And if, as I hope, there are any miners present, they will be able to understand me. Gentlemen, the Newcastle Programme is a conglomerate. (Laughter.) A conglomerate, if you look in the books—a conglomerate is a congeries of various fragments subjected to great pressure and friction and brought together from vast distances by many and various powerful agencies. (Loud laughter.) I see you catch the analogy. (More laughter.) The Newcastle Programme is, indeed, a heterogeneous congeries of various fragments of every programme under the sun, and brought together by the powerful agency of local caucus. (Laughter and cheers.) But, gentlemen, I tell you that this conglomerate—'pudding-stone' is the popular name—(Roars of laughter). . . ."

That extract from a speech delivered at Sunderland, October 22nd, 1891, is not an unfavourable specimen of Mr. Chamberlain's best platform oratory, and it is long enough to give one a fair idea of the "effects" he employs. It must be acknowledged that there is no great argumentation therein, and one will find not one whit more if one reads on for a column or two. Mr. Chamberlain has been accused of lacking humour; but the man who could so often convulse the audience simply by calling the Newcastle Programme a "conglomerate" or a "pudding-stone" must really be a wag of the very first order. And not only would Mr. Chamberlain appear to have the very best humour, viz., that which brings down the house, but he has a remarkable versatility in adapting his figures of speech to the taste of his hearers. For whereas in Sunderland he calls the Newcastle Programme a pudding-stone, yet in discoursing before a selected cultured audience in Birmingham he uses similes borrowed from the language of jugglery.

"We do not want Lord Salisbury to enter into competition with the authors of the Newcastle Programme—(cheers)—that bag of tricks—(cheers)—that inexhaustible hat—(much laughter)—from which Mr. Schnadhorst is to produce everything that can call for the wonder or tempt the cupidity of his moral audiences. (Renewed laughter.)"

One finds here the same incorrigible wag, the same shrewdness of mind, the same irresistible

mirth. But, again, there is no remarkable feat
of reason or art in dubbing the Newcastle Programme a " bag of tricks" or an "inexhaustible
hat." The best we can say is that Mr. Chamberlain has well gauged his audience, and that we
must always stand in respect of success. Elsewhere we get nearer to ostensible argumentation :

" If you support the Gladstonian party at the next
election, you will postpone indefinitely all social and
domestic measures. (Cheers and laughter.) Oh, it is
not a question. You may laugh now, but let those
laugh who win. (Cheers.) You cannot. No man has
ever been found to run three omnibuses abreast through
Temple Bar, and no man will ever be found to run a
measure like a measure of Home Rule through Parliament, and at the same time deal with anything else.
(Cheers.) And, therefore, so long as Home Rule is
adopted as the leading feature of the Gladstonian
programme, so long the Gladstonians are impotent—
positively impotent—for any other measures of political
reform. (Cheers.) "

Now without disputing the point about Mr.
Gladstone's particular difficulties, a logical mind
is curious to inquire the precise value of the
analogy cited. For after all three omnibuses
could be driven abreast through the Marble Arch,
and then, if we were to attach weight to this style
of. argumentation, we should have to sit down
and discuss as to whether Parliament resembles

Temple Bar very closely or inclines rather to the size of Marble Arch.

But why pursue the matter further ? We will do Mr. Chamberlain the credit to suppose that he does not arrive at his own ideas by the processes which he thinks good enough to set before his audiences ; but even as the whole system of party warfare has developed all sorts of absurdities, so the leaders find their great stock-in-trade to be fustian. Plod through the columns and columns of Mr. Chamberlain's utterances, or indeed (we say it with regret) of those of his rivals or friends, and endeavour to find any fine piece of wisdom, any sally of wit, any serious thoughtful line of reasoning, any noble appeal, any generous emotion, any superior flash of ideas : the search is a barren one. One of his speeches is very like another. There is much clap-trap, an aiming at points, a display on the platform.

But if we believe that Mr. Chamberlain has too much brains to be carried away by the force of the words that he utters, yet this does not imply that we think he arrives at conclusions by reasoning on the value of things in themselves. It was said—was it not of Lord Brougham—that it was a mistake to say he had no sense of truth ; he had much regard for truth, where he had nothing to lose. And so, since equity is an intellectual sense, Mr. Chamberlain would be just in all matters that did not infringe upon his own interests. But Mr. Chamberlain is not a very many-sided man, and there are few of his activities that have not emanated from, and returned again to, Mr. Chamberlain's self.

In order to understand a politician, however, it is necessary to study him in relation to the general body of politicians amongst whom his work is carried on. It is not fair nor in any way helpful to judge an ordinary public man by some ideal standard of pure and self-sacrificing patriotism, or to demand from him an unswerving devotion not only to the spirit but to the letter of his principles. Such a demand would be unpractical; and moreover it would happen in the hurly-burly of politics, in which great objects must be won by means of the co-operation of numbers of active men, each seeking his own point of vantage—it would happen that the rigid man of principle would accomplish less than the tricky politician; would accomplish generally nothing at all; would be submerged in the political ocean, or be ridiculed or hounded out of existence.

Politics is a question of strategy. Even to accomplish high purposes it is often necessary to resort to low means. It may be believed accordingly that the number of those who hold before their eyes, either some noble and attractive goal, or some definite utilitarian purpose, exceeds those whose conduct is entirely honourable, or whose course of politics has been fairly consistent. The great thing we can hope to demand from a politician is to hold to his *objective*; and then he may be allowed to work out his strategical lines and his minor tactics as skilfully as he can.

That there are politicians who are impelled to their work by high and noble ideals of public life will not be denied. That there are many politicians content to submerge their own personalities in the attainment of that ideal—that is a much more doubtful proposition. Every man's ideal springs out of his circumstances, his education, experience, and personal character; and so it happens that under cover of this furtherance of his ideal he flatters himself that he is the one person needful.

Accordingly it gives a strange impression occasionally to read of the moral outbursts of politicians who repudiate the suggestion of personal motives entering largely into politics; while at the same time in their private discourses, in which they estimate the chances of political combinations and their own prospects of advancement, the standard invariably referred to, without misgiving and without question, is that of the personal interest of the several men with whom they have to deal. Having summed up on this basis, they put on the accustomed gloss of cant for due presentation to the public. Sometimes, it is said, they mystify themselves.

Personal interests in politics, however, never move undetached from the interests of party. Party becomes the great fetich of public demonstration, and many a politician who has joined his party with the same sort of ideas as actuate the lawyer in taking his brief becomes at length seized with the spirit of forensic fervour, and by dint of oft-repeating the same formulas acquires a veritable professional sincerity. It is only when we find a man who withdraws himself from his party that we behold the analysis of motives practically demonstrated and discover the mainspring of a man's career.

A party man must work with colleagues with whom he has no more connection than that of general business interests, and no more sympathy than by virtue of a policy which it may be merely a formal duty to advocate. Nevertheless, since the combined force of the party is necessary to carry any one scheme, there is a continual interchange of little concessions. Hence we find politicians, whose intentions are honest enough, voting for and even advocating minor measures that are directly contrary to their convictions.

This is inevitable under the system of party government, for the purist, if such there be in politics, who would advocate or oppose measures according to his individual opinion would speedily find that in saving a clause of no great value he had wrecked the whole programme. Such a method of procedure would not be commendable. It would simply show a lack of grasp of parliamentary conditions. As to what is important and feasible, and as to what is unimportant or impracticable, that is a matter of judgment amid conditions that change from year to year, and of which the causes are often difficult to forecast; as to how much of one's own programme may be insisted upon, into what perspective the whole scheme of the party may be cast, that is a matter of calibre, authority, position. A man makes his way less by force of argument than by his weight—that resultant made up from a hundred different elements; wealth, position in the country, position in the caucuses, control of votes in the House, personal qualities.

In order to pronounce upon a politician's consistency it is necessary to consider in this manner the *milieu* in which he works. And especially is it necessary to take note of these circumstances in the case of a politician who makes his *début* in Liberal circles.

Mr. Chamberlain's guiding principle has been derived from the usages of commerce, and those usages—exemplified, for instance, in that monument of British common sense, the Law of Contracts—are above all things practical, and, moreover, as equitable as possible.

He is willing to give to every man a fair start and a reward according to his merits. And this principle, though at first blush not very inspiring, is the surest of guides in politics, and, moreover, when applied amidst the mass of privileges, traditions, superannuated laws, outworn prerogatives, and manifest injustices, which abound in the social system of Great Britain, that principle in all its simplicity becomes terrible in its revolutionary force, menacing in its candour.

That is the principle from which Mr. Chamberlain derived his early Republicanism, that is the principle that made him advocate Abolition of the House of Lords, Disestablishment of the Welsh Church, Home Rule for Ireland, Reform of the Franchise for Great Britain.

To none of these questions did he bring a mind burdened with the lumber of history and traditions ; to all of these questions he brought a mind singularly free from prejudice, and fair and statesman-like in the manner of expression. His early speeches on Ireland are remarkably well judged ; Liberal from the English point of view without being alarming, acceptable from the Irish point of view without demanding undue gratitude. Mr. Chamberlain wished to see a free and contented Ireland on the condition only of keeping the connection intact with England. He wished, in a word, to place Ireland in a position similar to that of Scotland—a programme that ought after all to have been acceptable to all Irishmen who, while desiring to see their native country as well favoured as possible, looked forward also to a final reconciliation with Great Britain.

While pursuing the main objects of his programme with remarkable energy and ability, Mr. Chamberlain was at the same time endeavouring to work smoothly as a good party man, endeavouring also to cultivate those personal amities that are necessary to party success.

And therein is the great problem of politics. A man may fight his political enemies with that energy which in its more exuberant moments rises into the *certaminis gaudia* of the warrior ; but to be reconciled to one's friends ! that is a more serious problem.

Consider the Liberal party. It is the party of reformers; and as parties, like everything else, have also the defects of their qualities, the Liberal party is also the association of the "faddists." A faddist is one who pursues without discretion an object chosen without intelligence. And of the sections, all afflicted with a quantum of faddism, of which the Liberal party is composed, a few may be mentioned—the official Liberals divided into several cliques, the Old Radicals, the New Radicals, the Nonconformists, the Irish Whigs, the Welsh Provincialists, the Little Englanders, the Puritans, the Fabians, the Social Democrats, the Labour Party divided into some dozen cliques, the Socialists of various colours, the Progressives, the Lord's Day Observancers, the Anti-Gambling League, the Local Vetoists, the Anti-Vaccinators, the Women's Rightists, the Parish Pumpers, the St. Giles Kitcheners, the Economists, and the Philosophers.

And one can well imagine, in dealing with this heterogeneous collection, a party in which each idea is represented by a zealous and often fanatical exponent—one can imagine the personal dislikes, grudges, jealousies, and rancours that are likely to grow up in the mind of an active politician; one can imagine the diabolical joy of being free from the restraints of party dis-

cipline, in order to pour out the bitterness of a
goaded and baffled soul upon the imbeciles, the
fanatics, the dilettantes, the snobs ! Add to this,
moreover, that there is no party more steeped
in the adulation of authority, titles, display, than
a certain section of the Liberals ; that their ambition in life is to climb to those ranks, to brush
shoulders with those personages, whose privileges
it is their official policy to curtail, but whose
half-disdainful recognition is more savoury to
their nostrils than the greatest of their forensic
and political triumphs. The arrogance of the
aristocrat ; the snobbery of the parvenu ; a
world divides them. Nor in the lower register
is the actual state of affairs encouraging. The
great conception of a Liberal policy, a Republican ideal, is ill-reflected in the Liberal newspapers ; the best of them insufferably smug and
Pharisaical in their bourgeois souls ; the worst,
ill-conditioned in their mean and yelping snap-
pishness. And, moreover, in none of the sections
of the Liberal party is the noble aspect of a great
civilising principle to be found ; the sections
advocate their claims each on the basis of their
own special interests, and indeed on their particular claims as a class. They demand reforms
not like patriots advancing under the banner of
a lofty and superior ideal of the State ; but like

discontented servants who wrangle with their "betters." The type of the Nation is that of the aristocratic house with its various degrees of servitude and privilege. And the whole style and title of the Nation, the manner in which laws are couched, the military and civil services maintained, the business of the Nation carried on, literature written, art patronised, amusements, manners, and morals fostered, and even the works of high enlightenment presented ; all this bears the stamp of a feudal tradition : The English are a Conservative people.

Here, then, is Mr. Chamberlain, a man of excellent principles, but also a man of considerable calibre, determined to force his way to the front, if only in order to find scope enough for the exercise of his abilities—the politician *par excellence* working amid these surroundings. In the House of Commons he is confronted everywhere with the vital importance of considering personal interests at every conjuncture ; and in the broad policy of parties he finds it tacitly accepted that there is no other ultimate standard of political argument than the material interests of the several sections of the community.

It will be therefore evident that without any special moral turpitude a man of Mr. Chamberlain's stamp might take his place in the Liberal camp, and yet feel himself but loosely constrained to its discipline. The opportunity arrives for jumping into the place of Leader, the great prize of his life is within Mr. Chamberlain's grasp; he crosses the Rubicon.

Yet in this Mr. Chamberlain might for a long time have affirmed that he had receded in no wise from his own principles; he might claim that his own view of the Irish question was more statesman-like, more consistent and saner than Mr. Gladstone's, and he might also truly claim that it was much more in accordance with the spirit of the English people; he might claim that in his secession his attitude was reasonable and dignified.

The final reconciliation of Mr. Chamberlain with the Tories was a logical consequence of all that had gone before. The playing the rôle of a Tory magnate presented no great difficulty to the Birmingham leader, for every politician, and indeed every public man, is to a great extent an actor, and that in a sense almost literal. He occupies different positions in turn, he guides himself by tradition and by his appreciation of the sum total effect, he endeavours to "fill the bill." And to any one who has seen Mr. Chamberlain make a "good debating speech" in the House of Commons the idea of the actor is brought very forcibly to mind. The type is that of the accomplished actor in Society comedy; he acts with *aplomb*, with a fine *tenue* which does not exclude the sense of power, with a *correction* (in the French meaning) which indicates discipline and virtuosity. As an example, Mr. Chamberlain is speaking on Mr. Balfour's measure of Local Government for Ireland—"I have known of corrupt councils in England"—(cheers from the Irish and Scotch members) . . . (pause)—"I have known of corrupt councils in Scotland"—(silence on Scotch benches; ironical laughter from the English; tumultuous applause from the Irish. Then, suddenly, at the first lull, turning half round and dropping his voice to a low forcible note)—"and in Ireland"!!

Mr. Chamberlain has sent home his point with a rapier thrust.

A man who could play in this style is not likely to be out of place in the "gilded halls"; not likely to be *gauche* at the tea-tables of the famous Duchesses. Nay, rather he would require to descend, to deploy his urbanity, to make them feel perfectly at ease in the presence of a gentleman so irreproachable and of such redoubtable talent.

In this respect, as in all others, Mr. Chamberlain is admirably fitted for his work. He is perhaps the most distinctively English of all the foremost politicians. He is English in his commercial ability, his energy, his common sense, his tenacity of purpose, firmness of temper, resistance to depression, his forcible ambitions, his practical aims.

Look at the man then; look at his career. A Birmingham scion of commerce, astute, persevering, successful, gradually enlarges his view. Provincial triumphs fall into his grasp. He is a Radical, and sincerely enough, for he can only gain his point by dislodging the Tories. His talents are above mediocrity, his training efficient in business, and he rather despises all else. Mediocrity is not an insuperable bar, and many men far below Mr. Chamberlain's calibre have risen to very high seats. Why not Joseph Chamberlain, a man of undoubted ability? He rises very quickly in Parliament, achieves a great reputation, acquires a force in the country behind him at one time not second to that of Mr. Gladstone himself. Then occurs the crisis, the separation from the G.O.M., the somewhat *naïf* expectancy that the others would follow; and now at length the pride of the Radicals has settled down as the henchman of that "armchair politician" whom at one time he wanted Mr. Parnell to help him to "dish."

Carlyle summed up Wordsworth by saying that he had led a "respectable life." We may say that of Mr. Chamberlain, but withal he is not an interesting man. Our sketch is grey and dull. But that is not inappropriate. How will he figure in history? Validly, he will not figure at all. Who would care to remember Mr. Chamberlain when he has lapsed out of the public arena? His friends must build their main hopes of his enduring fame upon a monument. What form should it take? Perhaps that epigram reported of him from his schooldays, "I'm Chamberlain, who are you?"—And the passer-by will repeat the inquiry.

THE rise of Mr. Stead is a certain triumph of Democracy. Those even of his friends who know him best would hardly venture to speak of it as a *great* triumph ; but, on the other hand, his enemies, even those who detest Mr. Stead, and they are not a few, even those who affect to despise Mr. Stead, and their opinions are not to be scouted, even Mr. Stead's political and religious opponents cannot, if they be true democrats, grudge a feeling of satisfaction at the contemplation of a career so well "*ouverteaux talents*." Nor will the satisfaction be less that whereas the career has been, in as far as is consistent with the dingy precincts of a journalist's office, astonishing in glitter and spangles and sawdust, yet the "talents" have been what Bret Harte would call somewhat "ornery." In fact, to borrow an illustration from another American philosopher, the immortal historian of the Jumping Frog, the first impression of Mr. Stead with all his record might be : I don't see no p'ints about that frog different from no other frog. The difference in both cases is in the internal machinery, the energy and dash, the steaming apparatus of nerves—in short, the jumping power.

Mr. Stead, we know, is fond of inviting comparisons between himself and St. Paul, Mr. Stead having the advantage of all the light and leading of " modernity," and also a pull in material prosperity, a thing never to be left out of account in this world. Whatever feeling the juxtaposition of these two illustrious names may evoke, will of course depend upon the opinions of the reader, his estimation of Mr. Stead, and his estimation of St. Paul ; but in any case, upon a consideration of all the circumstances a certain strong impression will remain of the evangelical character of Stead.

It would be spiritualising Mr. Stead and making him too unfamiliar to say that the atmosphere that surrounds him is impregnated with the odour of sanctity ; but his whole personality, his appearance, his style, his choice of words, and his mannerisms, have strongly the odour of that cloth which is the wear of the sanctimonious in spirit. Whatever Mr. Stead might have chosen to be, man of commerce, journalist, attorney ; whatever he might declare himself, Theosophist, Methodist, or Atheist, he could never escape from his nature.

Appearance, attitude, voice, style of utterance and of writing proclaim him a Nonconformist : if not parson, at least keeper of the conscience, the big man of a Little Pedlington Bethel. Mr. Stead's familiarity with the Deity is not excelled by that of the German Kaiser himself ; but whereas to the illustrious though as yet undistinguished "young man" it is the God of Battles, our powerful and terrible "ally at Rosbach," that is present to his imagination and holds some brevet rank ("*Gott mit uns*") in his army ; to Mr. Stead the Deity appears very like a great parochial guardian, interested in the details of a grocer's shop and in all the gossip of a Methodist back parlour ; and whereas the German Kaiser uses the name of Christ as a menace to those enemies whom he may desire to "shatter in pieces," Mr. Stead, with his business-like talents, does not hesitate to employ all the titles of the Saviour as a sort of advertising sandwich to his journal.

"The experience meeting of the Methodists," Mr. Stead has affirmed, "always seems to me so much more interesting and instructive than the mere word-spinning of essayists," and the whole of Mr. Stead's little world he converts into an "experience meeting of Methodists." His remark about the "word-spinning" is not unamusing to any one who has attended an "experience meeting" or "love-feast," or tea-gossip, or what-not of characteristic confabulation of Methodists, or even to one who has read the *Review of Reviews*. It is evidently not the "word-spinning" *per se* that is wearisome. It depends on the style. Mr. Stead has certainly found neither much interest nor instruction in the essayists, but with enviable self-satisfaction "spreads himself" in the rant and cant and preposterous jargon that he has found serviceable in the school of "experience." Nevertheless, or perhaps it is *because* of his neglect of the "essayists," Mr. Stead is very well satisfied with his own style and his own taste. The following, which appears in a political pamphlet, is astonishingly good; astonishing, if it were not from Stead : "And if there is one sentence or one word in this pamphlet which jars in discord with the keynote sounded by these Divine sayings. . . ." This passage gives us pause. It seems like rushing in where angels fear to tread.

Further on in the pamphlet we come across such flowers of rhetoric and "sayings" as : "What arrant drivel is this to be palmed off upon a community presumably more intelligent than a herd of microcephalous apes !" No doubt the intention here was to be forcible ;

but violence or explosion does not always imply effectiveness of doing, though to think so is a mistake with which not merely Mr. Stead's writing but Mr. Stead's whole constitution is imbued. He is a man of whom one could assert without more direct evidence than his demeanour that he had read and been "intensely" impressed by the Ecclefechan Sage. Carlyle has much to answer for, even in the fervent preaching of his doctrines of energy, and work, and purpose in life. He has a sad account to reckon with in the number of brains he has dislocated and the nervous constitutions his electrifying words have unhinged. Perhaps he is not to be held responsible at all for this, for it was not done with malice prepense. The storm wind from Labrador may serve the gallant three-masters, though it overturn the unballasted shallop.

However, just as in Byron's day there was a Byron cult, somewhat laughed at by Macaulay, and as in Deutschland there was a Werther cult, in which everything was done with "infinity," from the making of love to the drinking of beer; so in these latter days it is a commonplace to observe that not only is there a Carlyle cult, but that distinct physical appearances mark the disciples. One could pick out by the eye all the aspiring young parsons, for instance, who are imbued with Carlyle. There is a hard penetration in their eyes, staring like pebbles. This is the sign of "intensity." There is an awkwardness, an angularity, in their movements and manners, very uncomfortable to others (for they are "teachers")—a sort of mental as well as physical St. Vitus' Dance. They are "terribly earnest," they are "full of purpose," they are profoundly impressed not only with the awful responsibility of life but with their own importance, moreover ; and the more pronounced specimens are as absurd as if an old horse that ought to be pulling a coach were to devote the best part of his days to staring at the boards of his stall, with eye sore distraught at the conviction of everything being "all-wrang" in the regions of Horsedom. Well, one who has seen Helmholtz, whose work in science has been gigantic, does not observe the Carlylesque manner about him ; and, moreover, Napoleon did a huge amount of business while retaining an exceedingly plastic nature, and in the severest contingencies displaying not only complete presence of mind, but even at times an antique jocularity. We hold up such men as examples against the spasmodic school with its "sensations" and febrile excitements in matters of no remarkable import.

Napoleon describes the battle of Austerlitz with severe simplicity. Our newer journalists are capable of discoursing in dithyrambs over a vestry election, of writhing into hysterics over a street row, or dissolving into limitless "gush" over the birth or death of a princelet. There is something altogether unmanly in this; unsatisfactory too, in that it is but the indication—being the supply to the demand—of a weak and sickly state of Society, and the condition of what is called "culture."

Exaggeration in language is a sure mark of degeneracy in a nation. Nations which accomplish great deeds speak of them sincerely and gravely. The eras of the unheroic are the eras of extravagant and bolstered-up diction. This is a somewhat laborious instrument to put to work, one admits, to indicate that Mr. Stead's literary "monster demonstrations" are an unhealthy sign of the times; but we fear that those who have not found them preposterous already must be left to a surgical instrument. The German Kaiser, for example, according to Mr. Stead, is a Kubla Khan—a hair trigger,—the switchback of the Continent—a supreme type of the most vigorous type of latter-day journalist—in a word, an Imperial Mr. Stead. Mrs. Besant's spiritual developments—here is a great field for Stead—are through "agonies of doubt"—"horrors of great darkness"—"regions of political storm and stress in which she was hereafter to swell" (*sic*)—"for baby's sake"—"the struggle to believe"—Maurice, Robertson, Stopford Brooke, Greg, and Pusey, &c., &c., &c., up to the "crisis once more."

And here is another passage worth quoting, indicating Mr. Stead's character in a score of little points, and allowing the public to know of his "stalwartness" and his magnanimity—a magnanimity none the less admirable, perhaps, that it is only his amusing self-righteousness, his exquisite Pharisaism, that makes it magnanimity at all.

"Side by side with other stalwarts we marched across London with Linnell's corpse, in a funeral procession the like of which London had seldom seen, and at the open grave of another martyr to police brutality—a Secularist buried without religious rite or words of consolation—I publicly gave Mrs. Besant the right hand of fellowship in the name of Him who came to seek and to save the least of these His brethren."

Terrible engines, you see, and all manner of transcendental ecstasies and communions, have to be put to work in the soul of the "stalwart," after the funeral procession ("the like of which London had seldom seen"), before he could give his hand to Mrs. Besant or stand at the open

K

grave of a Secularist—for the eyes of the civilised world were upon him.

But how appears our modern St. Paul in the flesh ? for we must have more tangible points on which to rest our idea of his interesting personality. At first glance he is a very average man, and even at the last glance one has failed to discover any trait of genius or power or fine quality such as generally marks out a man born to lead. In fact, were it not for that "earnest" glaring eye and a certain nervous unrestful look, one could hardly suspect such an ordinary bourgeois of having a thorn in his side to buffet him, or hardly even a bee in his bonnet. There are a hundred points that might be in the countenance of a fine man, that we might even desire to see in the countenance of a man sympathetic to our view, that are not to be found in Mr. Stead. From the square uneloquent forehead, to the full brown or tawny beard, and the common lines of the features, there is nothing, except for the energy of that somewhat Carlylesque orb, that would not be found any day in, say, the picture the *British Workman* would give of a respectable journeyman carpenter. Mr. Stead's figure is wiry and serviceable, without being very strong or athletic. He looks as though he would be a healthy plebeian, were he not overwrought and overstrung. He is just the man to have been the editor of the *Northern Echo* at the age of twenty-two, with great ambitions for London, to be nine years afterwards fulfilled. In 1880 he was John Morley's assistant editor of the *Pall Mall Gazette*; editor in 1883; and author and publisher of the "Maiden Tribute" in July 1885. That was a great date for Mr. Stead.

It was the legitimate, or at least the inevitable, outcome of Steadism. For, no praise or blame being implied in the reference, we may see how all the characteristics of the man contributed to that remarkable production — the severe Nonconformist tenets, the fascination of London with its myriad forms of life, the sort of prurient activity of the champion of chastity, the vaunted outspokenness (that sort of bluntness of speech that, like the Alguazil's in "Gil Blas," wounds modesty more than does the fact it exposes), the horror, the hysterics, the journalist's instincts, the "sensation," the unlimited advertisement. If any one doubt this latter element, let him consider how a man just as "earnest" and "righteous" as Mr. Stead, with no *Pall Mall Gazette* to "boom," might have proceeded.

Mr. Stead was well-intentioned, no doubt. We are all well-intentioned, after our style. Zola is just as much well-intentioned; and, with remarkable genius and a depth of experience and thought quite beyond Mr. Stead, gives us very coarse matters in the midst—and to most people these are the pith—of his books. The judicial aspect of Mr. Stead's case seems to be that a very respectable man, and with the very best intentions, spread broadcast a certain liter ture, extremely nasty, flaunted and sold at a penny ; that he was thereupon sent to prison for a transgression of the laws of the land ; and that that imprisonment —"was about the best thing that ever happened to me in my life."

Since then Mr. Stead has proceeded from journalistic triumph to triumph. He has hob-nobbed with cardinals, and has reasoned with the Pope ; he has formed a romantic friendship with the Czar, and has half-patronised, half-yielded to hero worship of the Kaiser. There is something quite curious about his respect for great personages, their value as "copy," the desire for the "greatest show on airth," the instinctive reverence for titles, glitter and pomp, struggling with the democratic feelings (these, however, waning much of late in their stalwartness), the egregious self-esteem of the man who has risen to such dizzy heights. Perhaps it is the journalistic instinct which is really his *forte*. For a long time, before his recent mental diffusion, he could hardly go wrong. Every venture brought back even more than the expected return. Mr. Stead had well gauged the taste of the public ; that which greater men than Mr. Stead have often lamentably failed to do.

It is stated of Fox that he was in the habit of submitting a draft of any measure he had in contemplation to a certain lord who seemed by no means particularly astute. Fox, on being questioned about the matter, explained that he wanted to see how it would "strike the vulgar." There is much in this ; and without pressing the resemblance too particularly it will serve to give a hint of Mr. Stead's popularity and success. He is intellectually at the level of the great mass of humanity, and is enormously active within that range. Just as the desideratum in the theatre or in novels is not life, but what the majority take to be life, so the man who utters nothing better than platitudes may yet gain a reputation for profundity of thought. Many a man and many a woman to whom Herbert Spencer is an unknown quantity, or at best a dull pedant, might sit at the feet of Mr. Stead and believe his parochial dispensations of Divine ordinances to be the high-water mark of the wisdom of the race.

Then, again, the authority of a man of Mr. Stead's calibre is aided by contrast ; to wit, that there is in the popular mind a sort of distrust, not ill-founded, of learning and brilliancy. They are inclined to trust the ass that carries them rather than the horse that upsets them ; and if the ass be found to be full of vigour, endurance, and "go," they acquire for him quite an affectionate feeling. And again, Carlyle, insisting too narrowly upon the influence of body on mind, seemed to think that a man could hardly be a "great man" unless he were also a big man ; and sturdiness or "stalwartness" of character he expected to be associated always with a considerable *vis inertiæ* of the physical frame. A little reflection upon history or upon one's actual experience of life will play havoc with such slapdash determinants. But again with regard to the respect paid to that rare combination of qualities, "common sense," men of Mr. Stead's appearance and style get an unfair advantage.

So, after a hundred startlers, after a hundred displays of hysterics, veritable pyrotechnics of nerves ; after his "Truths," whether about Russia or Ireland, or the Church of the future, his Christmas Ghosts and various spooks, his proposal in practical politics for a sort of common supreme court for America and England, his Throughth, his Julia, his cancer cure, his opinions on literature, his opinions upon philosophy, and

the rest—after the ceaseless outpourings of rant
and cant, and so much of what it is unnecessary
to call balderdash, Mr. Stead is still admiringly
esteemed as a veritable Daniel in judgment. His
dealing with "sensational" questions calls to mind
the African woman beholding for the first time a
white man ; she pinched her belly violently, and
leapt ecstatically into the air. But that, no doubt,
appeared to her friends a very reasonable mode
of procedure. A careful consideration of all the
grounds of Mr. Stead's popularity would explain
why men of genius are so often accounted insane.

But with some people the word "popularity"
very faintly describes the feeling which Mr. Stead
has inspired. With women especially, or those at
least of more or less feminine minds, Mr. Stead is
a prophet, a centre of light and leading, himself
the founder of a cult. He is a benign person,
with a sort of molly-coddlish assiduity in women's
affairs, a sort of pottering about the washing-days
of life, the back kitchens, the baby linens, and
similar familiar domestic details. His mirthfulness
of spirit and jocularity is of that kind which sets
the Sunday-school mistresses into furious giggles.
And there is nothing more amusing than his
occasional lapses, or rather deliberate broachings,
of slang. There, again, it is like the curate who
is capable of using mildly explosive language in

order to give a hint of what a devil-of-a-fellow he might have been, and even is. Mr. Stead patronises slang to show that he is alive everywhere, and terribly up to date and broad-minded as well. For a like reason he occasionally patronises Huxley in his *Review of Reviews.* Huxley had occasion once to affirm that there was no better ground for assuming one God than many. Mr. Stead refers to this by the remark that Mr. Huxley was putting in a good word for polytheism ! It is the sly smirk of back parlour polemics.

After all, Mr. Stead is not a man to be pursued with any acrimony. It would be a hard heart that failed to acknowledge all the good qualities of "dear Mr. Stead." But one is entitled, once in a way, to set up against Mr. Stead standards more universal than his ; for it is only by concessions to his own little conventions, his own self-righteousness, the infallibility of his Little Pedlington purview of religion and politics, that he has any particular authority at all. He would shine especially in an epitaph where he would have it all his own way. He would be described as enthusiastic in the cause of "light and leading," as foremost in all "human progress," as incredibly brave, hysterically fearless, the defender of purity in the *Pall Mall Gazette*, and the Barnum of the *Review of Keviews.* He is a lover of England *à la* Stead. He encourages literature with that amusing "broad mind" of his, and with something of the style of a man who subscribes to an opera though having no ear for music. Of course this does not prevent his imagining—he of the essentially prose mind—that he appreciates poetry. For there are Pegasuses and Pegasuses, some without wings, some without wind, and some even made to order out of wood. Pegasus had, in Byron's time, learnt to take a "psalmodic amble under the very Rev. Roly Poly ;" and since then there have been Pegasuses husky-breathed, straining-eyed, and very spasmodic in gait. Mr. Stead would have a judicious, respectable, self-complacent superiority to Byron or Shelley. Keats would be an unknown quantity. Shakspere he would "take on" like the British constitution, not only as something to be proud of, but also as a duty. Martin Tupper would be too calm, though wise. Wordsworth would have many moods delightful to Stead. Tennyson is more than respectable : he is an institution under the patronage of the Court. Longfellow will fill up Mr. Stead to the brim ; and the shrewd Yankee, Lowell, with his 'cuteness and fervour, would rise to the height of a "teacher."

And so with Science. Science "in the abstract" must be something as foreign to Mr. Stead, even as dangerous to his peace of mind, as Socialism to the German Kaiser. Yet he sees its growing importance. He is heroic enough to praise it ; and even, when it produces something which he can touch with his hands, condescending enough to be enormously pleased with it and to wish to encourage it.

It is business that Mr. Stead is after. He is on the look out for novelty, for startling novelty. He wants something that will "sizzle" the public. The style he admires is a style with a "tang" in it. "Hev' the big bell fell yet ?" Lowell's farmer gasped, out of breath, as he ran up to see the fire in the church. Mr. Stead is always gasping for the big bell. Mr. Stead likes "snap" and "bite ;" that is to say in others, for his own style is tumid and vapid in its egregious rhapsodical bathos. But to hear Mr. Stead on business is really delightful. To hear him on poetry or science or "thought" is distressing—but on business ! He becomes masterly, felicitous, really pleasant in style. His scheme of the " Ideal Newspaper " is grandiose, but it will doubtless be one day a reality. It will have its Premier, its Cabinet, its departments, offices of administration—truly excellent. To hear him run rapidly over the strong points and the deficiencies of the London dailies is stimulating and full of instruction. Business, newspaper business, that is his *forte*. It would be worth

£20,000 a year to a great journal or a big firm of publishers to have Mr. Stead locked up on the premises, on the condition of rejecting nine-tenths of his suggestions—not that Mr. Stead would not suffer grievously from this restraint, and the British public also. For the range of Mr. Stead's activities is very wide, so wide that it would be difficult to enumerate them. He is full of zeal and full of work, none the less certainly because his mind is not very judicial and because his feelings are inevitably partisan. Everything that he believes to be a work of progress, everything that he believes to be an honest endeavour to do good according to the gospel of Stead, he is ready to encourage, to help, to show the way. We must make the most of Stead while we have him. "The evil a man does lives after him; the good is oft interred with his bones—so let it be with Cæsar;" and also with Stead. He is a live man, and his business activities and journalistic enterprises are more likely to be of benefit to the race while he is alive than are the records of those perfervid speculations of his after his death. When his planning, scheming, plotting, steaming, unrestful little brain shall at length have been brought to repose, then will remain of its alchemy, mainly—some valuable ideas of the New Journalism.

T. P. O'CONNOR

> " And what if here and miles away
>   We'd let a soaring fancy stray
>   To pick up chips to build a lay
>   With which to sing about Tay Pay?—
>   By nature warm and soft as day,
>   His shpirit's full of tender play,
>   Like billows on a slumbering say ;
>   But wrongs to wring a heart of clay
>   Have woke within the sterner trait—
>   Blow, breezes, blow, and trumpets bray—
>   He's bowld as lions in the fray ;
>   And yet throughout life's mixed display
>   The sowl is never far away—
>   What, arrah, more is left to say?
>   It comes to this in every way,
>   And which no other words portray,
>   *He is the only and the wone Tay Pay.*"

T. P. O'CONNOR is an Irishman. The phrase is
plain and full of information, yet on the very
surface it sounds redundant, not to say exuberant ;
and though given in perfect seriousness, and with
the intention of advancing the argument, it is
already apt to raise upon the reader's lips a smile.
Yet it is on this that we will continue to play in
making T. P. our document—T. P.'s Irishry,
T. P.'s exuberance, T. P.'s perfect seriousness of

intention, and yet withal the subtle something that prevents us from taking T. P. altogether too gravely. For even in an analysis of character it is not sufficient, we presume, to hold up mere blank symbols or formulæ. True it is that we can indulge in no elaboration ; but, with bold indicative strokes and with splashes here and there, we must endeavour to give relief, a little colour, a little warmth, and, if possible, a touch of the environment and a half-felt infusion of atmosphere. And with T. P. we can do this *con amore*, with a delightful feeling too of a relaxation from hard responsibility, and—for he is a sympathetic creature himself—with something better than a mere stern sense of duty.

Behold, then, T. P. in the flesh ; but not yet, for we will first describe another man, not T. P. but the great Dan, not O'Connor but O'Connell. And why ? Because we observe at a glance a very Irish look about T. P., and, trying desperately to find out where it precisely is, and not succeeding beyond a vague impression that it is there, *everywhere*, we look up for a " supreme type of the best type "—the phrase is Mr. Stead's—" of latter-day journalist," Mr. Stead's phrase naturally runs on ; but we mean of an Irishman at large. And we find it in Dan.

The Liberator from the mere standpoint of

the artist, to say nothing of the Documentator, is hardly less interesting a personage than Napoleon himself. Every moment of his life must have been a study for picture or statue or historian's scroll. The pose heroic was his natural attitude. Tall, stout, well-made, easy, healthy, as from a good stock, Dan was truly a " grand shtamp of man."   His fine presence is capable even of taking from our modern habiliments their usual appearance of vulgarity.   His cloak he wears about him like a toga.   The features are the genuine Celtic —the brow broad, not lofty, but heavy, pregnant, almost lowering ; the eye good-humoured, but dauntless ; the nose short, unclassical, but of no bad type ; the lower part of the face heavy, but not dull ; the mouth full of expression, pursy, humorous, voluble. O'Connell looks what he was—a man practical but eloquent ; not metaphysical, yet often influenced by intangible spiritual things ; apt to seize the salient features of great situations ; a man born to command and to debate, his skill for marshalling facts in argument being well matched by his capacity for organising a great popular movement. Yet withal he is overflowing with kindliness, shrewdness, humour, and good-humour.

Why have we talked of Dan O'Connell ? In order to come to T. P., for what the one had in greatness and adversity the other has in less of greatness but more of prosperity; Dan is the Liberator who crowned his life by the easement to some extent at least of the Saxon yoke; T. P. is the Liberated who begins his life fairly by beating the Saxon to some extent upon his own foggy ground; Dan, to be sure, had the faults of his qualities; T. P. has considerably less of the qualities, but *en revanche* a good deal more of the faults.

Carlyle has hammered into us so much about the hero as man of letters, and Mr. Stead has emphasised the suggestion of a latter-day journalist being a sort of St. Paul, and the retailing and wholesaling of gossip has reached such enormous proportions, and the leading articles are so packed with cant, and the age is so delicately cultured, that the stranger, more innocent than intelligent, coming to London, naturally expects to find the editors of famous penny and halfpenny sheets just like so many Jupiters or Apollos, or, to satisfy all susceptibilities, so many Moses's and St. Pauls. . . . But, alas, look on this picture and on that ! T. P., for instance, is not in the least like Apollo. He is much nearer to Pollux, and Pollux in his " off " days at that. He has the build of a coal-heaver or a prize-fighter, a torso that would have made Jem Mace " sit up " (the

phrase is one of the new journalism), and a
countenance that might have excited his professional envy. We note these things particularly,
for experience will show that in the " battle of life "
Pollux is the better fighting man, and Apollo finds
his lyre something worse than a bad second fiddle.

Or, under another figure, Pollux plays for the
pit, and if we inquire respecting the dress circle,
we cast our eyes upward, and behold there also
the friends mainly of Pollux. However, though
T. P. has such a fine breadth of shoulders, he
makes no very imposing appearance. He lacks
"carriage," or, perhaps, remembering how much
he is on the "big side" we should rather say
"deportment." A prize-fighter would grieve over
him a little as of a good man gone wrong. He is
too soft, looks as though he had never been
trained, lacks "steel," and walks with a loose and
unbraced knee. Physically, he is rather a big
man than a fine man. (And here is suggested a
great complaint against the sum total of our
civilisation, for Diogenes would need to search
just as diligently as of yore to find a *man*, a
man through and through. Would we were all
Afghans or undeteriorated Moors, or Crotonians,
for if genius be generally insane, so likewise
civilisation in many of its aspects is nothing but a
huge disease.) . . .

T. P.'s countenance is short and round, with a cast that marks him at once as Pan-Celtic, the forehead low but full, a good deal furrowed, however, too much so—for most of the furrows have the suggestion of mere worries and troubles, rather than of very deep thought. His eye is much less luminous than one would have hoped for, and the eyelids are tired and dragged. The nose is as Irish as Drogheda, but we have seen very many far better noses in Ireland. However, a nose too short is more than compensated for by an equally Irish and abundantly voluble mouth. His hair is dark and short, moustache the same. Such is T. P.—a fine broth of a boy, who has had a very tough fight in the metropolis of the brutal Saxon, and who has pulled through with a somewhat jaded constitution, rather a fagged look, and the loss in many ways of his Irish "original brightness."

T. P. has become a little Saxonised himself, and even affects, when he can, something of their cold, flat speech instead of that "large utterance" of his own native islanders that seems to come up from the heart and carry not a little of the human nature along with it. His voice is at times like the tinkling of a tin bell when you have been expecting, and even wishing, that he would vibrate and sound like a cauldron. Yet T. P has not entirely lost his brogue in his speech, and even in his writing it is still able to take the chill off the English. For the brogue is more than a mere accent—it is a rhythm, a balance, a cadence of the sentence. In Cork, at some little distance off—we are tumbling into it—when the mere sound falls upon the ear one could hardly suspect that it was English that the bhoys were "afther speaking," for instead of the English tone, abrupt, business-like, with a succession of hard little saccades with a slurring between, the speech of the Irish is chanted ; they call out in strophe and respond in antistrophe ; and, further, the language itself is a great part of the business—they love words as words. Hence has come about that rhetorical habit which has been one of the sources of woe to that unhappy land, yet, after all, to look on all sides, no undervalued little prize of consolement.

Rhetoric is in the air in Ireland, and one of the men in whom it was specially distinguished, and who has sent in turn much of his spirit abroad, was the famous, or at least in Ireland famous, Thomas Francis Meagher. Meagher had all the qualities of the hero of a romantic novel, and a good deal more besides, for he had brains, undoubtedly, and was able to give evidence of the same ; and lastly, or perhaps we should say firstly, he had also a "gift" of irresistible, out-

pouring, blood-stirring eloquence. Now many
of those who have come after Meagher have
caught the accent, and most of the tyros in every
debating club, or Celtic, or Nationalist, or in any
manner patriotic association, aim, if not at the
delightfulness and the exuberance of the ideas
of their hero, yet at any rate at the flow and
"shwing" of his stirring, billowy periods.—We
are not leaving T. P. altogether, but we are "playing round him a bit."—A lecture has been given
on Irish history, let us say, and when the lecturer
has ceased after having made their pulses beat
high, then one would think that the end would
never arrive of all the proposings and secondings,
and what not; and all the bhoys that rise to pro-
pose their votes of thanks are rough replicas of
Thomas Francis Meagher in the Dock at Clonmel.
They work themselves up as if they were winding
up a clock, and with blazing eye, and hair on end,
and vibrating voice, they thank the lecturer not
only for his "historical research," but also for his
"magnificent genius;" and not for this alone, but
also for his "pungent accuracy" as well as "dis-
perate instruction." *Pungent* does not seem to
fit in very well with *accuracy*, but when one was
well on the rising wave, the rhythm *had* to be
filled in, and something must give way somewhere,
and so the rhetorical phrase is filled up before

the mere cold term of precision. Besides, there
is much in that "pungent accuracy;" if it were
elucidated and made "limpid" it would be found
to be a very pretty idea, but what it loses in its
turbidity it gains in a delightful sort of—what
shall we say ?—shandy-gaffing of notions.

Now we come to T. P., though naturally in an
M.A. of Trinity College, Dublin, and the author
of ever so many good books, and the Sunday and
never uninteresting oracle of the best week's work,
we must expect to taste with no coarse and slapdash palate the delicious touch of the "stick"
amidst the hot water and lemon ; yet the aroma,
the Irish afflatus, will be appreciated, *just so, the
much more !*   Let us quote T. P. :—

"The cries . . . pierced not his ear and moved
not his heart" gives us just a squeeze.

"A common enemy is a great bond of friendship" is something to muse on, and "The tide of
Christian invasion floating against the East" has
a suggestion of the "billow."

"In both the one case and the other he employed the sacred name of religion and men's
spiritual instincts for the purpose of gratifying his
own desires."   If this be carefully tasted the
flavour will come out at a dozen little spots.

"To lead blind and benighted followers into
paths they did not expect" is something serious,

but something redundant. Why did T. P. make them benighted as well as blind ? To fill up this measure of rhetoric.

And there is not a little *pungent* accuracy in this :—

"But *here* are the Jews, dispersed over every part of the globe, speaking different languages, divided in nearly every sympathy—separated, in fact, by everything that can separate man, except the one point of race, but united in their feelings on this great contest."

The first and second phase show a very wide outlook, and the "divided in nearly every sympathy" brings us back again to a very fine point ; but that *except* is a gem in its setting.

"I am not the biographer," exclaims T. P. in another place, "of a creature of my imagination ; . . . and if I have to repeat myself over and over again, it is because Lord Beaconsfield is the same from the time when, as a stripling, he sought election in 1832, down to this *very moment when he is seventy-four years of age*, and the ruler of this great Empire. . . . In the instance just quoted I find him again making the most unfounded statements, although the Premier of England, and although every one of these statements *affected* the existence of millions of human beings in the present, and millions of human beings in the *future*."

Are we hunting in all T. P.'s most careless of writings for these little flowers of rhetoric ? Faith, then, no. We are but turning over casually the leaves of T. P.'s Life of Beaconsfield. But T. P. runs the great oriental conjurer very hard for the suffrages of posterity. "To such "—note the Demosthenean stroke—"To such it is given to sway by his single will your fortunes and mine, and even those of countless generations yet to come." The Jewish conjurer was indeed "superlative" then, and all with a *single* will. The whole passage is something unique.

Yet T. P.'s "Beaconsfield" is a great book. It is laborious, full of information, built up like the argument of a clever advocate, and in such a way as to carry conviction ; and, moreover, there is not a dull page in it. The so-called stylists, with their polish of verbiage, their "precious" mannerisms, and their superficial and barren ideas, are generally tedious enough, and are made the more intolerable bores because they are held up as exemplars ; but T. P., even in his nonsense, has something of the afflatus. He is vivid, without being *too* vivid, as some are with their spangles of dazzling words ; in T. P.'s vividness there is more of blood than of nerve. T. P. is something of an inspirational writer. He gives us not only the idea, but the thousand subtle associations and suggestions along with the idea. He contrives to give, or rather gives without contrivance, colour and odour and attitude and the "impulsion of

the ideas as they light" into his mind. He is
thinking of the thing more than of its symbol;
and then when he writes he is thinking of more
symbols than things.

There are styles that one may call "cham-
pagny." Schiller, though not illustrating the
idea, yet trusted somewhat to the beverage for
his nocturnal inspirations. Byron found a stimulation in the waters of Geneva, not merely his
" clear placid Leman," but the other "contrasted"
product of the place ; and, finally, if the proverb
be true, " Drink beer think beer," we may presume that the more vulgar liquor is in great
request at the offices of some great daily broad-
sheets. T. P.'s style, however, has more body
than champagne, and is elevated far above beer.
It suggests to us—what then ?—with its warmth
and its flow—with its round and generous flavour
—with its aroma, its inspiration ; yes, that can
lead but to one thing—what shall we say to be
very Irish ?—the mountain dew of his own native
valleys, where the very green grass has a flash and
a verve nowhere else in the world to be seen.

T. P.'s books are all readable, and all full of
instruction. He has a great idea of actuality, and
the palpitant association is never far away. T. P.
is seldom humorous. He is even always, or nearly
always, quite earnest. It is his readers who have

the humour, or at least who smile pretty often where T. P. himself sees nothing to keep them amused.

But pathos is T. P.'s real strong point. He is always sympathetic, but at times he is touching—more than touching, desperately moving. T. P. has a way of drawing you a *weeshy* sort of stroke with the tears in his eyes, "and the heart must be cold and the imagination sluggish which refused to be stirred" as one looks on the page.

This is particularly the case in T. P.'s latest book, "The Life of Parnell," an admirable book, moreover, well-balanced, just in perspective, written with genuine sympathy, and, as one would naturally expect from T. P., with plenty of his own pictorial vividness and interest, that never once flags. The little book was written at about twenty-four hours' notice—a great feat, even though it was not much more than a rearrangement of already published material.

His "Parnell Movement" is also a most interesting book, and to read T. P. with the glow on, one is carried away into thinking that his heroes are hardly inferior to Homer's. Yet in the light of common day they seem to resemble the Agamemnons and Achilles principally in their voluble mutual denunciations, antistrophe and strophe, and in their never yet doubted readiness for a general fray.

Singularly enough, or possibly naturally enough, it is to be remarked of late that T. P. is becoming more pathetic, and also that he is showing remarkable evidence of a strong ethical troubling. From the examples we have given of T. P.'s "pungent accuracy" it might have been inferred that he would be one of the last of men to solve subtle psychological problems; for these depend on exquisite introspection, and something, too, of analysis. We do not aver that T. P. has solved, or ever will solve, anything "in that line," but we affirm that the ethical purpose is there, and may be observed in all sorts of odd places giving off steam. T. P. probes the mysteries of time and space and the human soul with a blackthorn. Yes, there is lately an unrest about T. P. The days are past of "delicious anticipation and great and unsated longings; and there is the unrest of middle age, which is the product of disillusion and weariness." Poor T. P.; even less than "fifty years of Europe" has been too much for him. He longs, if not for a "cycle of Cathay," yet at least for a trip to Japan, "the enchanted land of *delighted* manners," or to India in spite of "its deadly perils and *circumambient terrors;*" anywhere, in fact, away from the "perplexing problems and duties and conflicts that surround one in Western lands"—anywhere; but T. P. goes *further* than that. For what can one think of this flight of his ?—

"If man be in his chief elements composed purely of matter ; if on matter depend health, happiness, genius, the proper resultant of the appeal of passion, duty, and conviction to the brain—then human endeavour to relieve man's estate may always go on with illimitable and enduring ardour. The amelioration of man's physical condition has no limits—save at the close of all our journeys, be they in health or decrepitude, in happiness or in despair, there ever stands dark Death as the end of it all."

There are a hundred little points of "desperate instruction" in this little meditation. The problem whether health depends on matter is not a bad one for a man of T. P.'s width of shoulders, for T. P. can hardly be like Plotinus, who was ashamed of his body. What the "proper resultant of the appeal of . . . conviction to the brain" may be one hardly knows, and perhaps, as Dr. Johnson once said when asked to explain his meaning, "perhaps no man will ever know." Has T. P. been reading his Plato, or his Spinoza, or his Kant in their originals, or in what remarkable fashion has his Hibernian brain evolved this point of pure reason, that *then* human endeavour may not only with *illimitable* but also with *enduring* ardour "*always* go on" ?

The last great sentence about dark Death being

the "end of it all" few would venture to dispute, but in another of T. P.'s musings we come across something that "would have *sacrificed the dead* to the reputations of the still living." So that T. P. is concerned not only about the "fortunes" of the countless generations yet to come, but presumably about the rights of those who have gone.

But we must leave T. P. the philosopher in order to consider the statesman T. P.; for T. P. is one of the most versatile of men, and from the airy heights of unfettered speculations can descend to the giving up "to party what was meant for mankind." T. P. in these latter days, it is said, has lost some of his old fervour for Ireland, and now should be ranked simply (*och hone!*) as a Radical and English.

There are many points of view for considering this. Stands *Ireland* where she did? Alas! it is too much fervour that is ruining her, too much historical and rhetorical "desperate instruction." And T. P. is the man who has in his own person done something, perhaps from his own point of view one of the best of things, towards solving the national immemorial trouble. For T. P. came, as we said, to the metropolis of the Saxon and beat him in his own Bœotian strongholds and with his own weapons.

T. P. must have been quite an heroic figure in

those days—young, handsome, and unfortunate, but with the fire of enthusiasm in his eye, a fierce, desperately clinging, *unscissible* resolution in his heart, and last, but not least, the key to the golden doors—the brilliant, the Sheridaine, the O'Connelique impeachment of the " Great Earl " himself. Therein T. P. has beaten them all, the other patriots ; and perhaps on the whole, to those who believe in a final reconciliation with England, he is a more commendable, and certainly a safer, guide than Thomas Francis Meagher himself.

It is hard to point out where T. P. has cooled in his love for all that is best in Ireland ; not that we pin our trust to T. P., or believe that he pins too much of that sort of thing to himself. He has been a new journalist for a good many years, and a newer journalist quite recently, and in this new sphere it is his Radicalism that is somewhat more dubious of late. To call T. P. an English Radical is not quite apt; he is rather an Irish Gladstonian. T. P. is a hero-worshipper. That might have been predicted of him—with his strong vein of sentiment, of enthusiasm, the billowy or tidal movement of his ideas, the softness of his steel, or what ought to be steel, and his lack of thorough-going faith in himself or his purpose. The great Dan whom we mentioned for a good reason at first would have been for

T. P. a complete hero. But Dan is dead, and
T. P., as new journalist, is great on "actuality."
Hence Gladstone's the man. His qualities are
those precisely that appeal to T. P., not only for
admiration, but for the strong smack of sympathy,
the boiling of the blood of enthusiasm. . . .
There is absolutely no word in English to express
what the Germans call *Schwärmerei*—the idea of
there being not a bee in the bonnet, but a thousand restless but not unpleasant little devils of
bees in the brain that completely buzz away the
judgment, but leave you their own humming
Schwärmerei, which seems ever so much better
than judgment. Now T. P. the experienced, the
weather-beaten, the road-dusted man of a not
very luminous world, the politician, the agitator,
the new journalist, the prober into mysteries,
can *schwärmen* like a blue-eyed, yellow-pigtailed
little German maid of sixteen.

And, further, there are many things that tend
to heat up T. P.'s admiration for the Grand Old
Man. For not only has he the qualities to sweep
over T. P., but if he have faults, there are none
of which T. P. is free. And not only that, but
just as every one thinks his own little sect to be
all of the "world," so in the eyes of T. P. the
whole business of politics and parties has a preposterous importance in the perspective of life.

He is, as Emerson wrote to Carlyle of Webster (a fine character in his way, interesting mainly to Carlyle for his "crag-like amorphous countenance"), "soaked"—one regrets it—"soaked in the rum of party." There is something very amusing in the importance, in the whole constitution of things, and particularly in regard to the building-up of our modern life, that T. P. assigns to the members — mostly "barren rascals" Dr. Johnson would have said—who have sat in St. Stephen's. But T. P. is very serious.

And so we are coming to the end of a very excellent subject, and finding T. P., as he himself said of Beaconsfield, "the *same* from the time when as a stripling he sought" his fortune in London down to the *very moment—when* we hope he will live long to enjoy it. It is true we have not beheld him in his rage, and T. P. can be terrible. But even then, whether it be in the good old Sheridaine invective, the biting, antithetical, Johnsonian sarcasm, the sirocco of his withering scorn, or in many a little vicious *swish* at "contemptible" personal enemies, T. P.—there is something not quite tragic in the fate of T. P. —T. P. fails to make an impression entirely and utterly grave.

And why go further? For it is not in the quantity of a man's products that we must seek for guidance, but in the quality. Every man can pour forth indefinitely at his own level. The thing to ascertain is the *scope* of his reticulating outpouring works ; then if we hold the little scheme of his mind and dip a sort of lactometer into his -blood, we can guess what he will continue to do in the "concrete." And of T. P. it remains to be said that, compared with the hide-bound brains of most men, he can pour forth more abundantly and more exuberantly in response to the like outward prod or probe.

ZOLA[1]

"WHEN I have seen the two others," cried I, after a visit to Zola (thinking of two, distinguished in quite other realms of intellectual exercise), "I shall have seen all the great men in the world!" And while I was thinking of great men, it was less on account, perhaps, of any shining example of well-balanced and amiable virtues than of those qualities which distinguish a man and his work from all others; which make his advent a particular incident in the march of civilisation and culture; which make him not merely superior in the path in which others are striving, but mark him out, original, unapproachable, incomparable—all that, to give it the word, makes genius, that something so hard to define, yet so unmistakable in its characteristic and confident display. And in the enjoyment of those ideas which brought the figure of Zola within a circle so limited of "particular stars" that I should hesitate to mention it, there came to my mind the saying of Coleridge, that

he had known many men who had done great
work, but had known only one great man—
Wordsworth being, I believe, the individual so
distinguished.

For what we seem to look for is not merely
one who has distinguished himself by a great
service or in the accomplishment of a severe duty,
or one who has in his own corner woven the
part that has joined on to the whole great woof
of civilisation ; we seem to look for the man
whose work grows out of the needs of his own
great personality, who is prepared if need be to
check and thwart and turn the current of civilisation towards new directions ; the man whose
work is thoroughly characteristic and identified
with himself, the direct output of his original
nature ; the man who becomes a critical point,
a node, in the way of some great human activity.
And of those who, in the whole course of literature, strike our attention and attract by a curiosity which continually grows and deepens into
a superior interest, prominently stands the figure
of Emile Zola. So one might think, at least, who,
having pursued his way through the vast tracts of
contemporary English literature, and finding so
much to admire and so little to satisfy, and who
had at length in the somewhat vaguely defined
wants of his spirit demanded a wider range, a

keener glance, a deeper experience, a more masculine grasp, and that something *derb*, as the
Germans say—the quality of tough resistance—
and who had at length lighted on a great passage
of Zola, and found his need realised, and with a
vengeance, and had been compelled to lay the
book aside stupefied by the onset of huge emotions, and had long afterwards returned to make
a study of these prodigious writings.

Therefore it is that I am urged to attempt a
documentation of this man, and to do something
perhaps towards removing such of the objections
to his work as spring from mere prejudice, or mis-
apprehension. For the impression I had at first
formed of Zola was that of a vehement, passionate
man, rebellious, iconoclastic, with a strong magnetic
personality, an on-driving dynamic energy, a certain "proud precipitance of soul," even in malign
things, a sort of Danton of literature, not unmixed
with Belial. And, behold, his portrait shows us a
countenance, even if less demoniac and disquiet-
ing, yet on the whole disappointing. The type
is Teutonic rather than French, the features
dragged and heavy-looking, the expression earnest
but slow, and charged with the appearance of
deep and not entirely sympathetic sadness. He
looks like a solid *bourgeois*, harassed and overwrought, with no indication of brilliancy, none of

those beaming lights and glancing changes which we always hope to discover as the external signs of genius ; but nevertheless of great tenacity, and with the aspect of one who could "toil terribly."

An encounter with the actual Zola in the flesh, however, makes us recognise that his portraits fail to do him justice, and indeed makes his whole personality more understandable. His countenance is much more full of energy and alertness than in any of the portraits ; the regard, though thoughtful and grave, has nothing of the wearisome look of mere melancholy. The head is well balanced upon a thick and heavy torso, suggesting, familiarly, an honest *bourgeois* of good original constitution impaired by a sedentary habit and the troubles of indigestion arising from the privations of early life. But though Zola is above middle height, and stands erect with broad shoulders and stout limbs in easy posture, and with a figure not even yet pronouncedly inclining to corpulence, he has nothing of a commanding aspect or of the suggestion of great muscular power, still less of athletic accomplishment. Rather he seems admirably fitted to withstand the evils of his own particular *metier*, those colics, stones, gravels, and all the list of atrocious things which Burton in his "Anatomy of Melancholy" assures us afflict great scholars.

And so in the comfortable negligence of his *bourgeois* habiliments, the nonchalant courtesy of manner, that absence of any form of affectation or pretension—the style of a man, in short, who has won an unassailable position in the great Paris—Zola makes an impression which, if not particularly striking, gives at least the assurance of abiding for ever with complete respect. His eye is rather short-sighted, but without that confused, uncertain look so often found with short-sighted people; his glance is direct and calm, conveying no small hint of the profound intelligence that is summing you up. Yet withal he looks at you benevolently. The voice is sonorous, slightly nasal, suggestive of the Italian in Zola's ancestry (it is in these terms, it may be mentioned in passing, that the voice of Napoleon is described), the *vox fusca*, the dark-coloured voice of the Romans, that accords so well with the deep, grave character of the utterance. The countenance is drawn into lines that tell rather of severe studies, patient labours, than of turbulent and distracting emotions. The complexion is pale, slightly sallow, but of an even sallowness that seems derived from race and constitution rather than from the distress of ill-health. The nose is short and well-formed, the lips full and firm, the moustache and short beard thick and coarse,

turning grey, the whole head, of size corresponding to the figure, strong and solid, not thin and
not soft. The forehead is neither very high nor
very broad, but, presumably, ample, and the
temples are peculiarly prominent and square—
this being perhaps the most striking characteristic
of the countenance—and this prominence is the
more marked by reason of the hair, coarse and of
a dark tawny colour, being drawn back from the
forehead.

Such, then, are the exterior aspects of the por-
tentous Zola. His moral and intellectual qualities
will perhaps come the better into relief if we take
a brief survey, with a sympathetic consideration,
of his career.

Zola was born near the Halles in Paris in 1840,
his father being an Italian, an engineer of ability,
his mother a Frenchwoman. The father died
when Emile was but seven years of age ; but the
mother, though sorely put to it, managed by dint
of self-denials and steady purpose to secure her
son a liberal education. It was in the South of
France, in that Aix which figures in his romances
under the name of Plassans, that Zola spent his
childhood and early youth. And it is scenes from
early recollections that are continually cropping
up in his writings, marking them indeed from
other descriptions by the greater ease and expan-

sibility, the greater sympathy of treatment. The
" Paradou " of *La Faute de l'Abbé Mouret*, for
example, arises from such delightful memories ;
for on a certain beautiful day in spring, Zola as
a boy had taken a peep over the wall of an old
neglected property, " Galice," between Aix and
Roquefavour. Nothing more congenial to him,
one may be sure—the beautiful earth, the lusty
growth of flower and shrub, their fragrance, the
unkept unartificial profusion. And all this and
a great deal more has Zola reproduced in his
description — the exuberance of increase, the
freedom of the wilderness, the native savage health
of the garden, all the forms of teeming lower life,
the aromatic perfumes, the incense, the freshness
of the air, the melodious sounds, the indefinable
sense of renewal, of fructification, in the atmosphere. Nor does he stop here, for with his inevitable tendency to symbolisation, with the artistic
impulses towards expansion, the earth becomes
infused with conscious life, a sort of energy of
dreaming, a feeling and a purpose of perpetual
reproduction. The nobly formed but mentally
undeveloped Désirée, sister of the Abbé Mouret,
is *Cybele !* The Abbé at length becomes *Adam ;*
his companion, Armine, *Eve !*

And so too in the first and one of the best of
the Rougon-Macquart series, *La Fortune des*

Rougon, one feels how much is wrought out from vivid early impressions. The characters live and move, and the story gives, without forcing or exaggeration, a glimpse at the whole agitated little life of a provincial town.

And, again, the description of the marching upon Paris of the Insurgents, bent upon resisting the *Coup d'Etât* of Louis Napoleon, and also the delightful story interwoven of Sylvére and Miette, are all replete with sympathetic natural touches ; but here too the artistic ardour of portrayal escapes the control of reason. The successive files of the Insurgents, with their improvised weapons, their scythes and their pikes, are named after the style of the Homeric catalogues of ships, and in the beautiful night the wild chords of the " Marseillaise " ascend, become repeated and re-echoed, and fill the valley, until, as almost by the seizure of a palpable Goddess of Liberty, the whole troop seems carried along and led to the strains of the magnificent music. And in another part the story of the two young lovers becomes gradually idealised, till at length it is no longer Sylvére and Miette that stand before us, but Daphnis and Chloë ; till at length, again, in another aspect the same Miette has become transfigured in her death even as the type of the young Republic slain.

All these matters are understandable in a study of Zola's personality and history. The future realist was, as a boy, serious, shy, not fond of sports, deeply emotional, subject to brooding fits, and, though gentle in disposition, not widely sympathetic nor sociable. A certain degree of short-sightedness contributed, no doubt—as some like limitation has so often done for others—to increase his bent towards meditation, and hence to aid in the foundations of his quiet, steady, plodding character. For how often is it not that success is due partly to limitations, and that the restriction of possibilities, of incitements, and hence too of distractions, serves to increase the capacity for enduring all the disappointments, the discomforts, the delays that lie in the track which the man of genius is destined to travel on the way to victory.

Zola's bent was in youth towards the natural sciences rather than to the orthodox studies of literature and history, and like so many of our greatest writers the future author of "The Rougon-Macquart" was a veritable "wooden spoon" of the schools. Behold him then at the age of twenty, a failure at the University, scarcely fitted to be a day labourer, destitute of any particular apparent skill, manual or mental, and faced with the problem of daily bread-and-butter. He was glad at that time to accept an arduous " billet " at the docks at the rate of thirteen shillings a week, but in the struggle of life found himself unequal to the hardihood of retaining it. For the next two years he lived a life of utter misery, almost at hazard, inhabiting the traditional " garret," and lucky no doubt to have even the barest of shelters and the most meagre of sustenance. It is said that he was even put to the invention of snaring sparrows on the roof for food ; but certain it is that not the Johnsons nor the Savages nor the most sordid denizens of Grub Street were ever more hardly beset by the difficulties of mere existence. But Zola, gloomy, raging, alternately depressed and furiously assailed by lower wants, a unit in that Paris, most beautiful and most terrible of cities, was yet young, resolute, and filled with the deep consciousness of power, of there being " something in him," even though at present too vague and vaporous, that would not fail to lift him from obscurity and give him pre-eminence even in the ranks of those who were in his eyes the most admirable and illustrious of men.

The *Confession de Claude*, a somewhat formless hysterical book, but one which already reveals that certain striving purpose, a longing for a wider scope of things, records closely enough, no doubt, the experiences of its young and gloomy author. There is felt through it all the tension of attraction and repulsion of that mysterious Paris which he was exploring almost less as a study than as with an irresistible bent, not with cool intellect, but with the hot breath and absorbed interest as of a bloodhound on the trail.

Consider now a young man, with no profession, with no credentials even of good education, but already filled with huge ambitions for literary fame, overwhelming possibly the lower desires of comfortable *bourgeois* existence ; a nature withal rather practical than soaring, strong in sensual impulses and seeing all things in somewhat sombre aspects, sombre even in pleasures ; intellectually not yet particularly well furnished except with a fair foundation in elementary science, and a respect for the scientific manner ; virtually with no access, of course, to any high stage of political or social life ; with no love for, and, to be sure, no lore of, the records of the past, whither Victor Hugo, or Scott, or Schiller, could freely turn to fill their pages with large figures, pomp, and panoply, and what Sir Walter himself cheerfully described as the "big bow-wow." And yet withal for Zola, with the characteristic demand for big panoramas, Jordaens-like paintings, *derb* (tough and thoroughgoing) effects, what was there left for him to do ?

To starve yet a while, to look deeper and deeper into the hearts and lives of the people whom he could best understand, to see every sight, hear every word, and smell every odour in that *milieu*, to despond, no doubt often enough, to project large work in his more energetic intervals, to increase the area of his observation, until the mass of his material, the sense of there being a body of large human life behind it, would give him the weight, the momentum, the calling-forth of power, the resistance of a task large enough for the grappling of his mind, the straining of his nerves, the whipping up of the hot passions and vehement impulses of a literary gladiator sworn to success.

It is beyond the purpose of the present document to detail the list of Zola's attempts, or the story of his slow success, or to criticise circumspectly any of his work. Suffice it to say that after much writing, and testing of powers, generally pretty well down in the lower register, there gradually arose in his mind the features of the Rougon-Macquart series. His dabblings in physiology and kindred subjects, particularly heredity; his predilections towards vastness and system ; his hope of establishing with his present experiences and powers a platform from which to project future work when the opportunities of studying other strata of society should arise ; his materialism ; the deep impression made upon his mind by Taine and by Balzac, both realists, both capacious, synthetic in plan, analytic in method, both thorough-paced workers ; all these factors determined Zola to the *Histoire Naturelle et Sociale d'une Famille sous le Second Empire.*

His training had been complete. Long afterwards he wrote in one of his essays that it is an excellent thing for your genius to starve, and rage, and boil up, even towards the bursting point : *facit indignatio versum,* wrote Juvenal of old ! *La Fortune des Rougon* was actually begun in 1869 (Zola, *æt.* 29), but, excellent though it is, and especially free from certain characteristics of Zola's writings that his adverse critics have so severely reprobated as objectionable, this first of the long series was not a decided success.

L'Assommoir was Zola's first undoubted triumph. Here he was on territory that he had explored only too well, and the theme—depicting the joys, the sorrows, the work-a-day world, through and through, of the artisan class in Paris —gave him the full scope that he wanted. Zola's descriptions of that Paris in which he had lived arise in great part from his own most intimate experiences, experiences that had bitten their lines —for pain is a rare mordant—and stained their colours upon his brain. His words often fall like dull physical blows upon the sense; but probably there is no exaggeration here. The Coupeaus, the Bibi-la-Grillades, the Gervaises, and all the *dramatis personæ*, one sees and knows in Paris continually verified to the life. And few are there of the characters, so true and understandable is the delineation, even in their misery and wrong-doing, entirely shut out of sympathy; and Gervaise, poor, weak, maimed human being, crushed by the Juggernaut of the mighty city, erring, foolish—her nature one of limitations rather than faults— is, down to the last, inevitable, hopeless scene, one of the most complete, and one even of the most lovable, characters in literature.

But perhaps the greatest of all Zola's works is *Nana*, for certain it is that *Nana* has become the most famous and most popularly successful, and it would seem invidious to reject in the appreciation of an author's merit the overwhelming testimony of the contemporary public. Yet *Nana* is, according to the prevailing canons that indicate what a novel should be, one of the least "artistic," and, according to Zola's own principles, one of the least "realistic" or "naturalistic," of all his books. But after all, if we look abroad we find that it is not those works which portray men and women closely and circumspectly as they are which survive the storms and trials of the centuries, but rather such works as exhibit in bold sign-painting some exaggerated type of which the potentialities, or, at least, the appreciations, are more or less to be found in the general run of human nature. If we pass in review the most renowned, and also the most characteristic products of different nations, we shall observe that Zola's naturalistic theories carry us but a little way in accounting for their qualities of popularity and permanence. Don Quixote is as remote from our " sense of the real " as Achilles ; and if we consider in turn the Tartuffe of Molière, the Lady Macbeth of Shakspere, or the Faust of Goethe, we shall rather become convinced that the fine and delicate shades of individual character are much less here in account than the portrayal in bold, exaggerated lines of pronounced irrefragable characters. And with these names may be associated Nana. " There were brave men before Agamemnon," but Achilles will remain for ever as the type of warrior. Lady Macbeth is not merely a woman impelled by an occasion of ambition ; she is the *ambitious woman* above all. And Nana is not to be described as a profligate woman in Paris ; she is the embodiment and the type of all that contribute to make a woman attractive by the lower appetites that spring from and accentuate the opposition of sex. And in such a work was naturally to be found Zola's field of predilection. Here he could exercise to the full, to the very top of his bent, that power which is probably his *forte*, and is certainly the most familiar explanation of his success, the power of inciting deep natural passions, of whipping up prurient desires, of portraying scenes repellent in their vileness and vulgarity, but "seizing" in their particular quality, of collecting in overwhelming array all those incidents and effects that are the delight of the coarse and sensual elements of our nature. Then again the field is unlimited for the tendency to exaggeration, to the continually piling up in *crescendo* scene upon scene, emotion on emotion, till finally the artistic forcing towards expansion finds its outlet in another need, the irresistible, the inevitable demand for symbolisation.

"I am not understood," said Zola, sadly, one evening to a friend—and this after twenty years of fame, and production, and polemics—"I am not understood;" and the half-eaten dish lay before him, and the almost-untasted wine, for it was at a banquet of his *confrères*, where his admirers were both numerous and loud in the expression of their homage. But the friend sought to comfort him, that *he* had at least comprehended the "true inwardness" of all these writings—for were not *La Curée* and *Nana* written to disgust people with the past *régime*, and *Germinal* and *La Débâcle* to inspire hope for the future ? ! Truly, after this utterance, I could imagine Zola, still more sadly, muttering under his breath, "I am not understood"! His complaint was like that of Hegel, who had but one solitary disciple who understood him, and he, alas! misunderstood him. At any rate, the motive-force suggested by the excellent friend seems inadequate to account for the work of Zola ; and the irony would have been almost too severe had Zola written with such sharply indicated purpose only to find his name a signal of horror to so many of the well-disposed and righteous. To write to instruct, and to be prohibited and branded as a corrupter of youth ! To flagellate vice in terms of more sombre aversion than can be found in Juvenal or Tacitus, and to be the favourite reading of so many whose delight in these books is but to whet inferior appetites, and to satisfy vicious and sordid appreciations of things ! And even with many who claim to be liberal-minded and "advanced," a confession of an admiration for Zola is met with the broad grin, the vulgar suggestion, and that sort of familiarity as if one were to be drawn more closely to his neighbour by a mutual low sentiment and degradation of soul. The explicit statement of the value of a serious study of Zola is received with the thin sneer and the distasteful cant of the cynic. From the same flower may be sipped honey and poison.

What, then, is the manner in which Zola would wish to be "understood"? Possibly as a sort of great historian, the historian of the lives, through and through, of the people of France of to-day. Throughout the whole great range of his works one recognises not merely the illustration of the characters of his *dramatis personæ*, but one assumes, without losing their well-defined characteristics, that these and their environment are but representative of a class; one hears the confused hum, and feels the hurried, irregular march of a whole modern world behind Zola's wonderful romances; and the intention of the author, exploring and expounding successive ranges of society, is surely here manifest. In the earlier works the interest of the narrative is more personal, more full of vivid personality, of the qualities of life and movement produced by the interaction of the characters themselves. The later works tend to exhibit more and more the mechanical structure, the plan, and the "mountain of notes" which have served the author in his studies; and this tendency is linked with, and perhaps helped on by another, that which the eminent Danish writer, Brandes, considers in fact to be Zola's most salient feature—his tendency to symbolisation.

In the earlier works the examples of symbolisation are appropriate, unstrained, and used to produce striking and brilliant literary effects. Miette, the little heroine of *La Fortune des Rougons*, has followed her lover to Paris in the stream of the insurrectionary provincials advancing, as we have referred to before, to the theatre of the *coup d'état*. At the barricade she holds up the flag of the Republic, supporting the staff upon her virgin breast; she has turned her red petticoat upon her head, and in a moment this becomes a Phrygian cap, and Miette, while the strains of the Marseillaise are rising, becomes transfigured and transformed into the figure of the Republic herself ; and her death, for she falls with a bullet crashing through her skull, signalises the downfall of Liberty.

Again, the name of Nana has become famous, and is bestowed by one of her admirers upon a racehorse which, while the original Nana is parading her beauty and her wantonness upon the lawn at Longchamps, carries off the prize against a redoubtable English competitor, and so becomes for the moment the heroine of France, the victorious carrier of the national colours of France ! *Nana ! Nana ! Vive Nana !* the name is vociferated and resounded in enthusiastic shouts until it reaches the Imperial box itself, and the Empress rises to her feet, and clapping her hands, re-echoes the triumphal name, *Nana! Nana! Vive Nana !* And with all this brilliant literary description, so full of verve, is felt underlying the author's suggestion, his symbolisation of Nana, her apotheosis as the Priestess of Vice. And so again in another guise when Nana dies, a mass of corruption, while the cry of weak delirium, *à Berlin ! à Berlin !* is being shrieked in frenzy in the streets.

But in *Germinal,* the incessant personification of the coal-mine, the insistence upon its nature as of a sentient being, becomes tiresome, and when a similar mechanical effect is reiterated elsewhere, as, for example, in the case of the locomotive in *La Bête Humaine,* the result is one of sheer tediousness. We begin to suspect that if Zola were to write a sea story he would devote a hundred pages, through which we anticipate him all, to vivifying the ship. Victor Hugo has done something of the kind before him in several places, and one wonders that Zola, who depreciates the "romantic school" unduly, should borrow and use so frequently one of the least inspired of their tricks.

In *La Débâcle* the strategical lines of the campaign play a somewhat similar part, and in certain episodes the tendency is manifest, as, for instance, in the personification of the cannon which holds together the little family of its "servants." The plan of strategy is felt to be superior to the group of personages in *La Débâcle;* they serve but to explain the onward progress of the campaign, and their characters are limited or stretched according to that design. We have the Parisian student, Maurice, who has joined as volunteer in a moment of enthusiasm, and who serves very well to explain the successive crises of emotion of his class according to the progress of the war. Then we have the peaceable *bourgeois*, Weiss, who knows more of strategy than all the generals together, and whose luminous discourses make the main lines clear. And then we have Delaherche, the shop-owner of Sedan, whose "inquisitiveness" and restless comings and goings obligingly fill up for us the details. And so with the soldiers.

Compare for a moment with *La Débâcle* such a book as Erckmann-Chatrian's "Conscript of 1812." There everything is envisaged from the point of view of the soldier, and the war forms but the series of vicissitudes that separate poor Joseph from the object of his affections. Even his cowardice becomes sympathetic. Not so with

Zola. It is rather as though he had studied a
treatise, such, for instance, as the admirable *Les
Combattants de* 1870–71, *par Commandant L.
Rousset,* and had vivified general descriptions
and picked out striking details by pictorial examples. The soldiers are finely portrayed ; but
after all they are only types served up again from
his other works, and, for the rest, but food for
powder. The war is the great thing which drags
them along in its unescapable chains and eventu-
ally swallows them up. Even the battle scenes,
the battles of Sedan, lack a full measure of anima-
tion. Our attention is invited rather to the great
plan, the lines of investiture of the Prussians, the
enemy so far off that they are like toy soldiers
" made of lead," the deadly effect of their cannon,
their inevitable advance. So that though the lines
of attack are even more clearly mapped out than
in Victor Hugo's description of Waterloo, there
is not felt as in that last the storm and stress, the
prodigious collisions, the force of movements, the
desperate struggles, the epic greatness of the play,
the feeling of battle itself.

In fact, in the progress of Zola's literary work
from first to last there has been a growing tendency
to develop the more intellectual appreciations of
things, and to depend less and less upon sympathetic emotional effects. And if *La Débâcle*

has produced a great effect in every country in Europe, and is already one of the most famous of all Zola's works, that is less, perhaps, on account of its peculiar qualities as a novel *per se*, but rather from the gigantesque aspects of a great historical event of which Zola is able to give an account free, on the one hand, from such details as make study tedious, and, on the other hand, enlivened by brilliant sketches. We may say enlivened here advisedly, for strained as the word may appear with reference to one of Zola's books, yet *La Débâcle*, though the misery depicted in its pages is profound, takes place perhaps after all as the least depressing of any of the Rougon-Macquart series. It is true that no distressing feature is omitted. We have the whole dismal litany of the woes of war—the faults of the commanders, the shortcomings of the preparations, the confusion of the mobilisations, the distrust of the officers, the want of discipline in the soldiers, the defeat already marked out from the first hour, the terribly long, hopeless, heartless, purposeless marches, the aching limbs, the famished, maddened soldiers, the fearful destruction on the field of battle, death in a thousand shapes, and mutilations and agonies worse than death, and all examples of cowardice, meanness, stupidity, brutality—yet shining above all, victorious and ennobled even amid disaster, the acts of high courage, self-devotion, manly valiance even unto the extinction of life.

Zola's work is all continuous ; continuous, perhaps, not so much for its much emphasised principle of heredity—for that plays but a small part in the coherence of the series, and is, as might be expected, so elastic as not to give any particular point to the developments—but continuous as showing, by dint alike of patient details and of wonderful luminous *aperçus*, a vast range of French national life, stage upon stage, from the very depths and foundations of society, up even to the *fine fleur*—so *fine*, in fact, that Zola's hand seems all too heavy and brutal to touch it.

Balzac, to be sure, attempted something of the same sort ; but not only is the field quite inexhaustible, but also the two masters, both realists as they may be, are so diverse in manner and method, that, even after Balzac, Zola holds his own perfectly original and unique position. Balzac seems to be attracted rather to the study of individual character in diverse *milieus*, and doubtless surpasses Zola by his stimulating verve, his delightful *entrain*. Zola makes us know better the nature of the whole surroundings in which, perhaps, individual characters seem somewhat submerged, and of less vivid importance. And all this, with Zola's passion for accumulating effects, for insisting on powerful impressions, together with his qualities of thoroughness of study and massiveness of style, makes one feel, as perhaps with no other, the confused presence, the hum as of a crowd behind all the scene, the irregular and motley march, march, march, of a world behind it all. He has set out with the intention, not certainly to " disgust with the past " or to " inspire hope for the future," but to exhibit with an entire objectivity the world as it is, insisting neither upon pessimism nor optimism, purpose nor moral.

Yet he has found it for ever impossible to adhere to his own tenets, and that indeed must arise in the very nature of things. Purpose and moral cannot be avoided, even in the very selection of details, the prominence in perspective, the throwing on of the colours, the attitude and temper of treatment. Indeed, Zola's gloomy temperament is felt everywhere in his writings. His pictures may all be true from his point of view, but he sees them through a medium which casts a dark, unpleasant tone over all. He delights in painting coarse and vulgar scenes, but he holds towards them an attitude of repulsion, an air of a sour and even impracticable Puritanism. Part of his power is really derived from his habit of holding up matters not unnatural or recalcitrant

to consideration, but which he forces himself
to impress with some repellent or perilous element. *La Terre* is a book which convinces by
its life-like pictures, its entire naturalness, its easy
and complete handling of the whole lives of the
peasant population ; but few, knowing even as
intimately as Zola every detail of rural existence,
would bring away a general impression so charged
with cruel, sordid, and disgusting ideas. Zola's
respect for truth may be always evident, but
respect for truth may consort with a coarse disposition, a proneness to discover and throw into
undue relief the drossy and abhorrent parts of
human life. For, on the other hand, as a contrast,
the respect for truth might be equally a delicate
matter with a Lamartine, whose mind experiences
a positive difficulty in contemplating the ugly and
vulgar, and finds itself filled with beautiful and
inspiriting images. Ideals, the creations of fancy,
the stirring of hopes, the freshness of enthusiasm,
are as real things, are as living things in human
life, as the feelings of disgust, despondency, or pain.
Yet Zola seldom cares to lift his eyes to the objects
that after all make life possible and desirable. On
the contrary, though the coarseness of his writings
is seldom extraneous to the purpose, yet he often
takes occasion, as if with sheer perversity, to assert
a Diogenes-like grossness of image and speech.

Nevertheless, in spite of himself, or rather in spite of his theories, the *moral* of his works is for ever cropping out. His power is more or less obscurely felt to depend upon a continual referring of the events and actions of the worlds he describes to broad and constant ethical standards, to a form of morality sound and in the main commonplace, but often overstrained and joined to a tone of perverse misappreciation and lack of sympathy. And it is in these terms, finally, that Zola must be understood. He puts us through a drastic discipline to teach us what human nature really is; but though painful be the process, we are continually compelled to thank him for his knowledge, his truthfulness, his desire of steady judgment; and it remains for ourselves to throw over the whole picture some more genial atmosphere than emanates from Zola's temperament, and by forgetting much of the grossness and ugliness, and rejecting much of the cynicism, to endeavour to gather from his wonderful pages the reward of his profound instruction.

Kipling is the Reporter who made himself King.
But in this designation the superlative position of
the "supreme type of the most vigorous type" of
latter-day journalists (*teste* Mr. Stead), the angel
Gabriel, and Julius Cæsar, or at least the German
Emperor, must be respected ; and, on the other
hand, the comparative lack of seriousness of our
fin de siècle monarch must be duly considered.

Rudyard Kipling came at a time when English literature had need of him. Dickens and
Thackeray had been the last of the masters, and
Dickens and Thackeray had long since passed
away. Literature had developed in several directions, and the general level of excellence was
higher, perhaps, than ever before in English
history. The name of clever writers was Legion.
Yet there was no great distinctive figure to give
a character to the generation as Shakspere had
given a character to his generation, as Johnson
had given a character to his, as Byron had given
a character to the literature of the beginning of

this hundred years. Nay, on the contrary, there were a number of highly respectable writers, both in prose and verse, through whose works it was a definite part of culture to toil ; and when the mind had travelled from Dan to Beersheba it had found all mediocre. The poets were getting old, even old-fashioned. Swinburne's swirling verses and empty metres had lost their glamour. Andrew Lang's futile poesies had been admired sufficiently ; William Morris was not quite convincing ; and Louis Morris as commendable, but really as slow as the ox that treadeth out the corn. Sir Edwin Arnold wrote like an official poet ; they were not poems, those verses of his, but rather massive pieces of furniture ; of the Georgian era, moreover. Austin was pleasant as a rosy sunset, and as fugitive in impression ; and Dobson's bric-a-brac had been partly forgotten, like blue china and other society "rages."

And in prose there was also an inhuman dearth of noble natures. Black was good, but he cannot be eternally on the shores of Ultima Thule. Blackmore was better, but the joy he gave us was serene rather than passionate. Haggard's enormities had grown familiar ; and Besant's work was laid in with the conscientiousness of a carpenter. Grant Allen, that excellent student of biology, was still brooding over his "Woman Who Did." Remained

Hardy, and Meredith, esteemed by the readers of culture, marvelled over by the feminine *élite*, but withal, and indeed therefore, not popular. And, moreover, there had grown up a new school, worshipping a master who shall be nameless, but whose affectations had worked like a ferment amongst his disciples and evolved strange neurotic distempers. These disciples, pale reflexes of a decadent power, had arrogated to themselves the titles of "culture," of "taste," of "æstheticism," and of "art," and had imposed upon the British public — that respectable *bourgeois* class ever ready to receive in dutifulness, if not in understanding, the guidance of "superior persons"—had imposed, then, their authority upon the British public, and by dint of insinuating themselves into the journals, had given to their opinions a mutual support by what is called "logrolling," and had formed a ring of malign influence against alien intrusion into "Literature"; the older and more conservative criticism becoming thrust into outer darkness, and the æsthetes held the day.

But the British public endured their sway not altogether contentedly. Æstheticism was foreign to its traditions, not only by reason of what was admirable in its spirit—the renaissance of art and the love of beauty—but also by reason of the puerilities, the affectations, with which it had

become sicklied over, and the mephitic atmosphere in which it became gradually enshrouded.

Another potent influence in literature must be
mentioned — the redoubtable "girl of sixteen."
For as every generation has its special physiognomy with regard to science, art, literature, and
"tone," it had come about for various reasons that
of the latter part of the Victoria age the "girl of
sixteen" was the despot. To produce this result
there had been a thousand causes in operation.
On the one hand, the lives of men had become
so crowded with occupations that the lighter
forms of reading were in their leisure moments
the sole desirable. People wished to be amused
after business. And the novel had become so
debilitated in tone, so far removed from any
rational exposition of life, that men had gradually
neglected to read. Women were the *clientèle* of
the circulating libraries. And again, it had ever
been either a tradition or an inveterate form of
cant, that the tastes of the feminine sex were less
hardy in the matter of exploration of difficult
subjects than those of men—an illusion soon dis-
pelled with a vengeance by the outcry of women
themselves. By refining them upon the assumed
conditions of feminine morality, the vogue had
been given to such anodyne productions as might
without detriment be placed in the hands of a

boarding-school miss, and the standard thus set up had determined, of course, the intellectual power of the works.

Herein was perhaps the pith of the whole matter. The generation preceding had seen the beginning of epoch - making works in the domains of science and abstract thought, and the ideas that had been started by the Darwins and Spencers would, naturally, gradually infiltrate into literature and make their way downward, translated into the vernacular of the people. It was those ideas that were especially dangerous in a decadent and cowardly age, and there had arisen an almost invincible body of sentiment threatening to stifle any production in art, science, literature, or in projects of social reconstruction, that bore the dreaded banners of Reason or Truth.

In a word, English literature had become provincial; mincing in form, canting in style, anæmic, and moribund.

It was upon this *milieu* that Rudyard Kipling descended. His earlier productions were not very remarkable, his verse especially giving little more than the promise of what he has since achieved ; but there was recognised in him a rude and vigorous health, a buoyancy of spirit, an exuberance of humour, a quaintness and unconventionality—a style, in short, that was like a breeze of

sea-air amid the chlorosis of æsthetical "culture."
The invalid critics and book-room gossips felt
their nerves a little braced in reading Kipling.
Andrew of the tactile fingers rejoiced in the vica-
rious enjoyment of virile power; gave the new
man a puff. Gosse, that finicking patron of
Shelley, patted the bold balladeur on the back,
half-encouragingly, half-timidly; and Sidney
Colvin, the cultured but uninspired biographer of
Keats, thought that Kipling really promised something great. The æsthetes hissed at him a little
suspiciously, but the man from the East had
evidently not come to usurp their dominions.
And Rossettian blue-stockings at suburban At
Homes ventured to use the awe-stricken word
"genius"! Kipling's boom had begun.

Kipling was the more easily recommended because he was evidently a "safe" man. His ideas
were all orthodox. He roared, but he roared like
a sucking-dove. And even if he did attack the
administration of his native country, he attacked
it for sins that were also orthodox, just the sins
to be expected in all well-regulated departments.
He satirised officialdom, but the verse had a
careless swank rather amusing than hurtful :—

> Potiphar Gubbins, C.E.
> Is seven years junior to Me;
> Each bridge that he makes he either buckles or breaks,
> And his work is as rough as he.

This was a new style of poetry, and the verse, though clear in intention, often displayed the amateur hand in his rhythm. Note, for example, the second "he" in the third line, an unnecessary word, that interrupts the metre and gives a false touch to the sense.

Here is another verse that Kipling printed. It is worth reproducing in order to indicate the development of his powers under the genial sunshine of success; for, after all, if adversity be a good school, success is a much better dwelling, and the warm and generous recognition of Kipling's early efforts made it possible for him to expand into the bold and breezy rhymer that we know :—

> Then a creature, skinned and crimson,
> Ran about the floor and cried,
> And they said I had the "jims" on,
> And they dosed me with bromide.

This was not good. It was bad; but it was Kiplingese, and pardonable.

Apart, however, from this jejune rhyming, Kipling's stories were excellent. He had discovered an India, and a Tommy Atkins of that habitat, redolent of amusement, abundant in interest. He had sat at the feet of strange Gamaliels, this vivacious youth, and he had absorbed their learning greedily. By no design could his lines have been cast in more fortunate places—a bright, intelligent, sympathetic lad, a mirthful, exuberant youth, with a *diablerie* of enjoyment of contemplation, laughing to himself consumedly at all the strange adventures, the quips, the cranks, the oddities of his Soldiers Three, the immortal Mulvaney, Learoyd, and Ortheris ; and hearing betimes in other quarters the gossip of the officers' mess, the scandal of the drawing-rooms and boudoirs. The field was, after all, a narrow but unhackneyed one, the opportunities excellent, the colours rich and flamboyant.

Kipling, like Martial of old in another sphere, was learning without perceiving his application in study ; and having acquired what Zola calls the invaluable habit of "loafing," he was profiting hugely by his lack of instruction. Or, to put the matter in another form, the artist had found his workshop, his material ; he pursued his work in his own fashion, finding his way by abundant experimentation ; and his mind was little distracted by the pressure of other pursuits. Like a Beethoven in music, a Rembrandt in painting, a Davy in chemistry, a Hannibal in war, Rudyard Kipling was "following game."

And, as almost invariably happens, these early impressions remain the fund of Kipling's "material." He may traverse the wide world, he may enter into a hundred phases of Society, see ten thousand forms of life, strike into new dominions of culture, yet the atmosphere, the aromatic smack, the surety of hand, the enjoyment of freedom, he will find nowhere as in his Jungles or with his Mulvaney.

So far, however, the description of Kipling might have been that applied by Artemus Ward to his favourite kangaroo—"An amusin' little cuss"; a eulogy that in these days of extravagant adulation of the humourists of life and the worship of "mummers" must seem a veritable blazon of fame. Kipling was "the born yarn-spinner of the lazy nights." He had absorbed his Mulvaneys and his Gobinds. He had tasted each redolent smack of their expressions, he had felt the weight and twist of each trick of their movements, he had seen unrolled before his imagination the brilliant panorama of their adventures ; and these, with his own billowy humour, his artistic throwing into perspective, his laughter-loving exaggeration, his *diablerie* of crescendo, Kipling was ennabled inimitably to reproduce.

Truly he had discovered India, and Tommy Atkins, Indian brand. Mulvaney is not a typical Irishman ; but he is a great type of the British soldier of Allahabad, late of Cork. Learoyd and

Ortheris are good, but they are merely the figures
on the pedestal of this gigantic creation ; Mulvaney
ranks with Sancho Panza.

Bon chien chasse de race.   Kipling was one of
the irritable tribe, indubitably.   He bore the
stamp in all his moods—the peculiar faculty of
sympathy, as distinct a thing as tone of physical
fibre, the love of quirks and turns, of bizarreries,
brusqueries, the gay *baroque* of lively phrase, the
Tang, the *Schweif*, the *ictus ;* the love of words
not merely as exponents of meaning, but as things
in themselves.   His vocabulary was already remarkably wide, and a graphic word was as dear
to him as a bronze of Benvenuto Cellini to an
amateur collector.

There is something in all this that implies a
dissipation of intellect.   And so it is.   The artist
becomes endowed by the disintegration of his
own character, and in that disintegration he makes
successively the discovery of its elements, he projects different capabilities of himself into overweening shapes in the perspective ; he understands
by the devastation of his own purposes.   In the
hierarchy of men, the artist, the author, the
histrion have in modern life been assigned too
high a position.   The old hierarchy of the Greek
gods is the one sane and durable : Jupiter is at
the head, Apollo and Vulcan below him.   And

in our actual life we must appreciate the force of
this to know the profound meaning of these lines
of Keats :—

> And only blind from sheer supremacy,
> One avenue was shaded from thine eyes,
> Through which I wander'd to eternal truth.

Attest it, Byron, the wittiest, most genial of
souls, over-clouded with the pall of sombre
thoughts ; Shelley ; Burns ; and Shakspere—the
teeming brain ; the shattered purposes ; the
glorious aspirations ; the ineffectual desires ;
creator of mighty types ; the laughing libertine ;
the demi-god ; the clown.

These reflections are occasionally suggested by
the somewhat preposterous idea of the " Hero as
Man of Letters " suggested to us by Carlyle. The
Hero as Man of Letters hardly exists ; at least he
is not to be found among the *litterateurs*. Look
around at our *litterateurs*. Their manners are those
of upper-class domestics. The Hero as Man of
Letters is Mahomet, carrying his burning words
to the outermost ends of the earth ; Bonaparte,
whose bulletins are Iliads in brief ; Darwin, whose
thought is more trenchant than a sword. The
words are but the instrument.

But in our day the writer is born to amuse us ;
at least it is for that that we care to esteem him.

He declares that to be the true function of literature. And when we acquiesce, he claims haughtily the rôle of a prophet, a seer.

When Kipling arrived in England he was still a youth, happy in the glow of his first success—a young man with just sufficient physique for the blank fatigues of a writer's life; not likely, as Horace of old said, to be distinguished in the Isthmian games as a pugilist, nor liable to be unduly distracted from his work by physical exercises. His countenance shone with good-humour and abundant good sense—a broad plebeian countenance in which the emotional characteristics seemed more in evidence than intellectual strength; the forehead and set of the features, however, showing the great capacity for production—high intelligence backed up by cheerful persistence in labour. There was in Kipling a suggestion of the honest, sonsie face of Robert Burns, and the finer, mobile countenance of Byron—all this, however, merely peeping out of that characteristic expression of his own, ever ready to "bob up serenely" from its plainer background. It was a countenance abundant in sympathy; and therein is named the Kiplinguesque quality, the "chief intensity" of his spirit.

The studies of Mulvaney had grown up with

the studies of the character of the country itself. The "Jungle Book" was hereafter the result :—

> "Where's the Poet," cries Keats—Show him !
> Show him !
> Muses nine ! that I may know him !
> 'Tis the man who with a man
> Is an equal, be he King,
> Or poorest of the beggar-clan,
> Or any other wondrous thing
> A man may be 'twixt ape and Plato ;
> 'Tis the man who with a bird,
> Wren or Eagle, finds his way to
> All its instincts ; he hath heard
> The Lion's roaring, and can tell
> What his horny throat expresseth ;
> And to him the Tiger's yell
> Comes articulate, and presseth
> On his ear like mother-tongue.

These lines might have been written after reading the "Jungle Book." They sum up its purport.

Keats himself in one of his letters speaks of spending an idle forenoon of watching a sparrow picking. He picked around with him he says ; and this little stroke is of the character of what the "Jungle Book" gives us in such marvellous abundance.

Kipling's tiger acts, moves, and speaks like a tiger ; at least, when reading we feel that he bears his credentials with him no less incontestably than Mulvaney himself. His wolf is a convincing wolf. His elephant talks, walks, and comports himself as an authoritative elephant. His mongoose is an authentic mongoose. His weasel is like a weasel. His camel is not merely like Hamlet's, humped like a camel; it is the "oont" itself. His whale is "very like a whale."

It is difficult to appraise work of this kind, for all who have spoken of birds and beasts, or made birds and beasts speak — Æsop, La Fontaine, Grimm, pale their ineffectual fires to Kipling. He has the quality that gave Buffon one of his most remarkable talents; but Kipling's graphic descriptions make a tame thing of Buffon. He describes a seal : the seal lives and moves, and has his being. And when he writes for the baby seal he is no less happy :—

> When billow meets billow, then soft be thy pillow,
> Oh, weary wee flipperling, curl at thy ease !
> The storm shall not wake thee, nor shark overtake thee,
> Asleep in the arms of the slow-swinging seas.

This fine descriptive power is what, in reference to Keats, Matthew Arnold called the "natural magic." "He speaks like Adam naming the creatures." But what Keats did occasionally and in searching and graphic phrases, Kipling has expanded into the complete elaboration of a world. The defect that always accompanies excellence

is with Keats an overstraining of expression, as
in the phrase :—

A palpitating snake,
Bright, and cirque-couchant in a dusky brake ;

and with Kipling an appearance of mincing affect-
edness, as when he speaks of being unwilling to
pull up his plants by the roots—"they squeak so."

Intrinsically the "Jungle Book" reads like an
original and wonderful fairy tale for children ; but
it also bears the evidence of a power that could
not but give striking manifestations elsewhere.

Accordingly, in his many voyagings and his
professional studies, Kipling has endeavoured to
fix "the thing's essential reality" of as many diverse
countries as he has travelled in. The most ambitious of these efforts are the story of Badalia
Herodsfoot of Gunnison Street renown, and
"The Light that Failed." Each of these in turn
is forcible, graphic, told with knowledge, power,
and energy, but each in turn gives the impression
of a *tour de force*. They are both simply instances
of picturesque and "supreme" reporting without
deep knowledge or deep insight. Hence they
are not quite convincing in the reading, and the
impression that they leave behind is not durable.

A clearer indication of what is meant by his
reporter's faculty is seen in his description of the
locomotives at Allahabad. He is full of informa-

tion, he speaks in detail, and with understanding ; but there is nothing in what he says that might not have been learnt, as probably it was, by a busy reporter in one crowded afternoon.

To understand first the principle of the steam-engine in general, and the life and work of a locomotive as an engineer understands it, is a matter of study of years. And when such a man speaks, he speaks with less anxiety to show an inventory of detail, and with a somewhat clearer perspective. And so, too, with all Kipling's sympathetic faculty, it could scarcely have been anything but a clever feat to have expounded the life of the people in the East End of London. It would require years of residence amongst them to give such an account of their mode of existence, their motives and thoughts, as would make their actions clear and palpable; in default of this, Kipling's stories of Western life lack the depth, the atmosphere, the riant confidence and richness of the wonderful themes of his early days.

Next to his successes in India must be ranked those of his stories of the Far North. He is almost as much at home with the seals as with the elephants; and there must be some special attraction in his temperament to the form of life he therein depicts. His Esquimaux, or rather Inuit story, Quiquern, is one of the most fascinating and delightful that he has written. The reason may lie partly in this—he is happiest when his *dramatis personæ* are few and of comparatively simple character, influenced by elemental motives, —love, fear, hope, courage ; and when the *milieu* is of a strange, remote, *outré* character.

Pari passu with Kipling's wider scope in the objective world proceeded his experiments in the technique of his art ; and accordingly his later productions in rhyme have been distinguished, not only by the graphic force which is ever his best characteristic, but by a firmness, strength, and resonance of metre of which his first verses had given men occasional hints. The " Lover's Litany" is good :—

> Eyes of grey—a sodden quay,
>   Driving rain and falling tears,
> As the steamer wears to sea
>   In a parting storm of cheers.

And in the "Galley Slave" there is not only the regular beat of a fine cadence in the lines, but he has mastered some of the tricks of the Alexandrine —the poise, and bold rush at the finish :—

It was merry in the galley, for we revelled now and then—
If they wore us down like cattle, faith, we fought and loved
  like men !
As we snatched her through the water, so we snatched a
  minute's bliss,
And the mutter of the dying never spoilt the lover's kiss.

So far that is excellent.   But there were higher developments to be attained, and assonance of words was to be added to the strength and elasticity of the metre :—

"A gift for a gift," said Kamal straight ; "a limb for the
    risk of a limb.
Thy father has sent his son to me, I'll send my son to
    him !"
With that he whistled his only son, that dropped from a
    mountain-crest—
He trod the ling like a buck in spring, and he looked like a
    lance in rest.

There is there a vigorous fibre and a strenuous lyrism not inferior to Byron, but there is a scope in the development of rhythmic effects considerably beyond anything produced by the "noble bard," with whom virtuosity in metre was by no means a strong point.

The deliberate study of metre is evident in Kipling, and his attention may have been specially directed to the American Poe, and also to a writer who has more points of resemblance to Kipling, probably, than perhaps any other, Bret Harte. The graphic force is the strong point of both, the sympathy with wild and rugged aspects of life, bathed, however, in the redolent atmosphere ; there is the same predilection for the reds and oranges of the spectrum, for the colours flamboyant yet sombred, for the deep register of the musical scale, for the broad fibre, for the quips and cranks of eccentricity, for the tambourine and trumpet. And amongst Bret Harte's little researches into metre are a number of happy *trouvailles*, one being the playing on the ā sound at the end of several successive verses. It is an effect reproduced in the famous "Ta-ra-ra-boom-de-ay," and also in Kipling's "Mandalay":—

Ship me somewhere east of Suez, where the best is like the
    worst,
Where there ain't no Ten Commandments, and a man can
    raise a thirst ;
For the temple-bells are callin', an' it's there that I
    would be—
By the old Moulmein Pagoda, looking rosy at the sea ;

      On the road to Mandalay,
      Where the old flotilla lay,
      With our sick beneath the awning
      When we went to Mandalay.

      O the road to Mandalay,
      Where the flyin'-fishes play,
      An' the dawn comes up like thunder
      Outer China 'crost the bay.

This is reckoned the high-water mark of Kipling by many of his admirers ; but an endeavour may be made to look at it temperately.

Its principal virtues are metrical, for otherwise it does not impress as having much consistency. There is a jolter-headed incoherence in the ideas that show that the writer has caught at the rhyme and the catch of words rather than at any sequence of association.

That it is a great production of genius may legitimately be doubted when we compare it with the above-mentioned "Ta-ra-ra-boom-de-ay," which has had at least a greater popular success —a supreme test nowadays—which, moreover, in the strain of ideas and dignity of language is not inferior. Even the once-famous "Never introduce your Dinah to a pal" cannot be overlooked as a competitor to some of Kipling's renowned barrack-room ballads and *genre* word-paintings. The "swank" and "ictus" are there also in the wonderful music-hall ditty, as well as a rare catchy swing and some original, striking metre.

Or take another example in which sense is entirely sacrificed to sound :—

> A star is slowly faring
> With fear to go through Erin,
>   His heart must be
>   Apart from me,
> Guarded and free his bearing ;
>
> A star of deeds unsparing,
> In darting spears, in daring,
>   Both large and leal,
>   With targe of steel,
> And barge of keel sea-tearing.

This is logically absurd ; but there is not only a fine metrical effect, but a marvellous play of words in their harmonious force and colouring. And this passage, moreover, gives us hints of the unexplored capacities of metre, rhythm, assonance.

The study of the actual technique of poetry, the study of the whole instrument of words with their associated melodic effects, is hitherto comparatively rudimentary, as evidenced by the works of some of our most famous poets. Yet that study should be definitely made ; for, after all, the very meaning of excellence in art can only be tested by reference to the difficulties to be overcome. The most glorious pictures are but feeble reproductions of nature's effects ; the most marvellous feats of poetry are but a pale reflex of the poet's thought. We admire by reason of a tacit comparison with standard productions. And in this view it will be found that the command over metre is not the essential characteristic of the poet. It is the thing of all others that can be taught and learnt ; it is the least inspirational ; it is the least divine of those subtle qualities that mark the poet. With respect to skill in this element of technique, the phrase is not true, *poeta nascitur non fit.*

Byron's metre was irregular, and not by reason of entire ease and confidence in its employment, but from the fact of his having paid little attention to the actual technique of poetry. In his later writings he is content with the octosyllabic stanza, in which indeed he acquired such facility that his irregularities in that case are either intentional or merely careless, and often serve to give piquancy to his meaning. The essential virtue of Keats was not the "singing" faculty at all. His poetry was in its meaning wrapped in the associations of feelings which he was able to intimate so subtly ; but Keats, intelligent in all things, was beginning towards the close of his career to develop some rare and exquisite metrical effects. Tennyson went to the Greeks with the deliberate purpose of correcting his style by the discipline of practice in metre—the " blackboard " exercise as Swinburne called it ; and Swinburne has a facility in metre which by the frequent lack of appropriateness becomes a fatal facility. Wordsworth was a master in metrical studies, and in the adaptation of metre to the sense and to the emotion called forth he is one of the best examples in English literature. To be convinced of this it is only necessary to compare the stately organ march of " Tintern Abbey " with the bursts of rapturous music in his " Ode on the Intimations of Immortality." And lastly, the man who insisted on most intelligently and expounded most lucidly the possibility of the development of rhythm, Walt

Whitman—that deep-mouthed Bœotian unfortu-
nately was deficient in the sense of metrical flow.

This exposition is by no means apart from the
consideration of Kipling's literary position. For
it would be doing injustice to his "Soldiers
Three," to his "Jungle Book," to his "Quiquern,"
and other products of his genius, if too much
weight were given to his *études* in metrical forms.

Something of the incense of his adulators
ascending to Kipling has probably affected him
a little ; it would be strange if it did not. And
having diverted him from the knowledge of his
own strength and of his own weakness, that adulation has induced the story-teller to pose, on occasion, as a youthful "seer." Else to what do we
owe these remarkable lines, forming an introduction to a very good book, " Many Inventions " ?

> Beyond the bounds our staring rounds
> Across the pressing dark,
> The children wise of outer skies
> Look hitherward and mark
> A light that shifts, a glare that drifts,
> Rekindling thus and thus,
> Not all forlorn, for Thou hast borne
> Strange tales to them of us.

What this portends it is difficult to surmise ;
and not even by anxious inquiry and by sage
reflections is it possible to be assured. It is
something like the oracular utterance of Shelley's

P

friend : " I have entered the sacred temple, I have eaten of the sacred barley, I have said Konx Ompax, and it is enough." On comparison, the Konx Ompax is better.

And then, finally, there is this amazing effort :—

There purged of pride because they died, they know the
  worth of their bays,
They sit at wine with the Maidens Nine, and the Gods of
  the elder Days.
It is their will to serve or be still as fitteth our Father's praise.
It is theirs to sweep through the ringing deep where Azraël's
  outposts are,
Or buffet a path through the Pit's red wrath when God goes
  out to war,
Or hang with the reckless seraphim on the reins of a red-
  maned star.

The metre is very shaky in this production, but the boldness of thought might well excuse any irregularity of execution. It is the Humourist's *Paradiso* " on his own," to descend for relief to a vernacular loved by Kipling ; and it must be taken seriously to be thoroughly enjoyed. Later on in the same poem are some rare examples of " ground and lofty tumblings." It is difficult to refrain from quotation. The red-maned stars grow pale before these effulgences.

And ofttimes cometh our wise Lord God, master of every trade,
And tells them tales of His daily toil, of Edens newly made ;
And they rise to their feet as He passes by, gentlemen
  unafraid.

That is very satisfactory. It sets the "upper limit," as they say in mathematics, to our Humourist's aberrations. It is a far cry from the region where "there ain't no Ten Commandments" to that height; but probably midway we find the habitat of the "real Kipling."

The Indian writer has affinities with most of the great ones of English literature—the abundance and vehemence of Byron, the Keatsian touch of picturing, the riancy and verve of Burns, the bold limning strokes of Shakspere, the humour and pathos of Bret Harte. But this only helps to define the matter. To say that Kipling has limitations is no more than to say that he is human, and no doubt his critics have from time to time indicated his deficiencies. Some of the criticisms appear to have piqued him a little, and he has a few verses levelled at the pretensions of "Art."

The "Art" that Kipling retorts against is a merely mechanical precision according to a classic model; and the fault of his critics is undoubtedly to attempt to restrict "Art" to certain rules and ordinances adopted as a mode of the time. The history of the development of literature, however, is that of a successive overturning of established canons. The tendency has ever been for the poet to find the form of expression that most forcibly reveals his own characteristics, and the result has been that of the many successive canons of art there remain now but little evidence.

Yet certain principles remain, for they correspond to our own very development. What, for instance, is it in the "Vicar of Wakefield" that gives us the sense of its completeness and artistic beauty? It is the sense that gradually grows up with us that it is a story taken out of a course of experience where at every turn new vistas and inexhaustible episodes might be opened up. It is a story that had lain long in the mind of the author, and had insensibly and gradually taken shape and colour from his own original nature.

Again, take Byron, whom it is the fashion nowadays to despise. His "Don Juan" is not merely a witty, lively, and variegated history, a succession of episodes; all that is expressed seems to be but a part of all that is thought and of which the mind has suggestions in the course of its progress. The episodes are but the precipitate of the life, philosophy, and record of Byron himself; and the lines, witty, humorous, forcible, are yet steeped in that subtle thing,—association, atmosphere. His letter of Julia, in the early part, throbs with the history of a woman's career; his slow but infallible deepening the shades of Adeline's passion for the young Spaniard; the theme recurring again and again with slightly stronger force amid myriad digressions—all that is unmatched of its kind in literature.

And again, with Keats this quality of producing with the actual living idea the hosts of its adumbrated associations—its atmosphere—this quality, rather than faculty, is marvellous. There are poems in his occasional words ; his phrases often have an aphorismal force, not revealing their full meaning at once, but developing as they lie long in the mind. That is no trick ; it arises from the thought itself, the form and expression of the thought, having been drawn from a fund of deep contemplation.

Another man whose words have that aphorismal force, and from the same pregnant cause, the summation of extensive thoughts into a clear idea, that is Napoleon Bonaparte.

And in pursuing this strain of thought we get clearer views of the standards of art—standards that should be omnipotent in criticism, simply because "art" should mean the form to which literature tends in its finest development. The grave pleasure we derive from the contemplation of a group by Theseus is not to be overthrown by any "new movement." It bears its own evidence ; it stands supreme even beside a clever sketch of Van Beers or a *Punch* black-and-white man.

The abundant but controlled energy, the power and tonicity of the opening chorus of Goethe's

" Faust," are beyond all mere *études* of metre ; the pause, and the vision, of the last lines of Keats' sonnet " On First Reading Homer "—these are the miraculous things that mean more than a talent, that mean genius and life both in one.

The theme is entrancing, but it would lead too far from Kipling. Suffice it to say that since excellence is but comparative, that it is in English literature in which cowardice and hypocrisy have produced this stagnancy and corruption ; it is only in this provincial literature of the end of our good Victorian era that Kipling proportions loom up as gigantic. But let the matter be cut short. Suffice it to say that it is not merely amongst those of an older generation whose reputation is world-wide, but amongst those of Kipling's own class that the fine examples may be found. Turn to the French.

Paul Adam can fling out a study, beautifully poised, beautifully expressed, exquisite in itself, and luminous in its *aperçus*, so that the theme seems veritably couched in its distinct colour tones.

D'Esparbes can tell a short story of a Napoleon episode that expands like an Iliad. Alexandre Hepp, in his *Minutes d'Orient*, gives us again the embalmed atmosphere of the Arabian Nights. In reading these we find no contempt of " Art."

And now to conclude : What will Kipling stand for ?

A man is remembered finally only for himself, for his inmost characteristic thought, expressed perhaps — even generally — in some objective image. " Cervantes laughs his life's regret " in " Don Quixote." Carlyle will be remembered for his " Sartor," for that contains the germ of all the rest. Goethe is " Faust " ; that gives us the centre and the promise of all of Goethe. Byron will live by " Don Juan."

And when we strip off from Kipling the excursions and alarms, the trappings, the suits, the studies, and the *tours de force ;* when we regard him as he will be seen in a dim perspective, when he will be defined by his salient features only— then we come back to the point we started from. He has discovered India. He has discovered the British - Indian soldier. He wrote the " Jungle Book"; and it is the latter that is most incontestably the work of genius, the unique thing that Kipling only could have done. His fame, however, has spread throughout the world ; he has filled the chronicles ; he has written much, and amazingly well; the Reporter has made himself King ; but his credentials are the tales he has brought from his marvellous Ind. And "even so," said Gobind ; " that is the work of the bazaar story-teller."

To have seen Sara Bernhardt is, of course, one of those events, or, as we may say, experiences, that not only interest us at the time, but form a certain notch in our memories for ever.

To study Sara Bernhardt opens up a world of ideas and speculations that lead far away from that personality ; suggestions that give us pause, that cause us to meditate upon the very meaning, " the end, the attribute, the evidence " of " culture," of civilisation, of the progress of nations, the rise and fall of empires. For Sara Bernhardt is the most exquisite example of that curious product of our latter-day civilisation, the *fin de siècle* Parisienne. (Already it seems necessary to express one's self in French idioms, for the very genius, the tone and style of the English language is foreign to this type, and gives us only the bluntest of descriptions.) And here, too, we must indicate a further explanation ; for it is as an actress, a comedienne, with her quick flashes of apprehension, that Bernhardt is the exquisite exemplar of this product. She has a coign of vantage in not being of the race. She expounds it. It is not that she formally analyses it, but rather that, with her intuitive artistic feeling, she seizes its characteristics and interprets and displays it.

`She herself is a quick, eager, daring little Jewess, or half-Jewess, with the best strain, the emotional power, the elasticity, the tenacity of that race; she has sprung from the *canaille*, from the class whose battle of life is the toughest, and she has their grit, reality, directness. She is the gutter-child of genius, and the *fine fleur* of Paris is but her study, and doubtless her amusement. She has pierced it to the core. A fascinating and sympathetic study it must be for Sara, for the Parisienne is truly an acme of art. She is un-approachable in the world in her own province and according to her own standards. She is the tiptop of "modernity," and from her dainty pedestal can flout and gibe at the Greek woman of Phidias or disdain with *elegante insouciance* the antique moral power of Portia. She gives the lie to the supremacy of the classic type, she offers battle with a thousand finicking airs and filigree graces to the antiquated models of womanly beauty, dignity, power. She lacks the supple, plastic fibre, with its suave strength of the noble dames of ancient story; and she lacks their largeness of nature. She has no concern for that. She touches the present hour at a thousand points, and she has a perfect magazine of nervous effects all ready to command. *Elle étale la femme* (she displays always the *woman*); she is sometimes the slave, sometimes the despot of the man, but not his companion. . . . In *l'Amour* there appears to be an idea of an incessant contest, and, according to the best connoisseurs, a certain piquant infusion of *hate*. The weapons of the woman are her weakness, her cunning, the whole range of her art, displayed under the permanent battery of her physical charms.

And, after all, why is the modern woman not the pinnacle ? Why should not her standards prevail ? These at least are questions to be asked. We presume that the age demanded her, that therefore she came. She must be the counterpart of our gilded youth. She must have been shaped and cultured to fulfil his aspirations. She could not exist irresponsible, detached. It must be he who admires her graces, her *desinvolture* (which is the lightest touch of French for what in English is, brutally, "go-as-you-please") ; he must admire her countenance with its thousand sophisticated expressions, its air *mutin*, its mouth *malicieuse*. It is he who finds her *finesse* so excellent, the imbecilities of her conversation so agreeable, so

charmant; and it must be greatly he who is interested in all the extraordinary displays of the
freaks of fashion in her costumes, her multiplicity
of fripperies, and who finds the most piquant
touch when he discovers that costume, as Victor
Hugo relates with enjoyment of the sweetest of
his heroines—*un peu indecent.*

In the novels of—not Zola, for his hand is too
heavy for the higher circles of society, but of—
Balzac, or Hervieu, or in the plays of Dumas the
younger, the whole aspect is to one not to the
manner born at first somewhat bewildering—every
sense is attacked, but in the manner of being
teased rather than delighted; there is a feeling
insupportable to the outsider, of glare, garishness,
glitter, shallowness, and insincerity. The eye is
dazzled, the ear is irritated, the nostrils snuff up
overpowering odours in which the sense finds
corruption. In the pleasant prattle of the French,
with its frequent nasal intonations, through the
elegant phrases, the wit and point, the laughter
and the *petits cris,* one becomes impressed at
length with a deep underlying feeling of *cochon-
nerie.* There is throughout an uneasy pruriency,
an itching, *démangeaison,* towards vileness, an
esuriency, a *relâchement* of appetites. Beneath
the gilt of the surface one comes at once to the
dust. The whole *milieu* is like a splendid house

of ill-fame. The refinement of life one would think coincided with the refining on vice. But then in the end there is that impression that caused Balzac in one of his most felicitous strokes of genius to call the whole series of his works *La Comedie humaine.* His smile of contempt or of pity is over it all.

Or consider, again, for example, Sardou's heroines, who have lived and moved and had their being in the famous Sara. They cannot be called tragic—no, not even in ruin. Of course, there is plenty of the gruesome contingencies of life ; but there is nothing of a great nature moving to destruction, or, as in the Greek tragedies or in some of Shakspere's, the braving of fate with a pride that seems but to complete its victory in death. A Fedora, a Tosca, or a Theodora, has the physique of a woman with the mind of a child and the appetites of a prodigy. Her fate is but the disaster of a life *déréglée*, a character ricketty, and mature only in vice. Her " tragedy " is but one of disorder, fury, and folly, passions not deep but unbridled and hysterical in their intensest display. In the ornate and elaborate exhibition of all that is in these favourite rôles Bernhardt cannot be touched. That is her *forte.* To be sure, she acts Cleopatra and Lady Macbeth and a vast range of characters between these and Frou Frou. To imagine her as the supple Egyptian Greek who captivated Cæsar and held Antony under her spell is difficult ; to realise her as the adamantine Scottish Queen is impossible. In *Frou Frou* or *La Dame aux Camelias* her part fits her as easy and naturally as the most perfect of her uncorseted vestures.

Sara Bernhardt is of middle height, slight, delicate of physique, but not, as in former days, very thin. Her gracefulness is like that of a cat or a tigress, for the gracefulness of a tigress appears less from the actual beauty of contour and correctness of lines than from the easy sinuousness of movement, energy combined with a curious softness of touch, activity with quietness masking a battery of feline and feminine power. "*J'aime le tigre,*" she lets out between her teeth in "Theodora," and with her velvet step and loose robe, her flat forehead, tawny hair, and lustrous eyes, cold and intent, she contrives to look something like one.

Her head is rather small, and well poised upon rather a short neck, sinewy but round, deepening into light though muscular shoulders and bust. Her figure in itself seems even a trifle ungainly, but with her ease and confidence and freedom of movement and pose even the long and rather awkward arms become undeniably interesting. Her loose-fitting garments are worn with admirable effect, and the figure not supple but *svelte* (which is the Parisienne paraphrase of supple), the *tournure* natural and untortured, the movements and poses—to recall them again—easy (*dégagé*), are delightful to observe in contrast with the stiff boxed-up figures and the deformities and absurdities of modern dress.

Her nervous physique is doubtless just the best adapted to its work—the wear and tear, the artificial excitements and exhaustions of the stage. The head is not highly intellectual, nor the features regular nor good. In that sophisticated countenance it is difficult to detect any determinative expression, but the total effect is redeemed, or at least made remarkable, by the brilliancy, the glare, of the eyes. To describe the eyes accurately would be impossible, for they themselves are full of change. At times they look like dark-blue beads in her head, at other times they shine like emeralds clear and large, or as though an electric light were kindled within. Often with their cold gleam they suggest a serpent, but then that again suggests Keats' " Lamia," in which the descriptions are perfect :—

> Eyed like a peacock . . .
> So rainbow-sided, touched with miseries,
> She seemed, at once, some penanced lady elf,
> Some demon's mistress, or the demon's self.
> Upon her crest she wore a wannish fire
> Sprinkled with stars, like Ariadne's tiar.

That is exquisite for Sara Bernhardt when (with the suggestion of a feat or in the display of her resources of weird " effects," rather than as a convincing piece of acting) she flings herself, in " Fedora," on her couch, and gazes basilisk-wise upon her audience, or on vacancy. This is the Parisienne—may we say it ? yes—for " Knock'd 'em in the Old Kent Road ! "

There are, by the way, many other passages in " Lamia " that are singularly appropriate to a Bernhardtesque performance :—

> Lamia, regal drest,
> Silently paced about, and as she went
> In pale contented sort of discontent—
>
> .   .   .   .
>
> Her eyes in torture fixed, and anguish drear,
> Hot, glazed, and wide, with lid-lashes all sear,
> Flashed phosphor and sharp sparks, without one cooling
> tear.

She seems unearthly in her pathos rather than irresistibly human, and again in her intenser expressions even of tenderness or devotion there is something suggesting the inarticulate rudimentary desires of some animal, as of a kid or a calf. This is a peculiarity of her power. Her art, though informed by remarkable intelligence, is not guided by any philosophic consideration, by analysis, or by any cold instrument of intellect. It is more or less instinctive, it is full of natural tact, and she presses home up to the last throb of the pulse and the last impulse of the nerves the power of the deep elemental passions. She flings herself into her part. And combined with her original genius for emotional displays is that faculty which is never wanting in high developments of genius—the ability to make use of all the resources of art, of schooling, of cultivation.

The qualities of personality, of hypnotic power, rest upon labour. In suffering only do we weigh and test feeling; in suffering only do we understand character; in suffering only do we gain the skill intuitively to read the souls of others. And herein is but one of the meanings of that many-facetted proverb, " Literature comes by blood."

We may see the striking force of personality, even if only in fugitive glimpses, in fine examples of acting, and finest of all in Bernhardt. She not only plays her own part; she keeps the tension of the whole of the action. The drama moves not by disconnected points, but in a broad continuous stream. Approaching a fine climax she is busy in a thousand ways, and from the changing ripples of her mouth, and from the glances of her eyes, a hundred invisible chords are moving the play like a living thing whose feeling has infected ourselves. All this is not " analysis," or at least conscious analysis; it comes from something that may be felt but which is not easy to express, the mysterious tact and sensations of a delicate nature. A glance carries its effect to the utmost extremity of the action. She feels the force and import of every movement on the stage, then strikes in with a master-stroke binding all the movements together.

An actress well schooled but without dramatic fire is simply mechanical and tame; an actress of genius but without training is wild, irregular, and frequently disappointing; but Sara's natural powers have been through a long course of assiduous effort developed to the greatest perfection. From first to last she has her eye upon a thousand things that would escape one less experienced and less intelligent. There is a kind of veritable necromancy in her art. She waves a wand, or at least waves her arms as though they were wands, and throws upon us a spell. Every scene and every passage, and even every word, is definitely related to her position on the stage and to her gestures, and of these she has an unending store, and none ineffective.

> She, like a moon in wane,
> Faded before him, cowered, nor could restrain
> Her fearful sobs.

That is Lamia again, and it does very well for Bernhardt.

> . . . So said, she rose
> Tip-toe, with white arms spread.

Q

And not only is her whole presence and manner always singularly appropriate to the action of the play, but particularly her voice is a treasure, for with its fine rounded *timbre*, its clear and perfect intonation, she has the control of all expressions, from a soft floating whisper up to one of her own particular little thunderstorms, or even down to harsh and coarse objurgations. There is music in her ordinary utterance, and there are a thousand *nuances* in the cadence of her words. And so, too, throughout the range of her several powers.

Her touch is so light that she has quite an arsenal of effects, a whole series of points and *tâtonnements*, all above the reach of a stock tragedy queen. A stock tragedy queen she can simply absorb in bulk, and then her range stretches out as far in the bolder as in the finer notes on each side of the scale. Her manner of engaging the attention of the audience, her necromancy, is irritative or electric according to the feeling of the spectator. She holds the reins of mastery in her hands, she brings in her daring strokes of acting with absolute certitude, and at the critical moment pours out cataracts of hysterics, ornate, elaborate, nay, pyrotechnic, and full of *éclat*. These violent humours—often the very abandonment in violence—may yet fail to sweep one away. The nature disturbed, though furious, is represented as shallow. Lady Macbeth would petrify Fedora with a look. Helen MacGregor would spurn her away in contempt with her foot, and her profounder nature, with the restrained though significant gestures, would stamp its superior seal on the mind. Perhaps the comparison is forced and unfair ; for the versatility of Sara Bernhardt is not to be paralleled, and she does nothing ill. Her "deaths" are amazingly vivid. One sees the countenance of the woman gradually becoming transformed into a hideous death's head. It is realistic, it is ghastly, but, on the whole, resembles a demonstration in anatomy rather than a high æsthetic achievement, and the suspicion arises that the performance is greatly mechanical.

Such, then, is the lady who holds audiences all over the world "spell-bound," or sways them with "magnetic" power, or stirs them with "electrical" touch, to whom the terms "startling," "thrilling," and "unspeakable sadnesses," and "tumultuous passions," and all manner of swoonings and "galvanic" displays are simply mere commonplaces. It is interesting, nay, delightful, to find so much fascination, so much charm, in one wicked-looking little Jewess. It gives new ideas of the possibilities of woman ; and of man. She knows a thousand stops in the whole grand organ of feeling, from the touches light as thistle seed

to the raging of dramatic cyclones. She throws
her body as well as her soul into her parts. The
emotions topple over at her command into wild
dégringolades, avalanches, *débâcles* of passion. She
throws out her energy, she presses on her *vis
viva*, all that she has, and every choreate impulse,
every febrile excitation, is swept along into the
work. She carries her point even up to the pitch
of panting for dear life or swooning in absolute
exhaustion. She deserves all she has won, and
her career has been her justification—the eager
little Jewess with the *diablerie* in her eyes, ungifted
in feature and rather awkward in frame, working
her way up through never - ending, assiduous
efforts, cultivating to its utmost every talent, and
developing the woman through all. And now the
terribly experienced *femme du monde* stands alone
at the top of the tree. The audience is a great
instrument of which she can touch cunningly the
chords. Her voice is thrilling in quality, her
figure interesting if only for the feline grace of
her movements, the amorphous features are almost
beautiful in the power of expression, the eyes blaze
with *diablerie* once more, and her verve and dramatic fire give the last stroke to genius.

BERNHARDT is the world's actress; Duse is the great Italian artiste; Rehan, the Irish-American genius. And possibly if the discussion be carried to a volume, the final conclusion and the pith will contain no more than that. For, after all, in the supreme sense, there is but one theatre, as there is but one literature; and France, ever the advanced guard of civilisation, holds the fief of both. Other countries possess great writers or great actors who rise almost like monsters from amidst their surroundings, great in their hugeness and their originality, but lacking in polish and refinement and perfect efficiency even by virtue of their isolation. Great acting—the subtle touch of exquisite emotional expression—is especially so rare in English communities, that, compared with Paris, London seems in this respect hardly more than provincial. To Bernhardt in tragedy there is no second; there is only a second class. After Réjane in comedy, we descend from the

delicate *nuances* of a fine picture to the coarse
effects of scene paintings.

Yet, after all, Rehan reasserts herself in the
memory and lives again in her own rare and
racy quality, her indubitable genius.

Ada Rehan was born in Limerick—a not insignificant fact ; for just as it was epigrammati-
cally expressed by Thackeray that Gil Blas came
from Cork, so also the stranger who takes a walk
down the streets of Cork or Limerick to-morrow
will see a hundred wild little Rehans, a hundred
untamed little Peg Woffingtons. And on seeing
Rehan for the first time my thoughts were continually being blended with the reminiscences of
the race from which she had sprung, and I rejoiced to behold in her the triumph of that fine
nature of which before I had so often beheld
the devastation.

The story of Ireland is written on the physique
of the children ; for at every turn, in the towns of
the South more particularly, one meets countenances bright, eager, and jovial in expression,
but showing at the same glance the deep underlying sadness, the haunting wistfulness of unattainable hopes. The eye especially is in these
children often of remarkable beauty ; for though
the contour of features is generally disappointing,
yet even in ugly faces there is often a power of

luminous and subtle expression that a Raphael, a Correggio, or a Titian might have started back to behold in delight.

And, again, even in the finest countenances there is a suggestion of a hungering, whether for righteousness or for points more material, it is not easy to determine, but nevertheless a suggestion that with its sharpness and its regrets makes one say—these eyes have seen hell. In the one glance we have the most attractive picture of the Irish character, the generous temperament, the faithfulness of their disposition, the tenacity of their affections whether of devotion or of hope or of pride, the warmth of indefinable sympathetic qualities, the blitheness, the pleasantness of their natures, the easy, laughing disposition where humour seems naturally to effloresce from the rich soil of the passions; and then at the next glance the evil passions, the devils of hate, the fierce thoughts that seem to have an edge of steel, the turbid feelings that vent themselves in the coarsest abuse.

And to these contemplations I was led immediately and spontaneously in looking at Rehan. For though she has received her education in America, her genius is Irish to the core; and though her qualities have been made effective by schooling, yet three generations of schooling would not have made her what she is, and happily all the schooling in the world could not have entirely unmade her.

What a great woman she was! Tall, easy, almost majestic, except that the geniality of her manner took from majesty its aloofness and pride. When she spoke her voice came out mellifluently, so that without forcing it seemed to pervade the room. It had something of the quality of a black-bird's note ; and also amongst the strange sequence of ideas that, after all, are not mere conceits but true associations, it made one think of liquid silver.

Ada Rehan is not at all of a classic type of countenance. She is genuine Celtic. To call her pretty would be ridiculous, for prettiness is something that seems to dwindle beside her. To call her beautiful would be neither completely expressive nor apt, for her features have the warp of too many conflicting irrepressible emotions, and the turn of what one feels tempted to call *rale ould Irish humour*. Yet the eyes, and the brow, and the head are beautiful—the eyes espe-cially, with their soft, lamp-like, mellow glow, with their sharp, fiery glints, with their gorgon direct-ness, or again with their innumerable little twinkles of fun and sly melting shadows, with the flashing from the lids and the eyelashes of light, or the deep still beaming that perhaps most eloquently of all speaks of soul.

To describe a lady with too delicate care may seem like trespassing over the line of indelicacy. Suffice it to say that Miss Rehan is of that fine type of womanhood that Phidias delighted in ; or, at least, that she would seem so were she not entirely modern, for modernity already implies a falling off from the type. Ah, where is the modern sculptor whose finest conception, whose most finished work, can compare for a moment even to a battered fragment of Phidias ? Consider, for instance, what must have been to him no extraordinary achievement—that Caryatid from the Erectheum which is now preserved at the British Museum. So perfect is the proportion and balance of that figure that even in the very stone it seems to breathe, and we behold it not in mere hard outline, but—one may dream for a moment—in an unpalpable atmosphere that in fine undulations floats around it. A Greek woman's shoulder is a volume in itself—one imagines the delicate flushing, suffusing, interpenetrating, its white and sculptured form, the perfect muscle beneath the soft and gleaming skin, the dimpled knitting of the hardy shoulder-bands, the lustre of the hair, with its aromatic odour and its touch that is like a deep draught of wine, the classic

strong repose, the bold sweep and the fulness of
the sculpturing stroke swelled up with a thousand
melting lines and stealing undulations in the ever-
present classic mould. But, after all, this has not
entirely to do with Rehan, though possibly, again,
not entirely apart from her. She stimulates fine
thoughts, and suggests distinguished associations.

To speak of Miss Rehan's acting fully, it would
be necessary to compare it in some detail with
that of her contemporaries on the English stage,
for, after all, excellence is but a question of degree;
but the task would be invidious. She differs from
other actresses not by surpassing them in their
own peculiar excellences, but by disregarding
entirely their methods. She is of another class.
Other actresses whom we have seen and admired
appear to be of meagre personality ; stiff, mechanical, and flat, compared to Rehan. We think, indeed, that we could never really have admired
before ; that we have always felt a certain disappointment and regret, as though at the curbing of
a generous impulse, in not having been able to
admire, in having been unable to give more than
somewhat cold concessions of appreciation. But
when Rehan walks upon the stage ! . . .

One could imagine her beholding the attempts
of the pretty and interesting ladies on the stage
to say their little say appropriately enough and

to make an orthodox pretty tableau. The acting
is feeble ; the tableaux are flat, discontinuous in
themselves, and discontinuous with the general
movement of the drama ; the dialogue lacks point,
because there are intervals in the acting and the
speaking that should be filled up with a hundred
lights and shades, a hundred half-discovered impressions ; but, most indefinably of all, there's
an absence of the broad unbroken sweep, the
tension, the life of the play.

She would know that her criticism would wear
an aspect of intangibility and that her instruction
would be futile. But she would burn to speak,
to tread the boards. Rehan is, then, more than a
circumscribed little figure ; she is a living, moving,
animating presence. She is the centre of all the
poetic harmonies of the play. She holds the
key ; she dominates the stage, and all the rest
are but in her train. No attitude is forced or
obviously studied. Yet each particular attitude is
complete and is in itself a triumph. Her voice,
manner, being, are swept into the spirit and swept
along with the passion of the play. She does not
act at her audience, nor, on the other hand, act
out of sympathy with them and apart from the
piece. The drama is real ; it becomes infused into
herself. It moves along without discontinuity,
without disproportion. It is broad and free, yet

through it all one is conscious of its tension, one feels interested, but not quite surprised or startled at the bold stroke, the electric touch of her truth. One is attracted to her, sympathetically bound to her, and borne along in the stream with her. The play fills everything. It presses on surely, inevitably, then hotly, to its outcome. We toil with her, wait with her, strike in with her, suffer with her, and in the last great effort triumph with her, and awake as from a hypnotic dream to find ourselves and our surroundings the real things; for so it seems. But the dream is a real thing too.

Seeing her as Rosalind one may admire her art the more just at the point where the limits of art are reached. For Rosalind, though one of the deepest in character of the heroines of Shakspere, yet is fresh, easy, and delightful as a day in spring-time, and her wit bubbles out from a well of good spirits; and there is in Rosalind no acting and no art solicitous to shine. And all this is included in the rare, indefinable atmosphere of Rosalind's beauty. So that more may hope to play the part perfectly; but a good actress may seek rather to interpret, to draw aside the curtain, to reveal it.

And Miss Rehan gives us luminous interpretations of the Rosalind she knows; she makes us understand the witching power of beauty.

Beauty is not of feature merely, for that is a

mask, nor of expression merely, nor of movement, nor of pose; though all these elements must doubtless be present in beauty. Nor is it the delight of intelligence only; and it is something more even than the affection of sympathy—yes, more than that. There are times when other aspects of human passion, and the struggles for distinction, the triumphs of intellect, the heroics of war, the delight of victory in great assembly —these things seem like the dusty fore-courts to another sort of world wherein lives beauty or love —for they are one, and they are the ripeness and the completion of life.

Then we can dream only of the warm sunshine, and the blue sky, and the soft cooing breezes that fan and linger on the cheek, and the glowing eye, and the ardent and languorous looks; and the earth and all her teeming fruits and her offspring seem to have but the meaning of swelling up into the universal and irresistible instincts of love. There is a beauty that subdues and entrances, that sweeps away resistances, that is a better thing than all the previous life, that is the apex, the "chief intensity," the "tip-top" of these, the "orbed drop of light." A beautiful woman knows her power, and rejoices in it; that is inevitable. And when others have been beautiful, and have charmed the sense, there is one that by a bold, swift stroke seizes the heart and wins the soul ; and there is a higher life in that long deep-breathing wonder in which all our senses and all our thoughts and all our rising impulses are blended.

Yet once again this is straying from Rehan ; but again not entirely, for there is something very inspiriting in her, in that free, expansive poets' soul. There is an amplitude about her—referring not to her physical proportions, but to the quality and range of her sympathies. She is grand but suave, with a fine womanly persuasiveness. She gives us new and impressive ideas of the scope and range of a woman's nature, while never anything but essentially womanly. She gives us the idea of there being a thousand kinds of beauty, even of pure physical beauty, and each with its characteristic charm. We feel the fascination of pure physical beauty, even of the beauty of a woman of thoughtless, untilled mind, whose beauty wantons merely in the atmosphere of sense, an infatuation the more intense because of its very limitations, because of the impossibility of meeting her on any other plane but her own ; and we feel the attraction in many characters restricted and helpless by virtue of their narrow intellect and want of stimulation to all ideas that lie outside their little world, if only in that there be enthusiasm, fire, and ever-fresh up-bubbling spontaneous interest—the infectiousness of strong and hardy native impulses. And there is an exquisite delight in the calm control of a woman of full and generous nature, but of good intellectual training, of well-tempered power. It is all within the range of *das ewige Weibliche*. All the thousand qualities of physical attraction, of the varied forms of intellect and the native sweetness of soul and all its fine culture, issue from the same source, and return again to develop and adorn it ; it is all contained in that large life of which *she* knows through and through the genius—the *woman*.

Great actress as she is, there are many parts that Miss Rehan could hardly attempt ; indeed, perhaps there is not one that she has made entirely her own. She is a tragedienne and comedienne ; but to call an actress a tragedienne or a comedienne is still to be remote from a definition. There are a hundred kinds as well as degrees of tragedy ; and in comedy also the greatest actress may find a hundred characters marked by their own peculiar tone which she knows can be shown better by others.

In the interpretation of Sardou's characters, for example, Bernhardt cannot be approached ; that is her *forte*.

Then, again, we come to another type at the

opposite extremity of the "powerful effects"—
Siddons. The critics were inclined to cavil at
Siddons at first. She was certainly not of the
"correct" school; and she was very little schooled
at all. She simply acted, as she herself once expressed it, "as well as she could." And she had
a peculiar way of jerking her arms back; it was
natural, but it had not been seen before, and
theatre-goers are full of "traditions." However,
Siddons could not be denied. She could not
meet the objections; she simply swept them away.
And of all the parts wherein she found her
triumphs none seems to have suited her better
than Volumnia, the mother of Coriolanus. Her
Lady Macbeth was not perfect, for Lady Macbeth
seems to have been of the type of the classic
Greek, and Siddons was rather of the Roman
mould. But in the scene in "Coriolanus" where
Volumnia, prevailing at length over the obstinacy
of her great son, saves Rome, there it was that
Siddons was at her greatest; for the various
accounts tell us that she seemed to totter and roll
and heave on the stage, like a woman intoxicated,
in her triumph; carrying off, however, at last all
suggestion of a false stroke by the magnificent
carriage with which she swept off to the wings.

Now, between these types, so unlike, so remote,
Rehan stands; yet, again, unlike both. She, too,

is undoubtedly of that classic type that "modern degeneracy" (so to adopt the phrase) has not reached. Yet she is entirely modern. She can be very winning, easy, familiar, as though bred merely to afternoon tea-parties ; but when beset by the intricacies of a difficult action, and teased by the weak chains of a tangling plot, she can suddenly *heave* out of it, and commanding the entire situation, and beating through unnumbered little billows that she heeds not at all, sail off in her pride.

Ada Rehan is of a superior race of women. She can be enormously interesting simply standing looking out of a window, her back to the audience, immobile, but with a "calmness" that sends off vibrations that stir the pulses very curiously, and make her always the magnet, the centre. She pauses, but it is the pause of a fine balance of strong feelings. She is all alive ; she whirls round and comes into the action with a bold ringing stroke that has been adjudged to perfection. She can stride—not like a man, for she is always a fine woman—but like the daughter of Fingal, the sister of Ossian. She can bang a door like a chord of martial music. She can precipitate herself headlong into a room, and seizing her opponent or her lover, for she is equal to all occasions, at the critical wavering moment,

R

sweep in with a wrestler's power and lift him metaphorically helpless off his feet. Yet in all these displays Rehan is never violent in a narrow way, or streaky or hard or wiry. Her limbs move with a tough strength, with a firm, well-tempered force. She can throw herself on a sofa in the most abandoned attitude of ease, yet she is always admirable, never coarse, or even luxurious—that is to say, not luxurious in a degenerate, idle, or weak fashion.

And with all these qualities the more regrettable is it to see this actress condemned by the taste of the public to exhibit herself, adorned with a curly flaxen wig, in a series of ridiculous German farces, and to amuse the populace by nothing better than the tomfooleries of absurd situations.

Let us forget these caprices, or rather these highly respectable, because successful, business transactions. Rehan is at base a woman of a sovereign type, delicate even while not mincingly cultured. She is hardy, toilsome, athletic, but patient. Her ideas run in no narrow line, but are submerged in vistas of associations. All her life is but an education to her, an education that develops and does not at all break down her original nature ; and a wide range of life seems natural to her in her plastic ease of sympathy.

She can move from the gloomy halls of death to the pleasure of a blue sky and the fresh air, the scent of flowers and blossoms, and the youth, ever renewed, of the bold, free earth.

`Laughter is there, and the sly twinklings of humour that peep out of the softest and murkiest corners of her eye, but also candour and directness, the outright burst of enjoyment. All these are natural to her ; so also are the tears, the terrible sobs wherein a living thing seems to escape from the breast, the deep sombre tones as well as the tender tones of remembrance, and the hot blaze of passions that sweep through the mind with fiery edge and buffet the soul up to the overleaping of all that is less than themselves—the cast of life or of death. The beauty of repose is delightful in her, the calm musing meditation, and the deep harmonious passion of devotion ; so also is the quick salient swerve of emotion wherein the soul is suddenly shaken to its depths by love, by fear, by admiration. She is a good woman always—able to meet the rude clang of earth and the unescapable pain of life, and to rejoice in the solid strength of reality ; for we find life and flesh and blood throughout, and everywhere the fire of the soul that animates it ; and she is one of those to whom the mind is specially drawn to speak of all the tender, beautiful, mainly ineffective thoughts that lie in a woman's world—the power of imagination, the power of hope, the power of love, genius, and the immortality of the soul.

HERBERT SPENCER is the third of the world's thinkers, if Aristotle and Kant be taken as the first two. For in the perspective of history these three figures will stand out clear and immortal beyond all others. That there were acute, zealous, and profound thinkers before Aristotle, goes without saying; but it was reserved for the marvellous brain of the Stagyrite to collect into something like a definite science, or sciences, the thousand hints and researches of his predecessors, and in turn to become the motive force of all the science of a thousand years.

It is true that later science has rejected much of Aristotle's work; that, in fact, the rise of our modern science began with the questioning of the Greek's overweening authority; yet it remains none the less true that in intellectual power the man was a king, even compared to most of those whose researches have eaten into his dominion. Aristotle is the great type of the thinker, the man who by dint of thought alone governs the world more powerfully than the conqueror clothed in imperial purple.

Kant, in turn, was not the first of those who in the modern *régime* of scientific thought have rendered Aristotle unnecessary. Nay, of all the great thinkers whose influence still persists, Kant is probably the man who was most impressed by the dicta of the Attic school ; and it is also true that the modern tendency has been to reject most of Kant's purely psychological work as decisively as Aristotle was rejected by the philosophers immediately preceding the German. Yet Kant also, the little Koenigsberger, poor in body, poor in birth, poor in possessions, stands out as the unique figure of genius in the world of the renaissance of philosophy just as decisively as, of old, Aristotle. The little docent's intellect swayed the life of Europe.

And now Spencer, the third in succession, has done not a little to destroy Kant's authority, beginning his work in the style and scope that tacitly averred what the German arrogantly asserted in words—There is no philosophy !

For Spencer, the continuator of the work of Locke, Hume, Berkeley, and Mill, is none the less a pioneer, an originator. The psychology of the future will date from him. The work of Locke, Berkeley, Hume, bears the same relation to

Spencer as the work of Van Helmont and Berzelius to Schwann, the work of Huygens and Fourier to Young, the work of Lamarck and Buffon to Darwin. The work of Spencer strikes so deeply and so broadly as to underlie and embrace all that has been done before, even while at the same time forming the platform to a new definite advance of untold possibilities. Or to give another glimpse of its vastness, it may be thus expressed : Kant expounded the nebular hypothesis, tracing the gradual development of the earth as we know it, from the original formless vapour of chaos ; Darwin in the biological world has traced the gradual development of the myriad kinds of life from one primordial form ; Bain has expounded the laws of the most delicate product of all that life—the human mind ; Spencer has traced the complete continuity between the formless vapour of chaos and the finest transcendental shapings of our thought. He sees the woof of existence whole, and sees no rent in the garment.

The *milieu* in which Herbert Spencer was born seems at first glance much less favourable to the development of a philosopher than that of Aristotle or Kant. The disadvantage of the Stagyrite was the deficiency of positive science in his day ; his advantages consisted in the unfettered freedom of speculation, the intense interest amongst his compeers in matters of thought, and the general reverence for and comprehension of the sublimity of the philosophic life.

The German was fortunate in being the scion of a race in which a backward state of political existence was to a great extent compensated by a free expansion of energy in science and speculation. Leibnitz, Kant, Hegel, Fichte, Lotze, are all University products, are all connected, even amidst their discrepancies, in a continuous hierarchy.

In England, however, the great thinkers have all been rebels—Locke, Hume, Mill, Darwin—and now Bain and Spencer. They are the enemies of Society. It is true that the makers of civilisation may become honoured after their death, and that by dint of the irresistible logic of facts Society is gradually forced to conform to their directions; but to each during his lifetime it has been his lot to find his work assailed with furious abuse and envenomed bitterness, none the less dangerous and obstructive because arising from ignorance and prejudice and enforced by the most pitiable arguments. The philosopher finds himself in the eyes of Society not honoured for his intellect, but degraded and ostracised even for the efforts of his thought. . . . Consider, for example, the work of Herbert Spencer in relation to the era in which it has arisen. Without aristocratic birth, without means sufficient even to secure leisure, without authority save in his powers of reason, it has been his fate to pursue his career in a country where the talismanic words are title, wealth, position. Distinguished as a philosopher alone, he has striven to make his influence felt in a nation where the respect for pure intellectuality, and where the general diffusion of culture, are far below that of the other two great nations foremost in civilisation—France and Germany. Attempting to establish philosophy upon a new basis, he has run counter to the prodigious prestige of the Universities with their stereotyped teaching, still locked in the absurdities of mediæval metaphysics.

Professing to have found in the conditions of nature and the constitution of Society the Data of Ethics, Spencer has been confronted with the dogmas of the Christian religion, and has found his life's work impugned and baffled by virtue of a legend which to his mind must have figured as a childish superstition. Setting no limits to the daring of his thought, and couching his speech in sincerity and candour, he has found the mind of his generation warped by the teachings of sophists dishonest or abject, the Mansels and the Newmans ; appealing to the light of reason alone, he has discovered his work crushed under the dead weight of vast vested interests, his voice drowned by the blatant cries of popular leaders. Nor in the world of politics has he been more fortunate. He has consistently taught Republican principles in an age when royalty with its trappings is adulated almost in proportion to the decadence of its actual power, and where movements of reform for the most part are directed to objects that must seem to him even more remote from the line of true progress. A poor scholar, Republican, agnostic, what should he do in a " nation of shopkeepers," monarchical, Christian ? These are the circumstances that give to Spencer's " Synthetic Philosophy " an air of unreality so far as touching the life of the nation is concerned, an impression of a monumental but intolerably dull study as useless but not so interesting as a problem in chess. As Keats found in another fashion the philosopher has " no depth to strike in," and his work has the sense of being written *in vacuo*. The vastest intellect, possibly, of our time ranks amongst us as a *caput mortuum*.

The detachment from interest, however, and the lack of that " scientific atmosphere " that is to be found in the cultured circles of Berlin and Paris, have been not without their compensations to some of the great English thinkers. Locke,

Young, Dalton, Darwin, to cite a few of the most illustrious names, were all somewhat secluded workers, and in the absence of the multiplicity of details of an active University life they found the leisure in which their minds descended to the depths of their subjects and elaborated fertile principles, each in his own domain, which have been the starting-point of all succeeding work. And that is doubtless the case also with Spencer.

His career, which may be summed up as a life of intellectual toil scantily recognised, has nevertheless been fairly well carried through with respect to the advantage of his work. Born of parents in a class of Society that permitted a liberal education while not dispensing with that keen goad to exertion, the necessity of earning a living, Herbert Spencer had in the first place a training very serviceable to one about to enter into the domain of abstract thought, viz., that of a civil engineer. It may safely be assumed that the time spent upon this study was by no means wasted even in view of his work as a philosopher. The practice of an engineer supplies that which is often wanting in the life of a scientific man, viz., the bringing to the test of actual experience the theories elaborated in the study or laboratory. And at the same time as distinguished from professions when empirical methods and rough

estimates are in vogue, as in the practice of
medicine, or professions that depend on forensic
skill, engineering brings to direct utilitarian purposes the results of the exact sciences, the highest
flights of which carry the mind to a limit where
the skill of the calculator is transported into a
region of exquisite thoughts that require for their
discovery the flash of intellect, the poet's subtle
fancy and flight.

After various tentative efforts, amid the uncer-
tainties of a young man's aspirations, Spencer at
length struck into his true course, and the intellectual campaign of his life has been probably the
most consistent, consecutive, and coherent of any
of which we have record.

Spencer is the true type of the English philosopher—a type not so ambitious, possibly, as the
German, but more sane and lucid; not so inspiriting in ethical purposes as the French, far
below in genius and charm of expression, but
more solid in judgment. And, singularly enough,
even in a country so little predisposed to philosophy, he preserves as an iconoclastic philosopher
the veritable national characteristics. In appearance the great thinker might be mistaken for a
respectable farmer or corn-dealer. The countenance is of a plain, *bourgeois* type, the features
being by no means so good as the setting of the

features—the lines of expression that characterise
the face and impress it with the aspect of deep
intelligence and power. The head is symmetrical and finely arched, and the dull mask of
the features is lightened by a look which tells
of the intense fire of intellect which has burnt
away their grossness and made the countenance
alive with sensitive feeling. At first glance the
physique seems to be that of a person inclined
to material interests; at a second view it is evident
that the light that guides that life is all compact
of intellect; the material power is there strong
enough to save the intellect from the mere
wastefulness of suffering; the emotional quality
has force enough to supply the motive power to
the highly developed and delicate instrument of
thought. Spencer is almost as various as Aristotle
in an age of greater enlightenment; he has that
candour which is Locke's distinguishing feature,
with a wider scope and greater illumination than
Locke; he is as subtle as Berkeley, without being
carried away by Berkeley's spiritual and baseless
enthusiasms; he is as keen as Hume, without
Hume's *tic* for sophistries; he is as earnest as
Mill, without Mill's tendency to fads and overstrained positions.

The name of Bain is heard in the Universities
of Germany, perhaps oftener than that of Spencer.

The reason is that Bain's work has been done more within the range of what might be called the technical study of psychology. Spencer's work gives us the deep base of the study, but does not present so many points of definite issue ; nor is it possible to behold without elaborate study the drift and scope of his work. His work bears the same relation to that of most other philosophers as the work of the engineer who lays down the framework of a ship and gives the principle of its design bears to the carrying out of the details of its furnishing.

Yet profound and vast as is the "Synthetic Philosophy," it will be seen to arise from one germinating idea—the principle of Evolution. That principle has become so familiar to us in common parlance that it is generally accepted rather than generally understood. With Spencer it has a perfectly definite and precise meaning. "*Evolution is an integration of matter and concomitant dissipation of motion, during which the matter passes from an indefinite, incoherent homogeneity to a definite, coherent heterogeneity, and during which the retained motion undergoes a parallel transformation.*"

And if we grasp the full import of every term and the meaning of the whole sentence, we have a sure guide to the reading of the "Synthetic Philosophy," for it then opens up like an exposition and

a series of corollaries of the original main proposition. Grasp the full significance of Herbert
Spencer's principle of Evolution, and the great
bulk of his work may, in outline at least, be
anticipated.

'By what processes, then, did such a mind arrive
at this fertile doctrine ? What was the original
suggestion, the innermost flame, of all this work ?
. . . We must assume a mind, to begin with, in
which the habits of analysis and generalisation
have become inveterate. Such a mind dealing
with question after question submitted to its intelligence, continually seeking causes and origins,
and continually seeking broad bases of similarity
of principle between things unlike in detail, must
inevitably at length be led to the attempt to relate
mental states first to physical states, and next to
the broad physical conditions of the world itself.
The irreducible things that we must take as the
ultima ratio of our analysis are Mass, Force,
Time, Space, and the relations that these necessarily involve. When we step from inanimate to
animate existence, we must add Sensitiveness to
external impressions related to internal adjustments consequent upon these impressions—the
most general expression, in fact, of Perception
and Action. Here, then, we are at the beginning
of a philosophy, and if we open our eyes upon

the world, we behold that our problem is to trace up the progress of life from the lowest stage to the highest—in other words, to enunciate the principle of Evolution from the most rudimentary to the most developed form of life. We may set to work trenchantly by comparing a man with an amœba, always in view of our fundamental position, and with the intention of giving to our enunciation of the differences the most general expression that will cover the whole ground. The doctrine of Evolution, as set forth by Spencer, results.

All ways lead Spencer to his fundamental doctrine, and from that fundamental doctrine conversely he can in successive routes attain any part of the whole domain of philosophy. Consider, for example, the proposition : Structure implies function. And consider also that the mind has its contact with the world only by the medium of the senses. It follows from these considerations that the evolution of mind must then be parallel to the evolution of the senses. And the evolution of the senses springs from the sense of touch. The evolution of all the complex motor apparatus in man corresponding to the complex sensory apparatus, similarly takes as its starting-point the automatic reaction consequent upon the rudimentary touch. In other words, we are led from man to the amœba again.

Or if we contemplate the nebular hypothesis and search for the dawn of animate existence, we find our problem in its simplest form, and we trace out from that point the history of the world. And the general expression of that history is infallibly again the doctrine of Evolution. The assumptions that underlie Evolution are that the mind depends upon the body, and that there is one material out of which all physical structures are formed. That material, protoplasm, appears to be built of elements which we find in other combinations in inorganic substances. The cell theory, one of the deepest generalisations we know of in science, is thus an explanation of an incident of Evolution, and Darwinism is one of its corollaries.

Bearing in mind the meaning of Evolution, it will be observed how luminous are passages like the following, quoted from a chapter in the first volume of Spencer's " Principles of Psychology," entitled " The Correspondences in their Totality,' the chapter being the last of a section entitled " General Synthesis " :—

" On comparing the phenomena of mental life with the most nearly allied phenomena—those of bodily life —and inquiring what is common to both groups, a generalisation was disclosed which proves on examination to express the essential characters of all mental actions.   Regarded under every variety of aspect, intelligence is found to consist in the establishment of correspondences between relations in the organism and relations in the environment ; and the entire development of intelligence may be formulated as the progress of such correspondence in Space, in Time, in Speciality, in Generality, in Complexity."

Guided in the same way we observe the depth and the purport of various phrases that occur in " Principles of Biology," as, for instance, that Life is adequately conceived only when we think of it as " the definite combination of heterogeneous changes, both simultaneous and successive, in correspondence with external co-existences and sequences."   Or again, the briefer and slightly looser form of the definition : " The continuous adjustment of internal relations to external relations."

Such is one of those pregnant sentences that are typical of Spencer, and which, though not couched in epigrammatic form, have the force of aphorisms by virtue of their containing the fund of a vast amount of thought.

And now we behold the basis and the principles of development of the " Synthetic Philosophy" itself.   The " First Principles" gives us the ultimate analysis, the reduction of all physical

science to the science of mechanics; the work
being introduced by a subtle metaphysical disquisition. It is the union of the philosopher
with the engineer.

In the "Principles of Biology" Spencer in-
troduces the special considerations of animate
existence, and foreshadows, in his studies of low
forms of organic structures, the principles of
ethics. His early "hobby" for field-naturalists'
work has here stood him in admirable stead.

The "Principles of Psychology" is but the
carrying the same principles of observation and
the same standards into the domain of human
beings. And gradually the ethical principle
is unfolded and insisted upon. The ultimate
standard of right and wrong is that which leads
towards fuller expansion of life, or towards
death, respectively; and the touchstone that
Nature has given for the direction of conduct
is that which in its more developed stage we
call respectively the feeling of pleasure or the
feeling of pain. From the contemplation of the
mechanical world from an indifferent standpoint
we rise then to the interest which finally gives
us our laws, our principles, our most exquisite
sentiments.

In the "Principles of Sociology," the individual
is placed in his environment, and the discussion

is enlarged with regard to ethical standards and tendencies.

In the " Data of Ethics " the results are summed up, in order to lay the foundation for a directive discourse following upon an expository discourse, which, however, has implied the principle of all that is to follow.

In addition to this vast work, truly a master-piece of human energy, Herbert Spencer has developed his ideas into a thousand corollaries, touching innumerable vivid interests of the social life of the nation. His work on Education may be cited as an instance.

Throughout the whole exposition of the " Synthetic Philosophy " one is astonished at the width and accuracy of the knowledge displayed, and the explanation is, of course, that Spencer, having early conceived the whole plan of his work, has ever had a guiding principle by which his acquisitions and studies have yielded the most effective result. But the mere accretion of facts is the least of the matters that stand to his intellectual credit. A fact or an incident never remains detached in his mind ; every phenomenon is made to yield the principle involved, and this is at once related by generalisation to a group of similar phenomena. At the same time his processes of induction are so active, that to ordinary minds his conclusions must often have the appearance of intuitions. Take for example the following, which, though suggested on very general grounds, seems to be borne out by the researches of the anatomists :—

" Much difference of opinion has long existed, and still exists, respecting the particular offices of these supreme ganglia (the *cerebrum* and the *cerebellum*); and especially respecting the office of the *cerebellum*. Without committing myself to it as anything more than a hypothesis, I will here venture to suggest a not improbable interpretation. The common function of the two being that of co-ordinating in larger groups and in various orders, the impressions and acts co-ordinated in the lower centres, we may fitly ask—Are there any fundamentally distinct kinds of order in which impressions and acts may be co-ordinated? The obvious answer is, that there are the two fundamentally distinct orders of Co-existence and Sequence. All phenomena are presented to us either as existing simultaneously or as existing successively. If, then, these two highest nervous centres, which together perform the general function of doubly-compound co-ordination, take separate parts of this function, as, from their separateness, we must conclude that they do, we can scarcely make a more reasonable assumption than that the respective orders in which they co-ordinate compound impressions and acts, answer to the respective orders in which the phenomena are conditioned. In brief, the hypothesis thus reached *à priori*, is that the *cerebellum* is an organ of doubly-compound co-ordination in *space ;* while the *cerebrum* is an organ of doubly-compound co-ordination in *time.*"—*Principles of Psychology*, vol. i., pt. i., c. iii.

Now this theory may be incorrect, but it is interesting to note how the mind of a man of great calibre proceeds even in its guesses ; and it is interesting to note also how in this passage, as in so many others, the neurologist or the biologist may find in Spencer food for reflection bearing on his own subject at its highest point. And this is true, with reference to other portions of his work, of the physicist also, the jurist, the educationist, the historian. For there is a range of thought at which the highest operations of the intellect in quite diverse fields are similar ; but apart from this Spencer in his luminous suggestions touches the subject of the specialist in its pith, and also gives the broad foundation for his work.

As an example of the clear statement of a proposition which contains, amidst its pregnant meaning, hints for educational and legal reformers :—

" To make my position fully understood, it seems needful to add that, corresponding to the fundamental proposition of a developed Moral Science, there have been, and still are, developing in the race, certain fundamental moral intuitions ; and that, though these moral intuitions are the results of accumulated experiences of Utility, gradually organised and inherited, they have come to be quite independent of conscious experience. Just in the same way that I believe the intuitions of space, possessed by any living individual, to have arisen from organised and consolidated experiences of all antecedent individuals who bequeathed to him their slowly-developed nervous organisations—just as I believe that this intuition, requiring only to be made definite and complete by personal experience, has practically become a form of thought, apparently quite independent of experience; so do I believe that the experiences of Utility organised and consolidated through all past generations of the human race, have been producing corresponding nervous modifications, which, by continued transmission and accumulation, have become in us certain faculties of moral intuition—certain emotions responding to right and wrong conduct, which have no apparent basis in the individual experiences of Utility. I also hold that just as the space intuition responds to the exact demonstrations of Geometry, and has its rough conclusions interpreted and verified by them, so will moral intuitions respond to the demonstrations of Moral Science, and will have their rough conclusions interpreted and verified by them."—*Data of Ethics*, c. vii.

Pursuing a kindred theme, Mr. Spencer replies to certain objections to his Hedonistic doctrines. The article is worth quoting in order to show the kind of argument used against his theories even by men of very considerable intelligence and habit of metaphysical speculation, and also to instance the calm adroitness with which the philosopher puts his finger on the flaw of his adversary's position :—

"The third argument states in the concrete that which is stated in the abstract in the preceding two, and is the sole argument. This argument is that M. Caro

thinks 'even an unhappy life is worth living.'   Now I
suspect that were M. Caro cross-examined, it would
turn out that the unhappy life which he thinks worth
living, is one which, though it brings misery to the
possessor, does not bring misery to others, but conduces
to their happiness.   If M. Caro means that life is worth
living even on condition that its possessor, suffering
misery himself in common with all individuals, shall aid
them in living that they may continue to suffer misery,
and shall beget and rear children that they, too, may pass
lives of misery; and if M. Caro means that misery is to
be the fate of all, not only here but during the hereafter
he believes in; then, indeed, and only then, does he
exclude happiness as an aid.   But if M. Caro says he
believes that even under such conditions life would be
worth living, then I venture to class him with those who
have not practised introspection."—*Data of Ethics*,
" Replies to Criticisms."

And finally, as an excellent example of Mr.
Spencer's dialectical skill, the following may be
cited, wherein he turns the table upon that subtlest
of philosophers, Berkeley himself.   He is criticis-
ing the " Dialogues of Hylas and Philonus " :—

" Had Hylas, as he should have done, taken the same
ground, the dialogue would have run thus :—
" *Phil.* Is your material substance a senseless being,
or a being endowed with sense and perception ?
" *Hylas.* I cannot say.
" *Phil.* How do you mean you cannot say ?
" *Hylas.* I mean that, like you, ' I know nothing ' of
any qualities of bodies save those I immediately per-

ceive through the senses; and I cannot immediately perceive through the senses whether material substance is senseless or not.

"*Phil.* But you do not doubt that it *is* senseless?

"*Hylas.* Yes; in the same way that you doubt my external reality—doubt whether I am anything more than one of your ideas. Did we not, at the beginning, Philonus, distinguish between things known immediately and things known mediately?"

And so the argument is continued, to the manifest enjoyment of Hylas.

This passage is written in rather a lighter vein than most of Spencer's expositions, and contains even as much wit and sparkle as may be duly allowed a Northern philosopher. As a matter of fact, the style in which the "Synthetic Philosophy" is written, though admirably lucid and correct, is deficient in the graces and turns of literary expression. It is formal and heavy and colourless, but at least it is well adapted to convey the author's meaning and intention, and to leave a durable impression on the mind. When one becomes immersed, however, simply in the endeavour to grasp his meaning and to contemplate the work in the scope he has in view; when its consistency, its circumstantiality, its vastness are considered; when the sense of its inevitable truth and surety of march is fully conceived; when the deep, pregnant expression is thoroughly compre-

hended ; when the spirit is alive to all its sugges-
tiveness ; then there are moments of meditation,
of enlightenment, of aspiration, in which to read
Spencer is like listening to the grand rolling music
of the mass of a mighty composer.

And all this may be said without involving the
necessity of accepting the whole of the Spencerian
philosophy. His work would remain great even
if a large part of the superstructure which he has
indicated rather than elaborated were destroyed.
For example, the theory of the functions of the
cerebellum and the *cerebrum* might be false, even
while his fundamental views of the development
of the nervous system remained impregnable.
And one might adopt not only the theory of
Evolution, but the great bulk of those portions
of the "Synthetic Philosophy" by which Spencer
illustrates that theory, without being committed
to the drift of Spencer's teaching with regard
to social structures. It is necessary to touch
upon this matter ; for even so acute a thinker
as Mr. Balfour has thrown out the opinion,
that if Weisman's theories of heredity were true,
it would mean the complete destruction from top
to bottom of the "Synthetic Philosophy"—an
opinion which indicates a failure to grasp the
"Synthetic Philosophy," or possibly even "Weis-
manism," or possibly both.

In ethical matters there does not exist an objective philosophy. There is not to be found in any of the great ethical writers, Epictetus, Epicurus, Kant, Mill, Spencer, a philosophy which is not impregnated with the temperament of the philosopher. There is nothing inevitable or final here, for ethical standards themselves must be finally judged by temperament and national disposition. And so it might happen that one who recognises the justice and depth of Spencer's objective philosophic positions might find his social schemes savour of a *bourgeois* environment, might find his temperament lacking in movement, in warmth, and colour.

It may be said that Spencer is the last of the system-builders, and it may be believed without disparagement that the " Synthetic Philosophy " is already becoming monumental and old-fashioned. The truth and force of Spencer's writings have of themselves brought about this result. He has convinced all those who have read him with intelligence and without bias that his main positions are impregnable. The doctrine of Evolution has come to be accepted among thinking men as one of the commonplaces, as incontestable as the theory of gravitation, or the theory of the circulation of the blood. It will yet be one of the principles invariably assumed even in the diffusion of knowledge amongst common people. And *pari passu* the corollaries, and the paths opened up during the discussions that form the bulk of the "Synthetic Philosophy," will be worked at in the special sciences upon whose province they encroach ; and so the work of Spencer will be superseded. Philosophy will become, on the one hand, a sort of logic, or methodology, of the sciences, and so lose the signification of the ancient name of philosophy ; and, on the other hand, it will regain that signification in a sphere where it will have scope in those psychical and speculative subjects untouched by the formulæ of objective science. Spencer will then become a name as Pythagoras, Zeno, Archimedes, Galileo, are names ; but his influence, as theirs, will persist, and it will have been his merit to have added to civilisation one of the sources of its perpetual enlightenment.

THE ruins of Thebes, the pyramids of Egypt, the tumuli of Troy, remain to tell of civilisations once flourishing and dominant, and now passed away for ever ; and casting our eyes down the abysses of time, these are among the few landmarks that remain as witnesses of the multitudinous activities of successive races and nations of men. And in the world of science, vast in extent, yet comparatively so close to our view, the great landmarks stand out no less impressively—Galileo's principle of the pendulum, Kant's nebular hypothesis, Harvey's discovery of the circulation of the blood, Oersted's discovery of the deflection of the magnet by the electric current, Newton's law of gravitation, Rumford's theory of heat a mode of motion, Young's undulatory theory of light, Dalton's atomic theory, Darwin's principle of natural selection, Schwann's theory of germs, Spencer's theory of Evolution. And in this company of *élite* we shall not fail to find Alexander Bain. For if we consider the march of the science of mind, we find in succession that the great links of the chain have been supplied by a few men : Locke, in his analysis of the source of our ideas ; Berkeley, by his analysis of extensity ; Hartley, by his doctrine of association ; Hume, by his analysis of cause and effect ; Kant, by his definition of the limits of analysis ; and Bain, by his law of relativity.

In this broad and general survey we found one great principle representing Bain's work ; but more truly than Napoleon said of his Austerlitz, there is something there that the enemy's tooth cannot bite into. The track of explanation of Psychology must ever pursue the same course, and inevitably each successive pilgrim shall halt at the same stages, and the work of the philosophers who have been named will remain more durable than the mighty monuments of the nations themselves. But beneath the minarets the life of the city surges ; and we may now descend more closely to the details of the work of Bain. In the second plane we have that profound work of his, " Education as a Science," and when we come nearer to the foundation we find an enormous amount of intellectual activity expended in the various branches to which his Psychology and Physiology have served as indicators—*Logic, Rhetoric, Grammar, the Senses and Intellect, the Emotions and the Will*, and a thousand other subjects of information, of history, and of exposition, that have lain within the scope of these main studies.

Bain himself has laid down the conditions for success in the field of philosophy, and these conditions are in part negative. It is not sufficient to possess the quality of subtle thought, the vivid flash of genius that illuminates a field of study; it is necessary also that the "objective" world as compared with the "subjective" world be small, that the vivid material and pictorial interests of a perfectly balanced mind be absent. Excellence implies restriction, and genius means the overthrow of proportion. In great types the bent of mind is as marked as an instinct, and genius is as definite a thing as breed.

An active habit of body, a mind attuned to poetic contemplations, a facility in the fine arts, a soul spurred on by ambitious thoughts—these are not consistent with the most exquisite metaphysical subtlety; yet equally certain it is that the great metaphysician shall possess no great excellence in physical exercise, in poetry, in art, in commerce, in society, in statesmanship. For since all human excellence has no other test than competition, it will be found that of two minds, equally keen in speculation and analysis, the work of that mind will be superior which is most deficient in the attractions of the objective world, if only for the reason that these attractions imply the use of time and energy. And so it happens that the idea of Plotinus is not altogether without justification— Plotinus who was ashamed of his body.

Under what strange aspects we find the greatest things of the world. On a certain fine evening, for example, outside the Athenæum Club a little man with a Scotch plaid over his shoulders might have been observed slowly pacing, head bent a little forward, absorbed in thought, not looking to the right or left, or at those who passed him by, not looked at by them—a plain, little, old-fashioned Scotch body, shrewd no doubt, but dry, self-contained and cautious, a decent little grocer of a small Scotch town—for if we turned to look again at him, so we might think him—with a possible seat amongst the elders of the kirk, and a respectable voice in the Parish Council's discussions. Such was the Alexander Bain I beheld. And if any one should imagine that there is a spice of irreverence in this description—any dear friend of Bain—then I will say that my admiration for Bain is not less than his ; nay, that as I looked my heart beat impetuously with the anticipation of his conversation, and I trembled, foolishly no doubt, in involuntary homage to the might of that little man's intellect. I smiled at the insignificant

figure, but smiling, I linked him in my mind, in regard to his stature, with Aristotle and Kant, whom indeed I reckoned to be among the few to be linked with him in genius.

The countenance of the plain Scotch type, irregular and little mobile, was yet made distinguished by the quick glance of intelligence—as if indeed Pallas Athena, descending from heaven with the splendid equipment of brains, had formed there and then the features from the materials at hand. The prominent thin nose, the straight dry mouth, the long chin and drawn cheeks, even the skull, long and well shaped, but not large, not particularly full in the forehead, though opening into an excellent arch at the crown and expanding into an oval contour—all these characteristics might have belonged to a little Scotch pedagogue; and the picture became completed by the baldness of the head, the stiff side whiskers worn a little long, fringing the keen, shaven face. The manner, too, was dry, reserved, and a little pedantic — decidedly, then, a quiet but deep-thinking little Scotch pedagogue. The eye alone gave hints of superior power, not that the eye was bright or Olympian in effulgent lustre, but on account of the keen, profound look of penetration, thought, and intelligence that beamed out in its subdued confidence and

its inveterate and disregardful speculative ab-
sorption.

The voice, as the philosopher spoke, was a plain
Scotch voice, a little hard in its sound, but with
the charm of the tone of a man of vast intellect
falling, without affectation, into an expression of
modest reserve, content, indeed, simply to follow
the truth and state the fact in its objective character, and solicitous of impressing his companion
only in so far as he wished to follow the line of
thought asked for, and to speak calmly out of the
fulness of his treasure. Truly the utterance of
that plain Scotch voice in its low tones, indifferent
to effect, and discoursing of impersonal concerns
—that was one of the richest on earth !

Bain's conversation is like his books, devoid of
charm except for their intellectual interest, yet to
those to whom that intellectual interest is sufficient more fascinating than the words of romance.
Ostensibly not emotional, giving no outward sign
of any emotional concern, and not solicitous of
any appeal except to the reason, and yet withal
showing in deep glints at times the well of deep
emotional feeling that lies below. That emotion
is not of the powerful, on-rushing character of
those who appeal to us by the force of their
feeling, or the rare sympathetic quality of fine
natures ; that emotion is secluded, not often

stirred, a sanctuary of private communings. And
so, too, with the sense of humour. For the sense of
humour exists in this keen, severe, precise thinker,
but of so subtle a character, so elusive and fine,
that one cannot point out definitely when it has
stirred the clearness of intellectual contemplation.
The emotional existence of such a man suggests
to the mind the thought of a Scottish tarn ;
secluded, awaking deep thoughts, but, when a
ripple moves on its surface, calling out in response the note of some of the deepest chords in
our natures. The emotion, thought, and interest
of the thinker are not those of the participator in
the *mêlée* of life ; he sits apart, quiet, watchful,
interested, even amused, and being indifferent to
the partisan feeling of the game, marks down the
" points " with an inevitable certitude of judgment
and genuine appreciation of value.

In order to consider Bain's intellectual work it
may be well to advert for a moment to a saying
of Huxley's. That philosopher contested the
idea that there was anything special in scientific
habits of thought, and he described science itself
as nothing but organised common sense. That
definition is doubtless correct ; but when we give
the full value to the word *organised,* we shall find
that therein is the crux of the whole position.
The difference between man himself and any one

of the inferior types from which he has become evolved may be expressed in a word, *organisation*. And so it happens that the mind of a man trained in scientific work moves in a different style to that of the current crowd.   Darwin, for example, declared that the chief characteristic of his own thought was "generalisation"—the elucidation of law by induction from discrete instances ; and finding that Carlyle was deficient in this respect, he had no hesitation in saying that the sage's mind was very ill adapted to cope with scientific problems.

Yet what has this to do with Alexander Bain ? Everything, for in discussing generalisation we are discussing a prominent characteristic of Bain's work ; and so marked is the influence of scientific training upon the whole body of that work, that in the years to come when our Psychology has reached such a pitch that we can reconstruct a mind from a few sentences, just as the anatomist reconstructs an extinct animal from a bone, then the sentences picked almost at hazard from Bain would suffice to establish his calibre as a thinker. Let us open his classic work, " Education as a Science," at a venture.   We find the following—he is writing a chapter on Discrimination :—

" Mind starts from discrimination.   The consciousness of difference is the beginning of every intellectual exercise. . . .

"We have by nature a certain power of discrimination in each department of sensibility. We can from the outset discriminate, more or less delicately, sights, sounds, touches, smells, tastes; and, in each sense, some persons more than others. This is the deepest foundation of disparity of intellectual character, as well as of variety in likings and pursuits. If, from the beginning, one man can interpolate five shades of discrimination or shades of colour where another can but feel one transition, the careers of the two men are foreshadowed, and will be widely apart."

Passages like these might be made the text for a small volume of criticism and elucidation. The intelligent but uninstructed reader meeting for the first time a sentence such as one of these quoted, has the impression that the words either express no more than "common sense," or that they are uninteresting because the mind has no grip of them and does not behold their drift.

Yet every sentence is an aphorism, and the argument moves on steadily in a continuous sequence. The peculiarity of the expression is that the dicta are the results of analysis, of the persistent and unavoidable habit of analysis in thought, and each sentence cuts down incisively to the depths of that analysis in which the structure and mode of mind have been examined. Consider the first: "Mind starts from discrimination." How abrupt is the opening; how uncompromising the thought. It stands like a mathematical formula, meaningless and therefore indifferent to one who does not grasp its full significance ; subtle and full of importance to one who understands, or puzzles it out.

Then the second sentence : "The consciousness of difference is the beginning of every intellectual exercise." Here we have a sentence abrupt like the first, and the sequence is an abrupt one. We have an intellectual nexus only, and in this nexus the second sentence strikes in as inevitably as the notes of a harmony. And so on throughout the exposition, if the full significance of each sentence be not grasped, the book will appear jerky, harsh, even disconnected, void of all style, and unconvincing in form. Arrive at these sentences, however, through an appreciation of the analytical habit from which they have arisen, then each sentence is pregnant with meaning, the argument is all consecutive, and there is an intellectual pleasure almost unsurpassed in the observance of the serried, onpressing, never-halting force of logical reasoning ; while on the line of march luminous *aperçus* open up in the general form of expression in which each particular thought has been couched.

Take the sentence : " This is the deepest foundation of disparity of intellectual character, as well as of variety in likings and pursuits." These words, their form and manner, alone would serve to indicate a high order of intellect in the mind who gave them forth.

So far we have touched but upon one of the phases of the mind of a thinker, but one which indeed prepares us to expect the others. For turn now to the index to note how the chapter on Discrimination occurs ; and here I will venture to say that a study of Bain's indexes forms one of the most stimulating and profitable intellectual exercises I know. The section on Discrimination is found in the third chapter, under the general heading, " Bearings of Psychology," and it is preceded by a section entitled, " All parts of Psychology applicable : the Intellect more especially."

All this is significant. There is nothing casual or merely suggestive in the index. The index is a plan of dialectical campaign ; the strategy is designed to cover the field of the subject of Education, according to a regular logical principle, and hence inevitably. The scope of the science of Education is fixed in the first chapter, and definitions are considered. Then the work is taken up in masterly style. Education refers to the individual and to the thing—that is to say, the whole complex intellectual character, physical and mental, and to the actual subjects of Educa-

tion themselves. Here we have the first basis
for a division of the broad subject ; and as we
proceed we find that the structure of the work
proceeds on the principle of continuous logical
division of the heads of subjects in turn, until
we come down to the actual details. The division
being determined, the principle of investigation is
sought for ; for example, in considering the physical side of the individual we resort to the teaching of Physiology. "Bearings of Physiology"
becomes then, appropriately, the heading of the
second chapter, and, as we might now anticipate,
" Bearings of Psychology " of the chapter succeeding. Then in the subdivision Discrimination
we have continuously further subdivisions. Discrimination is itself one of the ultimate facts of
the mind ; so therefore we seek the materials of a
further disquisition in the relation of discrimination to other mental processes. Hence we get a
section on the conditions of discrimination :
(1) mental watchfulness ; (2) absence of undue
excitement ; (3) interest ; (4) juxtaposition. And
each of these headings is elucidated.

Already it will be seen that there is scope for
making "Education as a Science" a monumental
work, and yet but a small glimpse has been given
either as to its excellence or the amount of learning
and thought upon which it has been based. It is

not enough to plan an extensive piece of strategy, and to elaborate the plan of the work in logical method ; each thought contributed in the progress of the work has some subtle quality of the thinker's brain, and these in due order sum up to an exploration of an immense field of thought, in Physiology, Psychology, and the various subjects of Education, with due regard both to their sequence and their proper proportion in the whole perspective.

"Education as a Science" may be considered the summit of Bain's teaching, just as the "Data of Ethics" may be considered as the crown of Spencer's philosophy ; yet the amount of subsidiary work is apparently more striking by reason of its vastness and variety. Physiology and Psychology, these are the bases of Bain's educational system ; the applications range into subjects as technical as English grammar and logic, as broad as the history of philosophical positions.

In all the works the same method is observable ; and the true way to study a book of Bain's is to search out the rationale of the index and to get hold of the contents by reference to that. In this manner we can retain the substance of the book with but comparatively small tax upon the memory, just as we remember the propositions of Euclid ; and indeed for the same reason, viz., that the treatment depends upon a consecutive logical exposition. And hence, too, it is explained how a mind so dry and so little exuberant has been able to give forth such an abundance of matter; for the infallible system of his exposition leaves behind, as belonging to a lower class, the work even of men like Mark Pattison and Matthew Arnold, who have brought active, acute, and earnest minds to the consideration of the same subjects of Education. The difference is as great as between a plan of campaign of Napoleon and the haphazard tactics of Blücher.

The intellectual interests likely to attract Bain are those of a fine metaphysical character ; a matter involving subtle introspection ; keen, exquisite analysis ; recondite resemblances ; trenchant thoughts that show a sort of hierarchy of science dependent on certain first principles ; then a broad generalisation grouping together a number of apparently separate things ; all questions of method, of principle, of law in science ; striking analogy, and the suggestion for developing a strain of thought ; the entire broad field of actual scientific discovery ; but especially the work done in the subjective world.

Even in dealing with matters of a more objective interest the same characteristics of Bain's mind are displayed. Witness his admirable monographs on the Mills. His work modestly

entitled " J. S. Mill : A Criticism," is to those
who care to extract from it its full importance
one of the greatest biographies ever written. Yet
to most it must read dry, formal, and pedantic ;
and truly it is so if Boswell's " Life of Johnson,"
for example, be taken as a standard. Bain gives
a clear idea of Mill, not by the gossiping relation
of his career, but by a remarkably extensive, cool,
and finely-judged analysis of his character, mentally, morally, physically ; and the reader who is
fascinated by the study rises from the book with a
clearer appreciation of Mill than even from Mill's
own autobiography, or from tomes of information
respecting his actual career. And though the
method be one of impartial scrutiny, and the
manner that of judicial estimation, and though
Mill's defects be in no wise spared, yet, again, the
reader rises from this book with an appreciation
of Mill far more solid and enduring than the most
lavish eulogy and the most favourable description
could possibly afford.

Bain does not scruple to weigh his man, literally
and physically. He estimates all his qualities in
order and eclectically, and allows the result to speak
for itself. How surprising in an English work, and
yet how admirable, is this passage, for instance :—

" I am not singular in the opinion that in the so-called
sensual feelings he was below average ; that, in fact, he

was not a good representative specimen of humanity in respect of these, and scarcely did justice to them in his theories."

And so he continues the theme ; not needlessly, for in passages of the like candour we are better able to appreciate that side of Mill's character to which the word "crank" might be not unaptly applied.

And the final words of the criticism of Mill are excellent :—

"Although, in order to a permanent reputation, it is necessary to produce a work great in itself and of exclusive authorship, yet this is not the only way that original power manifests itself. A multitude of small impressions may have the accumulated effect of a mighty whole. Who shall sum up Mill's collective influence as an instructor in Politics, Ethics, Logic, and Metaphysics? No calculus can integrate the innumerable little pulses of knowledge and of thought that he has made to vibrate in the minds of his generation."

The last sentence is exquisite in its intellectual quality. The peculiar collocation of the words calculus, integrate, pulses, and vibrate, indicate the breadth of the survey and the deep links of association in the thought expressed. Bain, herein referring to the life's work of a man, considers at the same moment not merely the mathematical force of *integration*, but the force of that mathematical expression in the domain of Physiology with regard to nervous stimulus, and moreover the peculiar harmonic movement in which that stimulation becomes intensified ; and thence in the same strain of association his mind has considered the meaning of vibration itself as referred to its ethereal basis.

Yet note the awkwardness of expression even in this wonderful passage. His words "in order to a permanent reputation" hardly make good English ; and there is an undesirable abruptness in the sequence of the phrases. In other parts of Bain's works, even in his works upon "Rhetoric" and "How to Teach English," the difficulty of the wording, the woodenness of the manner of expression, are rather below the standard of a provincial reporter. And even when the sentences give nothing very definite for criticism, yet a taste not at all too delicate in matters of style may detect the want of power and *maëstro* in the actual instrument of words. For instance in the following :—

"In the presence of a beautiful scene or a work of art, we derive great benefit from being shown when and how to direct our attention. We may chance to be misled, but it is assumed that we can find some one more advanced than ourselves in the conditions that regulate æsthetic pleasure. This is the rôle of the art instructor for all."

In this passage, as in everything that Bain writes, each particular thought is definite and clear, the

sequence is logical, but the form of expression is
not flowing and harmonious. And herein we
find an instance of the fact, so frequently ob-
truded in the perusal of Bain's works, that a
writer brilliant in ideas and lucid in statement
may yet be deficient in the power of expression
of his thoughts.

Bain's moral nature may be inferred from what
has already been said. His is a mind guided by
ethical principles even to the subjugation of the
warm emotional impulses, fond of questions of
casuistry, stickling for meticulous points—a mind
finding its highest enjoyments in intellectual pursuits, and little stirred by the many emotional
interests that passionate the multitude. His lot
has not been cast in conditions favourable to
the complete and harmonious development of his
nature ; for singular it is that Scotland, the nation
that has given to the world Hume and James Mill
and Burns, remains almost typical of a narrow
and rigid intolerance in matters of thought. Nor
in the wider scope of the national life has Bain
been able to find much sympathy. Our great
Universities are still struggling in the hopeless
morass of the theology of the Middle Ages, and at
the present time, as truly as ever, it may be affirmed
that in the direction of philosophic culture their
influence is either frivolous or pernicious, and

remains undisturbed by, and in turn devoid of influence upon, the march of intellectual progress.

In former days Locke, Hobbes, Bacon, Hume, the Mills, Bentham, and Darwin have been branded as rebels ; and no less severely to-day is the weight of orthodox philosophising bent against the teachings of the two great contemporary bearers of the light.

The life of thought is in itself and under the best of circumstances solitary and bleak. The philosopher must derive most of his stimulus from his own internal resources. Yet other consolations have at times been not withheld, as, for instance, to Kant, who so finely represents the German character of philosophy, and who wielded such profound influence in his own lifetime ; or, again, to Voltaire, that embodiment of the French spirit of candour and wit, who swayed Europe as from a throne. In the history of these islands the thinker has been the pariah of Society ; at every turn his mind hurtles against the solid buttresses of privilege ; and the very boldness of his effort of research, the luminosity of his vision, are the grounds of his *lèse majesté* of ignorance and prejudice.

Hence it must be confessed with sadness that the influence of Bain upon his generation has been but slight, slight even in the matters of intellect, except in regard to that quaint and meagre little class who are still content to search for truth.

One of the mightiest intellects yet vouchsafed to our earth has been in great part hidden and depressed amidst a community that esteems Mr. Balfour a great philosopher, Mr. Stead a great popular expositor, and Robert Ellesmere's balancing of fatuous doubts a great psychological problem, and which still listens to the doctrines of orthodox religion and orthodox education without the stirring either of laughter or scorn. In this miasma of intellect the vigour of the child has not been unimpaired ; he has grown up cramped, cold, and reserved, looking upon the world with keen though mournful eyes, aloof and superior, yet withering in that bleak superiority, understanding yet not feeling the play of passions that passes before his vision, yet charting down the web of human endeavour with calm and gnomic fatality.

THE END.

List of Books

PUBLISHED BY

BERTRAM DOBELL

77 CHARING CROSS ROAD, LONDON, W.C.

8vo.   Cloth extra, 324 pages.   6s. Net

Gluck and the Opera
A STUDY IN THE HISTORY OF MUSIC

By ERNEST NEWMAN

"'GLUCK AND THE OPERA' is an admirable study, not only of the great musical reformer's career and artistic work, but of the philosophy of musical drama, with more especial reference to its earlier manifestations.   The masterpieces of Gluck are carefully and sympathetically analysed in so attractive a manner as to increase every musical reader's desire to see some of them, beside *Orfeo*, on the modern stage ; the writer evidently possesses a remarkable degree of scientific and general culture, and his views on the æsthetics of the art carry conviction. The book is one of those rare achievements in musical literature that are likely to gain a certain amount of recognition from literary people as well as from musicians.   It well deserves it, for a more thorough, temperate, and right-minded piece of work has not lately been seen in England."—*The Times.*

Crown 8vo.   Cloth extra.   4s. 6d. Net

Like Stars that Fall
By GEOFFREY MORTIMER
AUTHOR OF "TALES FROM THE WESTERN MOORS"

"The theme of this story is music-halls and the careers of their artistes.   It is treated with evident understanding, as though the phase of life represented were observed at first hand.   Only within recent years have the halls been visited and discussed by respectable middle-class folk ; only recently have they been made the subject of novelistic enterprise.   The author of 'Like Stars that Fall' has produced a clear, and apparently true, picture of the people and their surroundings. From the time the reader is introduced into the back parlour of the small provincial greengrocer and his stage-struck wife, on to the time of her London successes and failures in a totally new walk of life, there is an appearance of reality.   'Lou,' in spite of her good looks, is not altogether our own idea of a winsome woman ; yet she is human, and the events of her life excite interest and pity, not only for her, but for the deserted child and the sturdy little tradesman husband, who has a kind of bluff dignity of character.   The sense of good-fellowship, the talk and chaff, and the occasional 'nastiness' of the comrades, their sordid lives, and at times dismal deaths, are conveyed in anything but a stupid fashion."—*The Athenæum.*

Parts I., II., and III. (64 *pages each, double columns*)
1s. *each*

Catalogue of a Collection of Privately Printed Books

COMPILED AND ANNOTATED BY
BERTRAM DOBELL

"Mr. Bertram Dobell has now issued the second part of his Catalogue of Privately Printed Books, coming down to the letter N. This consists, it may be as well to state, entirely of such books as are in Mr. Dobell's own possession; but as he has been collecting them for many years past, and as he appends copious notes to the titles, the work will always possess a permanent bibliographical value. We observe that he gives a large number of pieces printed at the private press of Charles Clark, of Great Totham, Essex, which possess little interest beyond curiosity; but he seems to have none of the dialect specimens of Prince L. L. Bonaparte, and the only examples of Mr. H. Daniel's Oxford Press that we have found, are under the head of Canon Dixon. The Appledore Press of Mr. W. J. Linton is fairly represented, and so is that of the late Halliwell-Phillipps. Among the rarities that have caught our eye is a volume entitled 'Literary Hours' (1837), which includes upwards of forty pieces, in prose and poetry, by Walter Savage Landor. Altogether, the curious reader will find here much to interest him in one of the by-paths of literature."—*The Academy.*

"The second part of Mr. Bertram Dobell's 'Catalogue of a Collection of Privately Printed Books' is, like the first, full of interest, to say nothing of its genuine bibliographical value. Mr. Dobell is not content with quoting the titles of the various books and pamphlets under notice, but gives in many instances the entire gist of the preface, which is usually the most explicit *raison d'être* of the book's existence; and in the case of poetry, the compiler both criticises and gives specimens, which are sometimes good and at others the reverse. Many of the books enumerated in this excellent catalogue are very well known to travellers in out-of-the-way regions of literature, but the identification of the authors will in several instances be a welcome revelation. That Mr. Dobell has spared no pains to make his list as complete in itself as possible, is patent to every bookish man, and the wonder is that he can afford to give so much labour for the small charge which he has affixed to the parts of this catalogue."—*The Bookworm.*

"Book collectors will be grateful to us for drawing their attention to Mr. Bertram Dobell's 'Catalogue of a Collection of Privately Printed Books,' in five parts, the fourth of which is about to appear. Martin's catalogue, of which the second edition was published in 1854, is the only book in English on this subject, and Mr. Dobell is no doubt right in saying that more books have been privately printed since that date than before it. The books in his collection are, in many cases, for sale separately, as he has duplicates of them, but he hopes to dispose of it as a whole, probably to some public institution. Certainly no collection like it is in existence, and it is very full in many of the rarest items in this class of books. We find a few omissions, 'The Feast of Bacchus, for instance, being the only work of Mr. Robert Bridges. Besides the value of the catalogue, however, as a work of reference, which is very great, literary interest is given to it by constant quotations of verses or passages of interest from the volumes themselves, and bibliographical and biographical information. As it is issued at a shilling, every bibliographer will be sure to procure a copy."—*The Daily Chronicle.*